The Naked Paranormal Investigators

George Ramsey

Copyright © 2025 by George Ramsey

All rights reserved.

All rights reserved. No part of this publication may be reproduced, distributed, or transmitted in any form or by any means, including photocopying, recording, or other electronic or mechanical methods, without the prior written permission of the publisher, except in the case of brief quotations embodied in critical reviews and certain other noncommercial uses permitted by copyright law. For permission requests, write to the publisher, addressed "Attention: Permissions Coordinator," at the address below.

Attention: Permissions Coordinator

George Ramsey

750 Concourse Circle, Suite # 103

PMB 379

Middle River, MD 21220

Contents

Prologue		V
1.	Johnathan's Unit	1
2.	Johnathan and Samantha	7
3.	Private Watts	15
4.	The Paranormal Team	23
5.	Samantha	29
6.	Research on Moon Bay Cottage	40
7.	Amy and Watts	51
8.	Investigation of Moon Bay Cottage	61
9.	Moon Bay Cottage Evidence Review	79
10.	Military Seperation	89
11.	Amy and Watts New Nudist Club	94
12.	The Naked Paranormal Headquarters	107
13.	The Naked Planetarium Club	114
14.	New Contracts	121
15.	Investigating Mike and Destiny's House	129
16.	Investigating The Haunted Aviation Museum	142

17.	The Aviation Museum Evidence Review	155
18.	The Reveal	163
19.	Mike and Destiny Join the Team	173
20.	The Naked Paranormal Team Promotions	182
21.	Traveling to Savannah, Georgia	193
22.	Investigating the Moon River Brewing Company	204
23.	Crybaby Bridge	219
24.	Back Home	232
25.	Epilogue	239

Prologue

Johnathan was reaching his third year in the Army and had just met Samantha at the NCO club one Saturday night. He was there almost every weekend except when he was out doing field training with his unit. Samantha, on the other hand, had only been to the NCO club a handful of times, as civilians needed to be signed into the club by a member of the military. Johnathan was sitting at a table over in the corner right beside the DJ so he could just look around the room. He loved to watch people, especially on the dance floor, looking at all the funky ways the soldiers were dancing with civilians. Most of the soldiers in the club were single, and the single civilians, especially the women, were in there to try their luck hooking up with soldiers. Some got lucky, but most did not, as the soldiers were smart and knew exactly what the civilians were up to.

As Johnathan was sitting there, his cell phone rang, but because the music was so loud, he did not hear it ring. He felt the vibration, even though he was not sure if was his phone ringing or if the base from the music. He took it out of his pocket and looked down at it. His mother was calling, but he decided to let it go to voicemail as he would not be able to hear her because of the loud music. Putting it the phone back into his pocket, he decided he would call her the next day when he had a chance. As he looked up at the dance floor, and he noticed Samantha.

She was beautiful. About five feet six, blonde hair, and blue eyes, she was thin but not too thin: just the perfect size. Samantha glanced over in Johnathan's direction, and she caught a glimpse of him looking at her. She didn't pay him any attention, as she had always got stares from guys all the time in the clubs. Instead, she just went back to dancing with the guy she was dancing with. Johnathan wondered if that was her husband or her boyfriend or if it was just some random dude that she had just met. The song played on and then ended, and the noticed that they went in separate directions. Johnathan immediately thought now was his chance to walk up and strike up a conservation with her, but his nerves started to get the best of him. *Ahh come on,* Johnathan said to himself, *what do I have to lose?*

Samantha headed to the bar and was standing in line, waiting her turn to order one of those flowery drinks that girls usually order. Johnathan decided to wait in line right behind her to order a drink as well. As Johnathan got in line, he started small talk with her, at first just saying hi.

"Are you from this town, maybe in the military?" he asked, but to Johnathan's surprise, she was not.

"Really?" he said. "It totally looks like you are in the military here. What do you do for a living?"

"I am a ghost hunter," she responded.

Johnathan was now very intrigued with that answer. "Would you want to accompany me back to my table? I want to learn more about that."

She agreed, so he paid for both of their drinks, and they headed back to the table Johnathan was originally sitting at. They found the music was too loud, so they decided to find another table away from the DJ. They both got up and walked around until they found a table outside in the courtyard. That area was much quieter and less crowded and had other bar goers and couples that were sitting out there talking. Despite that they could still hear the thumping of the music through the door, that area was much better suited to have a conservation in.

As they sat there, Samantha with her girly, flowery drink and Johnathan with his pale ale, he started the questioning. "So, what's your name?"

"Samantha," she said.

"Ahh, nice to meet you, Samantha. I'm Johnathan Smith."

"Nice to meet you as well," Samantha said. "Are you in the Army?"

"Yes, I am in the Field Artillery Unit here on post. I think I heard you say that you are a ghost hunter. Is that correct?"

She took a sip of her drink. "Yes, I am a ghost hunter. I have been doing that for the last ten years and absolutely love it. I had some spooky stuff happen, and then I didn't have so much activity. It's just a hit or miss where you go. Sometimes, people just say things because they want to believe that they have a haunted place."

"Wow, that's so crazy!" Johnathan said. "That's weird some people just say things to get you to come out for nothing. I'm really interested in doing that one day. Are you sure that you want to do ghost hunting because there's a chance that something can attach to you that you don't want attached to you."

"It can be a hazardous job, for sure," she agreed.

"I am totally ok with ghost hunting. I've always been interested in doing that, though I never thought in a million years that I would ever meet anyone that did that for a job. It's so exciting!"

After a while of talking, Samantha loved their conversation. "I have a job coming up in October, if you are able to get some time off. You are more than welcome to accompany me. Oh, and there is one thing that I forgot to mention."

Johnathan asked, "What's that?"

Samantha had a little blush on her face. She hesitated to answer that question.

Johnathan encouraged her. "Come on...you can tell me."

"Well," Samantha said. "When I do these ghost hunting jobs, I always do them naked. I'm a nudist."

Johnathan was very shocked and even more excited. "Really? I'm a nudist as well! I keep it hidden just because I'm in the Army. There have been times that I ran around naked out in the field during training, but it has always been at night."

Samantha laughed, excited to hear that. "All my other ghost hunting teammates would always join me investigating while being naked."

And this is how the naked paranormal investigators were born.

Chapter One

Johnathan's Unit

Johnathan Smith was a staff sergeant and the section chief of the first section in Alpha Battery 2nd of the 77th Field Artillery regiment with the 4th Infantry Division at Fort Carson, Colorado. He oversaw a crew of seven soldiers and worked on a piece of artillery called the M109 self-propelled howitzer. Private Alex Watts had just joined the unit and came directly from basic training. Since Private Watts was new, he was placed as the advanced party where all new recruits start off. As the new recruits rank increased, so did their position in the section. The section knew that Johnathan was a nudist, and no one cared about that. In fact, they all were intrigued, and each one of them wanted to try the nudist thing, maybe at a nudist beach. However, because there was so much training happening with the unit, no one had the opportunity to do anything outside of post in several months. There was plenty to do on post for all the soldiers for their rest and recreation. There was the NCO club, as well as a gym, indoor and outdoor pools, a movie theater, and a rec center that also had a military travel center inside.

Johnathan told his crew about his nudist lifestyle when he became their crew chief seven months ago. He had a sit down pow-wow with all his soldiers to get to know them. He asked where they were from, why they joined the Army, and why they joined Field Artillery. Once all his soldiers went around telling their story, it then became Johnathan's turn. He proceeded to answer the same questions, then told them the rest of his story, including how he liked to run around in the field when they go out for training in the evening if they were not doing any live fire. None his crew said they would have an issue with that. Furthermore, he told his soldiers that they were more than welcome to do the same thing if they wanted to, but that it was totally up to them. One by one, they said they would definitely think about it.

Besides talking about the nudist lifestyle, Johnathan also asked his section if anyone had ever been ghosting, which meant hunting ghosts, or if anyone encountered a ghost in their lifetime. All said no, except for Watts. The private said it was at his home back in Louisiana where his parents lived. There was a ghostly visitor in his room just about every night, one that was demonic in nature. After another hour of talking about what all Watts had encountered, it was 2200 hours, and it was time for the lights to go out for the evening. It was time to hit the rack for the night. They didn't have to go to sleep, but the lights must be out. PT was at 0600 hours each morning, so they had to be rested.

Early the next day, at 0530 hours, the CQ went around to all the rooms, knocking on the doors for wake-up calls to get ready for PT. All the soldiers had to get up and dressed into their PT uniforms. The uniforms were black shorts and a light gray with a reflective U.S. Army logo. As they all lined up into the field right outside the barracks by section, the sergeant that was running PT for that morning yelled for fall-in. Every soldier immediately lined up according to rank. They had to report, so each section chief raised his hand to salute and gave the morning status report on each of his soldiers and where they were at. Johnathan's section was all present. Then, the leader gave a command of left face, and then another command was given to extend to the left march. All the soldiers put both their arms up at shoulder height, and everyone except the first row went to the left. A all the soldiers finally stopped moving, another command was given arms downward-move. Everyone dropped their arms by their sides, and then the command of right face was given. Everyone turned right. The leader then announced from front to rear count off. The first row counted off one, the second row called out two, and so they went until all six rows sounded off. Another command was given for even numbers one step to the left march, and then rows two, four, and six took one step to the left. The first set of exercises were for stretching, then moved to cardio with the side straddle hop then run in place. Once all that was completed, it was time for muscle building with pushups, sit-ups, then elevated push-ups and the bicycle.

After that was completed, the command was given assemble to the right march. The soldiers all got back into normal formation, then went on a five-mile run. Once PT was over and everyone was back at the barracks, they had two hours to spare. It was enough time to take a shower, get dressed for the duty day, and hit the chow hall for breakfast since their next formation wasn't until 0900 hours. Inside the barracks, most of the soldiers were just running up and down the hallway with just a towel on to and from the showers. Of course, this did not phase any of the soldiers because they were all use to seeing each other with just a towel on or even naked. When 0900 hours came around, everyone was in the days uniform. There was another formation, and once again, a status report had to be made. This time, all soldiers were present and accounted for, and they all headed down to the motor pool to do maintenance on the howitzers.

While working, Johnathan started talking about his nudist lifestyle with his section again. He mentioned Samantha, the girl he had met at the NCO club Saturday night. He excitedly told them about her job as a ghosthunter, and that he had been invited to a ghost hunting trip with her in October. He asked if any of his section if they would like to go, too, but immediately realized he was totally out of line with asking, as Samantha did not say anything about inviting other people. Luckily for Johnathan, everyone said no except for Watts. Johnathan said he needed to call Samantha and see if he would be able to go with them. As Johnathan stepped over to the fence line, he called Samantha to ask. It was a pleasant surprise that Samantha had agreed to let Watts go. Johnathan called Watts over to him away from the rest of the section and said he was more than welcome to join them in October, but that he needed to put in his leave time for that today.

Right after lunch, Johnathan let Watts go to the orderly room to fill out his leave request for October. Once he filled out his paperwork for his leave and handed it back to the clerk, the clerk tried went to file it under first section and came across another leave request for SSG Smith. The clerk had seen that a request had already been put in for the same time, so he denied Watts request. The private explained to the clerk that Johnathan had told him that he could put in for the same time, but the clerk did not want to believe him. After a tense conversation, the clerk told Watts to wait for a second, and he went in the back to the first sergeants and the battery commander's office to ask them if Watts could be approved for the same leave time as SSG Smith's leave time. The commander told the clerk that he wanted to ask Johnathan if he approved Watts's leave request and sent Watts back to the motor pool so they could both come back to the orderly room. Once they arrived, they had to take a seat and wait for the commander to get off the phone on a very important call. When he finished on the phone, the commander had the orderly room clerk send both SSG Smith and Private Watts come back at the same time. As they entered the commander's office, both of them raised their right hand to render a salute. The commander saluted back and told them both to have a seat. The commander asked SSG Smith if he had given Private Watts permission to take the same leave time as he did. Of course, Johnathan said that he did and told Watts to come her right after lunch and fill out the leave forms. The commander responded that he usually does not let two soldiers take the same time off in a section, but he was going to make an exception to this for this one time because he knew that first section was totally squared away. Then the commander took Watts leave request and handed it to the clerk in the front and advised the clerk that both of their leave requests were approved and to go ahead and do what he needed to do to make that happen. The commander dismissed both soldiers, and as they stood up, they both rendered another salute and then left the office. On their way out, they stopped at the office clerk's desk to make sure that there was nothing else that he needed. When the clerk said no, Johnathan and Watts headed back to the motor pool.

As SSG Smith and Private Watts entered the motor pool, they noticed that the section was on top of things, as Sergeant Garret was there leading the way. They had already greased all the fittings, punched the tube, and performed Preventive Maintenance Checks and Services. The first thing that Johnathan asked was if they used the -10, as they couldn't do a proper PMCS without the -10. The guys started laughing, but he knew that his section was good at their jobs, and he trusted every one of them. It had gotten to be 1600 hours, and it was time to march back to the barracks for final formation and mail call. In formation, they listened to the 1st Seargeant and his instructions, then the mail clerk was starting to hand out letters and packages to the soldiers that had received mail. Once all the mail and the 1st Seargeant were finished, everyone was released for the day.

Chapter Two

Johnathan and Samantha

Samantha called Johnathan and asked him to accompany her to the nude beach that was an hour away from Fort Carson. She even offered to pick him up from his unit. Johnathan accepted the offer, and after they had talked on the phone for a while, Johnathan had to hang up so he would be ready when she got tom his unit. All they had to do was just drive down to the beach. Samantha had gotten to the unit 15 minutes late, and she honked her horn to let Johnathan know that she was there. After a few minutes, he came out, hopped in her SUV, and they headed to the post gate to get on the road to the nude beach. Johnathan was made small talk with her as they headed out the main gate until they were off of the post, heading for the highway in the direction of the beach.

Johnathan asked, "How long will it take to get there?"

"About an hour, so if you need to stop for anything, to let me know." She glanced over at him.

"I think that I'm good. I did everything I needed to do right before you got to the barracks. If I need to stop for anything, I will let you now."

Samantha asked, "Have you ever been to a nude beach before?"

"Once or twice, but I never knew there was a nude beach down where we are going. I been at Fort Carson for over a year now, and I usually research the places I go just to see where there may be nudist activities in the area. I have not seen or heard of this beach. This is great."

The rest of the way to the beach, they both were kind of quiet and just admired the view of the mountains along the way.

Arriving at the parking location, they pulled up to the park ranger guard shack, and a ranger had stepped out. "Good morning. How can I help you?"

"We are here to go to Conundrum Hot Springs," Samantha replied.

Johnathan said, "Hot springs? I thought we were going to a nude beach?"

Samantha explained. "There is a nude beach down here as well, but it's in the park where the hot springs are."

The ranger laughed at them. "Well, there is a $20 fee to get into the park."

Johnathan asked if there was a military discount.

"With a military discount, it will be $10 off. We only take electronic payments now as the National Park Service did away with cash payments."

Johnathan took out his military ID, showing the park ranger for verification. As Johnathan put his ID back into his wallet, he pulled out his debit card and paid the park fee.

The ranger gave them a receipt and a map of the area, then gave them directions. "Follow this road all the way to the end, and you will run into a parking lot for the beach. You will pass the hot springs on your right. Once you see the sign for the hot springs, it will be about another quarter mile down the road. Just park in Lot D, and you will have a little walk to get to the beach. Enjoy your visit."

Both Johnathan and Samantha said thank you to the ranger, and they started heading down to the beach. The speed limit was only fifteen miles per hour on the park road, so it took them about five minutes to get to the end. Once they passed the sign for the hot springs, they started looking for Lot D. Two minutes later, they saw the sign for parking, then pulled into the lot and found a spot and parked. After they got out of the vehicle, they both stretched like they had just gotten out of bed in the morning. Johnathan took his shirt off, getting ready for the beach, but Samantha kept her shorts and shirt on, despite wearing a bikini under her clothes. Samantha brought a foldable wagon to tote all their stuff for the beach with them.

Johnathan and Samantha walked through the parking lot and up to the entrance to the beach. There was a small snack shop that sold burgers, hot dogs, fries, and potato chips, which had some reggae music playing as well. They passed the snack shop, and right behind the snack shop, there were the large rest rooms. They both decided to stop at the rest room. Samantha was pulling the wagon, so she took the wagon into the restroom with her, and they both met each other out front when they got done. As they both started walking towards the beach entrance, they started seeing signs that read, *Warning! You May Encounter Nude Bathers Beyond This Point*. With that, they knew they were in the correct location. As they hit the sand, there was a walkway that was put down to make it much easier to walk down to the beach and made it much easier to pull the wagon. At the beach, there was the lifeguard shack, and guests could go either way to the left or to the right of the shack and find a place and plop down and stake their area.

They found a nice spot just behind and to the right of the lifeguard shack, set up some beach chairs, took their clothes off, and broke out the sunscreen. They sprayed each other with it and then placed towels on the chairs and stretched out, enjoying the sun.

After about a half hour of laying in the sun and taking a nap, Johnathan woke up and headed down to the water's edge. At first, he walked into ankle deep, just to see how the temperature was. To his surprise, the water was cool but not cold and seemed to be very refreshing. Then he went in up to his waist. As the waves washed up to the shoreline, with each wave that passed Johathan, he jumped up as if the waves were lifting him up. After a short time in the water, Johnathan decided to that he had enough for a while, as he just went into the water to cool off and headed back to his spot on the beach. When Johnathan returned to the spot where him and Samantha were, he saw that Smantha had woken up from her nap as well.

"How's the water?" Samantha asked.

Johnathan replied, "It's very refreshing."

"I think that I will go and cool off, too." Samantha got up and headed towards the water.

As Samantha was walking away, Johnathan watched her, thinking that she was absolutely beautiful. As to not stare at her, he looked around the entire beach at the crowd. Samantha was swimming for ten minutes, and then she had enough and decided to go back to their place they steaked out on the beach with Johnathan. Once she returned, Johnathan, he asked if she wanted to take a walk with him along the shoreline.

Johnathan and Samantha started walking the shoreline, and he asked her questions about her nudist lifestyle.

"Well, I been a nudist all my life. I was raised in a nudist family. Both my mother and father and my brother are all nudists. When we were growing up, my mother and father had a nice house out in the country where our closest neighbor was at least a quarter mile away, if not further. We had a four-bedroom, two bath house with a really nice porch, and we had a hot tub in it. It was a glass enclosed porch that had windows that opened, and it also had heating and air conditioning as well. Our family ran around the house totally naked all the time, all four of us. Then, my brother ended up getting married and is now raising his family as nudist and is doing the same thing with his family as what are family had done. I was the youngest, so I didn't leave the house until later. When I graduated high school and went off to college, I studied parapsychology, and that's why I now have a job as a ghost hunter."

"That's interesting," Johnathan said. "Have you ever caught anything when you do ghost hunting?"

"Oh, yeah!" Samantha said. "I've caught several things, numerous times. Sometimes, ghost hunting can be extremely scary, and that's why you shouldn't do any ghost hunting unless you know exactly what you are doing. But what about you? When did you become a nudist? And why did you join the military?"

Johnathan said, "That's a good question. Like you, my family were nudists all my life...probably before I was born. My father owned his own nudist resort, so that is where we lived. I don't have a sister, but I did have a brother. He passed away when he was fifteen due to drowning in the lake at our nudist resort. My parents warned us not to go down by the water. Of course, as we were young, we didn't listen. Then one day he and I went down to the lake and decided to get in to do some skinny dipping. It was fun at first because we have not been skinny dipping in the lake, but we were allowed to at the pool since there was a lifeguard on duty. The lake got to twenty feet deep in the middle, but just like this ocean, it starts out shallow and gets deeper as you go out. We were both pretty good swimmers, so we did not worry about swimming out to the center. Once we got out to the middle, both of us were ok, and then all of a sudden, my brother ended up getting a stomach cramp. We both tried to swim back to land. Unfortunately, I made it back, but my brother didn't. As I got back on land, I turned around just in time to see my brother go under. I ran home to tell my mom and dad, but by the time they got to the lake, it was too late. My brother had already drowned. My parents were distraught. I still blame myself for not doing more to help him, and now I am living with that and will live with that for the rest of my life. As for joining the Army, my brother and I made plans to join the Army together and stay together as cohort. At first, I did not want to join once I got to enlistment age, but because my mother and father knew that we wanted to join together, my mom talked me into joining, saying that my brother would still want me to join. That's when I went to the recruiter and did all the processing and enlisted."

Samantha was so emotional that she had tears in her eyes. She stopped walking and gave Johnathan a big hug.

"Wow," Johnathan said. "I haven't had a hug since I left home. I'm glad to have been able to hug you."

Samantha smiled. "If you ever need more hugs, I give them out for free."

Johnathan thanked Samantha as he took her hand into his and started walking again. While holding hands and walking, Johnathan asked Samantha what type of equipment she has for ghost hunting.

Samantha started rambling off all the equipment, such as digital voice recorders, ghost box, emf detector, laser grid, Boo buddy interactive bear, rem pods, and night vision cameras, just to name a few things. "I have more than that, but it would take me forever to name everything."

"I am so excited to go on this ghost hunt in October!" Johnathan said.

Samantha agreed with him. "Like I said, I do most of my ghost hunting completely naked in the good weather, so I hope that you are ok with that."

Johnathan was even more excited for this trip but told Samantha that he was perfectly fine with that. Johnathan once again asked if Watts was still able to go. Once again, Samantha said yes, as long as he is ok with everyone being naked, because it's not only her that was naked but her whole crew as well. Johnathan was sure that would be perfectly fine with Watts because from what Johnathan remembered, Watts was also a nudist and said so when he had his little powwow with his section. Johnathan took Samanthas hand, and they started their walk down the beach at the water's edge, people watching and enjoying the water washing up on their feet.

Johnathan and Samantha continued to walk down the beach, and suddenly, they walked into a part that where hardly anyone was on the beach. There was a run-down house and lifeguard shack up at the top of the beach that looked like it has been abandoned for years. There were signs stating, *No swimming. Lifeguards not present.* In all actuality, that section of the beach looked like it may be privately owned, although there was not a sign stating that it was private property.

As the sun was getting lower in the sky, Johnathan and Samantha turned around and started heading back. Although there was only three or four naked people on the beach, they were not swimming in the ocean but lying on the soft sand on their towels. After some time walking back, they started to see more people, and that's when they knew that they were getting closer to their spot. Still holding hands, both Samantha and Johnathan finally reached the place where all their stuff was. It was getting late in the afternoon and both decided to pack up and head out and take Johnathan back to Fort Carson. The drive back seemed to take less time than it did coming out as there was not as much traffic that they ran into. Once Samantha pulled up to the barracks, and before Johnathan got out of the car, Samantha unbuckled her seat belt and nearly jumped over the console to give Johnathan a kiss. Johnathan was pretty shocked but did not pull away and kissed Samantha back. When Samantha told Johnathan that she wanted to see him again, he was extremely excited. There was just something about Samantha that he loved about her but couldn't point out exactly what, but all he knew was that he just loved Samantha being around him.

Chapter Three

Private Watts

When Monday came around and another work week, Sergeant Johnanthan Smith and his section were doing the same old routine: up at 0500, getting ready for and doing PT. As the PT instructor assembled the unit for the morning run, he asked if there was a sergeant or higher that would like to call cadence for the run. No one sounded off until Private Watts said that he would. The PT instructor asked what section he was in and if it ok with his chief. Johnathan sounded off in the group and said that was fine, that if wanted to call cadence, he could. That was how he would learn: by doing. Once they got started and running at a mild pace, Watts stepped out of formation, took his place in the outside center, and started calling cadence. *C-one thirty rolling down the strip, airborne ranger on a one-way trip.* He kept singing other cadences until they got back to the PT field. Once back, the PT instructor took over again and did some cooldown and stretching exercises. Once finished, he had told Private Watts to get with his chief. Then if his chief did not have anything for him to do, he could take the day off.

After the battery was dismissed, Sergeant Smith held his section up for a few minutes to give them a breakdown for the day. "Get showered and dressed. Chow is from 0730 to 0830 hours. Everyone out front for formation by no later 0845, which is First Sergeant's time. Watts, enjoy your day off, but I do want to meet up with you later on."

Private Watts agreed.

Johnathan said, "Let's meet up at 1300 hours in your barracks room."

After the section got ready and had their first formation, everyone went down to the motor pool to do maintenance once again. They all worked throughout the morning while Watts went to the rec center to watch some tv and play a little pool. He was the only one there because it was a workday, so he could practice his pool shooting skills. As the morning seemed to fly by, it was soon 1100 hours and time to head back to the barracks.

Once Watts was back at the barracks, he waited in his room until 1130 hours, then he headed over to the chow hall. When he went in, there were only two other soldiers in front of him, so he pulled out his meal card, gave the soldier that was at the desk his last four of his social, and signed the roster. He went through the lunch line, got his lunch, sat down, and ate. He sat there for a little while, waiting until 1230 hours, took his tray to the tray drop, and headed back to his barracks room to wait for 1300 hours. At 1315 hours, he finally heard a knock at his door. Watts opened the door and invited Johnathan in.

Watts asked, "What's up, Chief?"

"Nothing much," Johnathan said. "I just wanted to have a little talk to you about October but didn't want to do it in front of the entire section. This is a conservation is between me and you only, so if the rest of the section or even the rest of the unit finds out anything I am about to discuss with you...well, I will know where it came from."

Watts said, "I won't say anything to anyone."

"First thing is that you know that I am a nudist, right?"

Watts nodded.

"Ok, so I have met this girl that's also a nudist. She is also a ghost hunter. We went to the nudist beach this past Saturday, and I had a wonderful time with her. I guess that we are dating now, which is beside the point. Just wanted to tell you that for our ghost hunting trip in October is nudist ghost hunting. Not only are Samantha and I going to be naked, but her entire team is also going to be naked. Is that something that is going to bother you? I know that you said that you were a nudist as well, but I just wanted to make sure before we go. Don't want to freak you out when we get there."

Watts told Johnathan, "No problem at all, I think it's going to be great and can I be naked as well."

"Absolutely you can...that would be perfect. It may be a little chilly, but we will be inside a historic location. If I'm not mistaken, it still has electricity and heat in there, so we should be ok and not freeze."

Private Watts was a little relieved. "I can't wait, and I can't wait to meet Samantha, as well. I just want to let you know that I have been a nudist all my life and grew up as a nudist. I absolutely love doing nudist things."

"Wow! You sound just like me," said Johnathan. "If Samantha and I go back to the nude beach, would you like to go with us? Of course, you will need to keep that hush hush as you know that lower enlisted is not allowed to hang out with NCOs."

"Yeah, I know, but I do want to go with you guys."

"Cool. I will call Samantha and see if we can go back to the nude beach this weekend unless you have other plans."

"What other plans would I have? I am a private, living in the barracks, with no car to go anywhere."

Johnathan laughed. "I know. I was in your position when I first joined the Army." He then took out his phone and dialed Samantha's number. She answered, and he put it on speaker phone. "Samantha, I am here with Watts, and I have you on speaker phone. I just had a talk with Watts, and he informed me that he is and has been a nudist as well. I—well, we —would like to know if all three of us can go back to the nude beach again Saturday?"

Samantha chuckled, and then said, "Sure we can! I had a great time with you this past Saturday."

Watts yelled out, "Yay! I can't wait. It's been years since I was able to get back to a nude beach. This is so exciting."

The next Saturday, Samantha pulled up to the barracks once again to pick up the guys and honked her horn. They both came out with their beach towels.

Their friend, Sergeant Garrett, saw them and asked, "Where are you guys going?"

Johnathan said, "We are just heading to the pool with my girlfriend."

"Oh, ok," said Garrett. "Have fun!"

"Whew!" Johnathan said. "I am so glad that I can think on my toes! That wouldn't have been good."

Watts agreed climbing up in the back of the SUV. "How long will it be before we get there?"

"Roughly half hour to forty-five minutes," Samantha replied. "Nice to meet you."

"You, too. Would it be ok if I take a nap?"

"Of course!" Samantha put the Jeep into gear. We'll wake you up once we get there."

After a lot of driving and conversation, they finally arrived.

Johnathan woke Watts. "Come on, soldier. Wake up! We're here."

As Watts opened his eyes and looked out the car window, he saw people walking towards the beach entrance. "Oh, wow. This is nice. How long is the walk to the beach?"

"It is about a five-minute walk, so let's go." Johnathan swung the door open.

They all grabbed everything out of the rear of the SUV, loaded it up in the wagon just like the last week, and headed off towards the beach entrance. Once they got to the beach entrance and walked down what looked like a runway, they finally reached the end of the walkway. They found a nice spot just to the right of the lifeguard stand in the middle of the beach. There were more people there this weekend than last weekend, but according to Watts, he loved that. The more people the better, he had said, and Johnathan agreed with him.

When the three of them got situated and settled, Samantha asked both of the guys if they would like to go swimming with her. Watts said yes.

Johnathan did not want to at the moment. "You guys go have fun."

"We'll be out there in the water if you decide that you want to join us," Samantha replied.

As Watts and Samantha went out into the ocean up to their waist deep, they were talked.

Samantha said, "Johnathan said that you were a nudist pretty much all your life, as well."

"Yes, I grew up in a nudist household and totally loved it. My mom and dad ran around the house totally naked all the time, and once I got old enough, they instilled the nudist lifestyle in me, as well. Johnathan told me that you are a nudist ghost hunter as well?" he asked Samantha.

"Yes, I am a nudist ghost hunter! My ghost hunting team are nudists, too."

"Cool. You don't mind if I go in October? Johnathan said that you said it would be ok." Watts knelt down in the water, so it came up to his chin.

"Yup. You're more than welcome to come. We are doing it naked as well, so is that going to bother you? I know you're a nudist, but I'm not sure what your limits are." She walked out a little further, so the water went up to her shoulders.

Watts swam out to meet her. "I'd try it. It would be fun going to do the ghost hunting naked."

"Awesome," Samantha said. "I can't wait till October. I had my researcher look into this location, and it turns out that it's very dark. Not dark as in light and dark, but dark as in demonic spirits."

Watts's heart started racing, as he never did any ghost hunting before. "I can't wait."

Samantha and Watts were still in the ocean floating around with the waves making them bob up and down like a fishing bobber and kept talking about the upcoming trip. Samantha was going over the equipment and what each piece of equipment does. Even though there was not a piece of equipment there, she thought it was best to at least explain it to Watts. Since this was Watts very first investigation and never worked a piece of ghost investigation equipment, he paid close attention to Samantha and what she was saying.

"That is so awesome," Watts said. "Can I use some equipment when we go?"

"Yes, you can use some of the equipment. When we get there, I'll have my tech guy go over everything with you again. You can actually see how things work since we'll have all the equipment there."

Johnathan come out to join them finally. "What are you guys talking about?"

"I was just explaining some of the ghost hunting equipment to Watts," Samantha told him.

"Thats cool. So what do you think, Watts? Are you still interested in going on this ghost investigation?"

"I'm totally interested! I'm going to do it naked, as well." Watts paused. "I'm going to research on how to do a ghost investigation. That way, I'll be completely ready."

Samantha smiled. "That's good, but don't stress over it too much. We will be with you and teach you. But like I said, my researcher said that this location is rumored to be demonic. Are you both sure that you want to go?"

"Absolutely!" Johnathan and Watts said in unison.

Samantha laughed.

Johnathan said, "I wouldn't miss it for the world. Well, only if the Army sends me away to a war zone or new duty station, and I don't think that's going to happen for quite some time."

Watts agreed. "I wouldn't miss that for the world, either...the same as Chief said."

"Well, it's settled then. I'll let my team know that we'll be investigating Moon Bay Cottage. So get ready, because I haven't investigated anything like this before. Hotels, trains, restaurants, yes...but nothing like this. There's no guarantee what we will find in there or what evil we may encounter. Make sure that you two want to go with us. There's no shame in backing out."

Both men nodded, with Johnathan adding, "We're not scared...we are soldiers."

"That doesn't mean anything," Samantha said. "No matter what work you do, there can also be a chance that something can attach to you. You can bring it back, and your life can be a living hell if that happens."

Later in day, the three of them packed up the car. On the way back, Watts was in the back seat again, which he did not mind at all. That way he could take another nap. It was nearly dusk, and they were getting back on the road. Watts laid back down in the back seat, just staring up and out of the car door window. It was a clear night, and the quarter moon was high up in the sky. He was just looking at the moon and admiring how pretty it was, and he was thinking about home and how he would sit out on the front stoop of his house, just looking at the moon for hours at a time. Watts finally drifted off to sleep, but it did not seem for long before Johnathan woke him up and said were back.

"Ugh. Already?"

"Yeah, already," Johnathan said. "And now that we are back on post, we need to go back to military bearing."

"I know," Watts said. "I am well aware of that." He said goodbye to Samantha, then headed into the barracks.

Johnathan stayed at the car for a few more minutes. He and Samantha both got out, and Johnathan gave her a hug and a kiss and said good night.

When Watts was back in his room, he decided to go ahead and get naked once inside the door. He didn't even let the door close all the way before he started taking off his clothes. Then, he grabbed a towel and his hygiene items and headed to the showers to wash all the sand, sunscreen, and ocean salt off. Once the shower was over, Watts headed back to his room, wearing only his towel. Once back inside his room, he took the towel off and got into his bunk totally naked, not even caring if his roommates saw him naked or not. He drifted off to sleep, dreaming about the upcoming ghost investigation.

Chapter Four

The Paranormal Team

The next day, Samantha called Johnathan at 0900 hours and told him that she was going to pick him and Watts up at 1100 hours to meet her paranormal team and that one of her team members said that he was going to treat everyone to lunch. Johnathan said that was very nice of him, but he could pay for himself and Watts. Samantha said that it was all settled and that they didn't need to worry, but to just be ready at 1100 hours. At 1030 hours, Johnathan went up to Watts barracks room, then knocked on the door. Watts roommate answered the door wearing only his physical training shorts, and when he saw SSG Smith standing there, he told Watts that his chief was there. Watts jumped down from the top bunk.

"Ready?" Johnathan asked.

"Yup. I am all ready."

Johnathan said, "We better get downstairs. Samantha made me promise her that we'd be ready for her when she gets here."

When Johnathan and Watts went down and outside, there was a cast iron bench that was installed right outside the barracks, so they utilized the new bench and sat on it, waiting. Watts said that it was a great idea someone had to put this bench here, and Johnathan agreed.

At 1100 hours, right on time, Samantha pulled up. Johnathan got in the front seat, and he leaned over and gave Samantha a kiss, while Watts got in the back seat.

Samantha said, "My team was going to meet us at the pizza place we went to the other day. They are going to get the party room for us."

"I didn't know that they even had a party room," Johnathan said.

"Yes, it's in the back, and it needs to be reserved. Tom called in yesterday and lucked out that no one had it reserved for today, so he got it for us." Samantha pulled through the gate and onto the main road.

"That's cool. I'm excited to meet your team."

As Samantha drove to the pizza restaurant, they talked about the upcoming paranormal investigation at Moon Bay Cottage and how and what it was going to be like. When they reached the shopping center where the pizza restaurant was, Samantha drove past the front, looking for a parking spot. She saw her team walk in the front door of the restaurant. As she rode by, she beeped her horn, and they all turned around and watched them ride by and waved at them. Samantha waved back.

Tom led the team inside, waiting for them to come in.

As everyone walked in, the hostess asked, "How many in your party?"

Tom said, "There's going to be nine, and we are just waiting for the other three to come in. They are parking right now. I have reservations for the private room."

"Sure thing," the hostess said. "Just give me a minute to make sure everything is ready for you."

As Samantha, Johnathan, and Watts came in, they greeted the rest of the team at the hostess podium.

Tom said, "We're just waiting to see if our room is ready. The hostess said she'd be right back."

A few minutes later, the hostess came back and told them to follow her. She led the way, with everyone following her to the private party room.

"Here you go. Have a seat, and your waitress will be right with you all," she said brightly.

They thanked her, and then they all took a seat. Johnathan sat right next to Samanth. Everyone else took their seat, and Watts sat next to one of the girls that was on the team.

Samantha started to introduce everyone. "Team, this is Johnathan, my boyfriend. He is a staff sergeant at Fort Carson. This is Private Watts, who is in Johnathan's section. They're in an artillery unit, so they shoot cannons for a living. Johnathan and Watts, this is Tom, my tech operations for all the equipment. This is Julia, my researcher for the locations that we will be investigating. Then, we have Amy and River that are with me during the investigations. And last but not least, we have Ryker and Grayson. They monitor the equipment and our command center. We always have a command center with camera monitors."

"Hello, everyone. Nice to meet all of you." Johnathan said, then turned to Samantha, who was talking with the team.

It turned out that Watts sat down beside Amy, which was on purpose because Watts thought that Amy was very pretty, and deep down, he wanted to talk to her.

Tom told them to order what they wanted as he was paying for everyone.

As the waitress came over, she asked, "Can I start you all off with some drinks?"

"Sure," Samantha said. "I'd like to have a sweet tea."

Tom, Johnathan, and Watts ordered sodas, while Julia, Amy, River, Ryker, and Grayson ordered water with lemon.

"I will be right back with your drinks." The waitress put her notepad in her apron before walking away.

It took maybe three minutes before the waitress came back with another waiter who was carrying trays with their drinks. "Are you guys ready to order now?"

"Yes, I think we are." Tom responded.

They placed their orders, and the waitress told them that she would get the order right in. As the team continued to talk, Watts and Amy were talking amongst themselves.

Amy twirled her straw in her drink. "Watts, have you ever had been on a paranormal investigation?"

Watts said, "No, but I have had some paranormal encounters when I was younger at my parents' house."

"Wow. Was it scary? I do ghost investigations, and I never had any bad encounters as of yet, knock on wood."

After that brief talk between the two of them, they turned their attention to the rest of the group having the conservation. They were talking about the upcoming investigation of Moon Bay Cottage. Julia chimed in and told everyone that during her research, she came across some information about Moon Bay Cottage. It was rumored to have some demonic spirits in and on the property, but that was something that they would have to find out when we they did their investigation.

The waitress finally came back with the same waiter, carrying the trays of food. She asked each one of them who ordered what again, as there were nine orders, and she couldn't remember who ordered what. After all the orders were given out, the waitress asked if there was anything else that she could get for them. No one needed anything else at that time. As the team was eating, they continued their conservation about the upcoming investigation.

Watts finally got the nerve up to ask Amy out on a date while all the other team members were involved in talking about the investigation. Watts was nervous about asking, mostly because he did not have a car to get around, since he was basically right out of basic training. He felt embarrassed about it.

"It is perfectly fine. I totally understand. Don't be embarrassed about that. I get that it takes time to get settled in and get things." Amy said, smiling.

Watts was really excited, as he has not been on a date in several years even before he decided to join the Army.

As lunch was winding down and everyone was finishing up, Tom asked for the check. The waitress came back with it, and Tom gave her his credit card. She went to run the card in the machine. The waitress came back with Tom's credit card, and he handed her a cash tip. They all got up and headed out. When they all got outside, Samantha gave her entire team a hug goodbye, and her and Johnathan headed to her car. Watts told them that he would be right there.

As the rest of the team headed to their car, Watts and Amy were finishing up the plans for Friday.

"Well, what do you think about Friday around one, the day before our investigation?" Watts asked.

"That sounds wonderful. I'll be at your barracks at one on the thirtieth."

Watts asked, "Would like to go to lunch? Then, there is a planetarium at the science center, if you would like to go."

"Of course! I absolutely love planetariums. I love learning about space, and sometimes, I wonder why I became a paranormal investigator instead of an astronomer. I guess I could still do that."

Watts said, "It's a date, then. I can't wait to go out with you."

As Amy and Watts finished up the date plans, they both headed to the prospective cars.

When Watts got in Samantha's car, Johnathan grinned. "I thought I heard you ask Amy out on a date."

"Yup, I sure did," Watts said.

Samantha said, "That's great! Amy deserves to go out on a nice date with a nice guy. She was put through the wringer by her ex-boyfriend. She's such a nice girl. I'm glad that you two are going to see each other. When are you going out?"

"The day before we go on the investigation. But we're going during the day, so we aren't up late before we head out to Moon Bay Cottage."

"That's nice. Where are you two going?" Samantha pulled out of the parking lot.

"We're going to lunch, then I am taking her to the planetarium."

"Oh, wow," Johnathan said. "I haven't been to one of those since I was in school on a field trip. That sounds like a wonderful date, better than what I ever could come up with. You'll have to let us know how it turns out."

"I definitely will," Watts told them. "I haven't been on a date in several years...since before I decided to join the Army."

Johnathan grabbed Samantha's free hand. "It's like riding a bike. You never forget how to do it."

Watts laughed, thinking about the upcoming adventures.

Chapter Five

Samantha

Samantha had been ghosting for years and already had the equipment that would be used for the upcoming ghost hunting trip with Johnathan and Watts. Some of her equipment was older and could have used an update to the latest and greatest technology, but the equipment was expensive. She did not have the funds to purchase anything new. She wanted a new SLR mapping camera and new electronic voice recorders. The SLR mapping camera was about $1,500 for a really good one, and the electronic voice recorders were $700 a piece. Samantha needed at least one SLR mapping camera and at least two electronic voice recorders. All, together, it would cost nearly $3,000 to upgrade her equipment. Since her credit cards were maxed out, there was no way that she would be able to pay for the new equipment. With the investigation was fast approaching, she was really hoping that the equipment she already had would be ok and last long enough to get through the night. She definitely wanted to make Johnathan aware of the equipment issue. Not that she wanted him to buy anything; she just wanted to make him aware of the condition.

Samantha got her phone and dialed Johnathan's number.

After four rings Johnathan answered. "Hey, Samantha. I was just thinking about you."

"I just wanted to talk to you about the equipment that I have."

"Sure," Johnathan said. "What about it?"

"Well, you realize that I have been ghost hunting for a while now, right? I was going through and checking the equipment out. The SLR mapping camera is pretty old and so are my EVP recorders. When I went to do a run-through on the camera, it broke, and I wasn't getting any pictures on it. As for the electronic voice recorders, I also checked them. I was not expecting them to go kerplunk as well, and as I was testing them, my voice came in all broken up on both of them. I took the equipment to be repaired, and the tech got the camera kind of working, but he told me that I need a new camera. As for the EVP recorders, he couldn't get them working correctly. He told me that because they are fairly old, there's no parts available for them. He recommended that I buy new upgraded equipment. I don't have the money to buy the new equipment. While I do still want to go on this investigation with you and Watts, we may not be able to do any EVPs. I'm so sorry." She paused. "Do you and Watts still want to go?"

"Of course we do," said Johnathan. "How much would the new equipment cost?"

"With everything, the SLR mapping camera and two electronic voice recorders, it will be roughly three grand. I'm not telling you this for you to buy the new equipment...I just don't want you to be disappointed."

"I know you're not, Samantha, but I want to help you out. After all, the investigation is only three days away. Tell you what. Why don't you come and pick me up around 1700 hours this afternoon, and we can go and look at the new equipment."

"Really, Johnathan...that is a lot of money for the equipment."

"It's ok, Samantha. Just come to post and pick me up. We'll go look at new equipment, and I'll also treat you to dinner."

"Aww, Johnathan, dinner would be awesome! But I'll feel terrible if you buy the equipment."

"Don't worry about it, Samantha. Just be here at five."

Johnathan was super excited about seeing Samantha that afternoon, and the rest of the day, he could not get her off his mind. It seemed like he was falling in love for the first time in a long time. Johnathan continued throughout the rest of the afternoon, wishing that 1600 hours would hurry up and get here. Once 1600 hours came and Johnathan had final formation for the day, he hurried to get a shower. He dressed in a nice pair of khaki pants with a form-fitting black shirt and waited outside for Samantha to pull up. Samantha pulled up at 1710 hours, late as usual. Johnathan couldn't help but to laugh at her.

"Late as usual," he said, grinning at her.

Samantha was embarrassed. "I'm so sorry."

"It's perfectly fine," Johnathan said. "I'm just joking with you. I couldn't wait to see you this afternoon."

"Really?" Samantha said shyly.

"Yup, for sure. Let's go and look at the equipment that you may need first before we go to dinner."

"Ok," said Samantha, and they headed to the paranormal equipment store.

As Samantha and Johnathan entered the store, they noticed a younger gentleman standing behind a display case with a numerous amount of EVP recorders. "Can I help you?"

Johnanthan looked in the case. "We are looking for some equipment. Samantha, what will you need?"

She walked over to the EVP recorders where the clerk was standing. "I am looking for a couple EVP recorders, and I need a SLR mapping camera."

"Sure," the clerk said. "Since we're already here with the EVP recorders, let's have a look." The guy pulled out several different models by price range from least expensive to most expensive. He started to explain what the difference is between each one and what other benefits that each one has.

Samantha still thought that even the cheapest one was way too much money. The ones Samantha had were bought years ago, and even the most expensive one was not even close to the price of the cheapest one today. Samantha weighed her options.

Johnathan asked her, "What do you think, sweetheart?"

Samantha didn't want to offend the salesperson, so she whispered, "These are very expensive. I don't want to get any of these."

"Well," Johanthan said. "You're not buying them, I am. So, what do you think?"

"I really like the one on the end, but it's a thousand dollars."

Johnathan said, "Good. Sir, we'll take two of those, please."

Samantha was shocked because she did not want Johnathan buying her those. She started to protest.

Johnathan just smiled at her, then asked the salesperson, "Now what about a SLR mapping camera?"

The salesman took them to the other side of the shop. On the wall behind him were several different cameras that had a huge difference between them.

The salesman pulled out four different SLR mapping cameras in the display case that was on the wall behind him. As with the EVP recorders, the guy also explained the difference between the cameras and the price range. Samantha picked each one of the cameras up and tinkered around with them.

After about ten minutes, Johnathan asked Samantha, "Do you know which one you like?"

Samantha pointed to the one she liked.

Johnathan asked the salesman, "How much is this one again?"

"This one is $2,100," the salesman said.

"Ok, we will take it," Johnathan said.

Samantha turned around and told Johnathan, "There is no way, I can't let you buy that...it's way too expensive."

Johnathan once again told the salesman, "We'll take that one."

"Let me go in the back and grab you one." The clerk wrote down the model number and headed in the back storage room to get one.

While he was gone, Samantha tried to talk Johnathan out of buying it. "We can use what I have now. It's way too much."

"It's a done deal, so there's no more discussion about it."

"Oh, Johnathan," Samantha said. "I really appreciate this. I'm starting to love you more and more each and every day."

"I love you more each day also, Samantha."

After a few minutes the salesman came back out carrying a box with the camera in. The salesman asked if there was anything else that he could help them with.

Johnathan looked at Samantha. "Is there anything else that you need? Speak now before we leave the store."

"Umm, I don't think so."

Johnathan asked her, "Are you sure?"

"Yes, I'm sure. All my other equipment is pretty new. These things I had for several years, and they're beginning to break down."

Johnathan looked at the salesperson. "That will be all for now."

"Sure. If you wouldn't mind stepping over here, I will check you guys out." As the salesman started scanning the item barcodes, he asked them if they would like a two-year warranty on the EVP recorders for and extra $60.

Samantha said no, but Johnathan said, "Yes, we want the warranty."

The salesman added the extended warranty to the bill, then he scanned the camera, and the camera rang up as $1,900. "Oh, look the camera is on sale for two hundred off.

"Thats awesome!" said Johnathan and Samantha at the same time.

Then the salesman asked if they would like an extended two-year warranty on the camera for an additional $70, to which Johnathan agreed.

Once the salesman finished ringing up the EVPs, the camera, and the extended warranty's, the total came out to be $4,335.

The salesman asked Johnathan, "Are you in the military?"

Johnathan nodded. "Yes, I am."

"Thats great. You know you can get a fifteen percent discount, right? All I need to do is scan the back of your military ID, and it will automatically apply."

"Sweet!" Johnathan got his military ID out of his wallet and handed it to the salesman.

The salesman scanned it, and it automatically put the discount on the total price. So now instead of everything being $4,335, it brought the total amount down to $3,684.75.

"Wow," Johnathan said. "That's one hell of a discount!"

"Yup," the salesman said, as he grabbed a big bag with handles and packed up all the equipment.

As the salesman did that, Johnathan got his credit card out of his wallet, and when the salesman was ready, he handed it to him. The salesman put the card into the chip reader, and the pos took a minute, but it eventually came across as approved. Johnathan signed the electronic display. The salesman handed Samantha the bag and wished them a nice day and thanked them both.

AS Samantha and Johnathan were walking back to Samanthas car, she asked Johnathan if he wanted to come over to her house. Johnathan didn't want to turn the invitation down but wanted to grab a bite to eat first.

"Absolutely," Samantha said. "I'm getting hungry because I did not eat any lunch. I was saving my appetite for this evening."

Johnathan asked Samantha where she wanted to go.

"I think we could do Carrabba's. After all, I do love their dread and oil dip."

Johnathan gave a chuckle and said, "That sounds great. Carrabba's it is, then."

"I'll treat you, Johnathan, since you just put out three thousand and some odd dollars for my ghost hunting stuff."

"I don't mind treating you," he responded.

"No, I'll treat you. Johnathan, I owe this to you."

"Ok, if you insist, I'll let you treat. Afterwards are we going to your house?"

"Yes, I invited you over to my house, and I would love you to come over. We can hang out naked and watch a movie. Not like you haven't seen each other naked before." She laughed.

"I can't wait." He reached for her hand.

Once at Carrabba's, Samantha and Johnathan were seated by the hostess and were handed a menu. While looking over the menu, their waiter came over with fresh, warm bread and the oil dip seasoning. "Can I get you something to drink?"

Samantha said, "I would like a glass of Chardonnay."

"And for you, sir?"

"I'd just like a coke, please."

"Are you ready to place your order, or would you like a few more minutes?" The waiter looks at each of them.

"Can you give us a few more minutes, please?" Samantha said.

"Sure, let me grab your drinks, and I'll be right back." Once the waiter got their drinks and came back to their table, he said, "Are you ready to order?"

"Sure, you go first, Samantha." Johnathan stared at the menu.

"I would like the chicken fettuccini Alfredo," she said.

"And for you, sir?"

"I would like the same thing, please.?

"Sure thing," the waiter said. "I'll get that right in for you."

Once Johnathan and Samantha ate dinner, they paid their tab and headed out to the car to go over to Samantha's house.

When they arrived at Samantha's house and walked in the door, the first thing Johnathan saw was a sign that read, *Warning! You May Encounter Nudity Beyond This Point.*

Johnathan laughed, then said, "That is so cool. where did you get that?"

"I ordered it off the internet. I love it."

"Thats awesome," Johnathan said, and then he asked Samantha if he could take a quick shower.

"Of course you can, Johnathan. I will get you a towel and wash cloth. The bathroom is the second door on your right down the hallway."

"Sweet," Johnathan said, "I won't be long." Then Johnathan went in and took his shower which he only took maybe ten minutes.

Once he was done, he walked out into the living room totally naked, and he saw Samantha sitting on the couch naked as well.

"Looks like we had the same idea," he said.

"I was just waiting for you to get done so I can go and take my shower."

"You should've said something, and you could've gone first."

She said, "No, you are my guest, so you go first. And after I'm done taking a shower, we'll pick out a movie to watch."

When Samantha was done with her shower, she came out and joined Johnathan on the couch, and they both tried to pick out a movie. After they both agreed on a movie, Samantha went in to make some popcorn. After she got back from the kitchen, Samantha put the movie on. The movie took an hour and forty-five minutes, and after the movie, Samantha offered for Johnathan to stay overnight.

"Sure, I will stay."

"You are more than welcome to sleep in my bed with me."

That caught Johnathan by surprise. "I will just sleep on the couch and be a gentleman."

"Are you sure?" Samantha asked.

"Yes, I am certain."

Samantha went and got Johnathan some sheets, a pillow, and a blanket, then put them on the couch for him. "Once we wake up tomorrow, I would like to ride past Moon Bay Cottage just to get a glimpse of what we are in for next week."

The next morning at nine, Samantha finally woke up and tip-toed into the living room to not wake Johnathan up. He was already sitting up on the couch with the blanket over him.

"Good morning. Would you like a cup of coffee, Johnathan?"

"Absolutely!"

"Ok. I'll make the coffee and some breakfast for us. How do you like your eggs?" she asked.

"Scrambled."

"Would you like sausage, bacon, or both?"

"I would like bacon, please."

"Ok. Coming right up?"

After they got finished eating breakfast, Samantha cleaned up with Johnathan's help, then they both got dressed and headed outside. Johnathan asked if they were going to do a ride by Moon Bay Cottage.

"Of course we are! I'm interested to see what we'll be walking into next week."

"Me, too," Johnathan said. "This is going to be so exciting. I can't wait to do this ghost investigation with you and the brand-new equipment we got yesterday."

"That reminds me! I need to make sure that I charge all the batteries up. When I get home, I'll connect all the batteries to the charger. Everything will be ready to go when the time comes to do the investigation."

After they got in the car, they headed towards Moon Bay Cottage. As Samantha was driving, Johnathan was trying to do more research on his phone. Every time he tried to pull up Moon Bay Cottage, he would get an error message that would pop up on the phone screen.

He was confused. "Samantha, every time I try to pull up Moon Bay Cottage, there is always an error message no matter how I try and word it."

Samantha gave Johnathan a suggestion to try and type in myths and legends and see what comes up. When Johnathan typed that suggestion in, a whole slew of things came up. There was an option in the search bar that to type in something specific. So, Johnathan typed in Moon Bay Cottage and hit the search. Moon Bay Cottage finally showed up with several paragraphs and a couple pictures as well.

"Here we go. It finally came up," he told Samantha.

She was driving so she couldn't read it. "What does it say?"

Johnathan started to read what it said to Samantha. "Here it says that Moon Bay Cottage has been around for decades and has been rumored to be haunted by the Vanderbilts. It also says here that people passing by have reported seeing a lady dressed in 1800s period clothing standing in the window, and then, she just vanishes."

"This is really going to be interesting. I can't wait to investigate with my boyfriend!" She gave him a smile.

Chapter Six

Research on Moon Bay Cottage

Three weeks had passed since the three of them had visited the nude beach, but Johnathan and Samantha kept in touch daily. Whether Johnathan called Samantha or Samantha called Johnathan, they talked on the phone daily. The last time that they had talked, Samantha told Johnathan that he and Watts needed to do some research on Moon Bay Cottage. Johnathan told Samantha that they would do the research since the investigation was only a week away. She reminded him that her researcher discovered that Moon Bay Cottage was extremely haunted and that it could even had some demonic entities in it. While she totally trusted her researcher, she was curious what they would come up with, to see if they would find out the same thing. Johnathan told Samantha that he would be honored for them to do research for her. After Johnathan hung up the phone, he immediately went to Watts room, knocked on the door, and waited for an answer.

Watts's roommate answered the door and saw that it was Sergeant Smith, and he immediately yelled for Watts. "Watts, your chief is here. Come in, Sergeant."

Watts sat up in his bunk. "What's up, Chief?"

"I need to holler at you for a minute. Can we go to the day room?"

"Sure. Let me grab some shorts and a shirt. I'll meet you down there in a minute." Watts jumped down from the top bunk.

After Private Watts got dressed, he headed down the hall to the day room and saw Johnathan playing with the bumper pool table.

"I'm here, Chief." What's up?

SSG Johnathan put the pool stick back on the table. "Let's sit down."

They both sat on the leather couch that was over on the back wall facing towards the pool table and the tv.

"Samantha wants us both to start researching Moon Bay Cottage. I'm going to start tomorrow, but I'm open to doing the research together if you want to."

Pvt Watts said, "I would be glad to do it together, Sergeant."

"Good. Let's start tomorrow after work. Since today's Friday, we can work on the research all day then."

When Saturday came, Johnathan went to Watts barracks room around 0900 hours. He knocked on the door. Watts was already up and dressed but was being quiet as his roommates were still sleeping. He went to the door to meet Johnathan. Stepping out of his room, they then headed outside to Johnathan's car.

Watts was shocked that the sergeant had a car and asked, "Is this your car?"

"Yes, this is my car...why do you ask?" Johnathan unlocked his door.

"I always thought that you didn't have a car and that's why we rode with Samantha when we went to the nude beach."

"Oh, that's because she wanted to drive, and Samantha's vehicle has a lot more room than mind does." Johnathan laughed and told Watts to hop in so they could get to the library.

The first library that they stopped at was on post, and as Johnathan found a parking spot, he asked, "Watts, well, are you ready to go learn some things?"

"Absolutely!" Watts said.

They headed inside. As they walked inside the post library, the first place they went was the information desk.

The lady at the desk asked, "Can I help you gentleman?"

Johnathan said, "Yes, do you have any reference materials on Moon Bay Cottage?"

The lady at the desk said, "I've heard of that place, but I'm not sure if we will have anything on it." She typed into the computer. "Hmm. We used to have a lot of books and reference on that place, but seems like we don't have them here anymore. I don't know why we don't, and the computer doesn't explain it. I'm sorry, guys."

"That's ok. Thanks anyway." Watts said, and the two of them headed back to Johnathan's car. "What do we do now?"

Johnathan said, "There is a public library just outside of post, right in town. We'll go check there."

"Sounds good," Watts said. "I hope that they have information there. They should because it's a public library and not like a cheesy library like what the post has."

Johnathan and Watts passed through the MP gate, and once they got past the guard shack, Johnathan picked up speed to the posted speed limit. After a few short minutes, they found the library, and once again found a parking spot, parked, and went inside. Johnathan went one way, and Watts went the other way, both looking for the reference section. They both must have passed it because neither one of them saw where it was. They both met at the information desk.

Johnanthan asked the gentleman behind the desk, "Excuse me, but do you have any references on Moon Bay Cottage?"

"I believe we do...give me a minute to check our database." He searched the computer. "Oh, yeah. We have a lot of information on it." He took out a pen and grabbed a piece of scrap paper, then jotted down the reference numbers. Once he was finished, he led Johnathan and Watts to the area where the information they were looking for was and showed them the entire area.

"Thank you," Johnathan said to the information clerk.

The section that had all the information on Moon Bay Cottage was a fairly large section, so large that it took up two complete shelves.

Watts said, "Awesome! This is exactly what we need."

They both started grabbing the books that they thought would be beneficial in their research. Once they got all the books that they could carry, they headed over to one of the tables that was set up in one of the corners of the library where they could have the privacy and be away from prying eyes. Johnathan sat on one side of the table while Watts sat on the other side across from him.

"Dig in" Johnathan said, like they had a pile of steamed crabs in the center of the table.

The first book that Johnathan picked was called, *The Mystery of Moon Bay Cottage*. Johnathan flipped open the book to the table of contents and ran his finger down as if he was feeling for something, but then came to a section that read, "Mysterious Hauntings." He then flipped the book to the beginning page. Once he got to the page, he was read the information in paragraph two. *There have been many sightings of apparitions in the windows of Moon Bay Cottage. No one knows who* the ghost is or even if the sightings are real, as there have been people that just passed by and reported on it. To date, there have not been any paranormal teams that investigated Moon Bay Cottage. "Interesting."

Watts said, "What's that, Sarge?"

"Here it says that there have not been any paranormal investigations by any paranormal teams to date. If this is true, we'll be the very first." Johnathan took a piece of paper and jotted down some notes on it.

The next book that Watts picked out of the pile was called, *The Haunting at Moon Bay Cottage*. Unlike Johnathan, Watts skipped over the table of contents and just started flipping through the book when there was a chapter that caught his eye. The chapter title was called, "Ghostly Apparitions at Moon Bay Cottage." As Watts read through the chapter, he also took his spiral notebook and wrote down his notes.

Watts looked up at Johnathan and said, "Here it says that there's a rumor that says that Moon Bay Cottage was built back in the 1800s, and there have been recorded deaths in the house and on the property. The deaths are believed to be of a girl named Mildred, age 12, who died of diseases in 1812. Then Ryan, age 16, who believed to have died back in 1815 from an accident. They were brother and sister, but it doesn't say what the accident was in here. Till this day, no one really knows what happened to their parents."

"This is starting to get really interesting," Johnathan said. "Let's see what other information we can gather here. If we can't get much more information, I'll call Samantha and see if there is anything else that we can do."

Johnathan and Watts stayed and looked through the rest of the books, and when 1300 hours hit, they both decided that was enough research for the day. They got up from the table, left the books there, pushed in the chairs, and walked outside.

Watts rubbed his forehead. "I have a small headache from looking through all those books, and I'm hungry, too."

"I'm hungry as well," Johnathan said. "Let's go get some lunch, my treat."

"Are you sure?" Watts asked.

"Yes, I'll treat. Where do you want to go?"

"I have no idea, Sarge."

"There is a great pizza place just down the road, if that's something that you would like."

"That sounds great," Watts said. "I absolutely love pizza."

"Pizza it is," said Johnathan.

Once inside the pizza parlor, they had to wait for the hostess to seat them.

The hostess finally came up to the front. "How many in your party?"

"Just the two of us," Johnathan said. "We would like a table, please. Preferably somewhere in a corner, if that's ok."

The hostess nodded, looked on her seating chart, marked a spot off, and told the guys to follow her. They went to a small table that was over in the corner and asked, "Will this be ok?"

"Perfect," Watts said

When the waitress came and took their drink and food order, Johnathan pulled out his phone and gave Samantha a call. After three rings, Samantha answered.

"Hey, Samantha. It's Johnathan. Watts and I went and did some research on the Moon Bay Cottage, and we got a little bit of information. First, we found out that there may have been a couple deaths in the house and on the property. It was nothing really specific, but we did get a couple names of children. Then, we have some information that there have been reports of apparitions in the windows by people walking past at night. That's about all we came up with.

"Ok. How about I come get you guys this afternoon? I have an appointment with a historian, and she has a lot more information that she can give us.," Samantha said.

"That's fine. Watts and I are at the pizza parlor that's in the shopping center in town," Johnathan said.

"Are you talking about Pizza and Wing's that's in the Colonial Shopping Center?"

"Yup, that is the one. We just ordered, so you are more than welcome to come up and join us for lunch."

"Sure thing," Sammantha said. "I can be there in like ten minutes. Sounds great. I can't wait to see you again!"

Ten minutes went by, and Johnathan looked at his watch. "Hopefully, Samantha will be here before the food is ready."

Johnathan's back was towards the entrance, but Watts was facing the door. "Don't look now, but here she comes."

Johnathan got up from his seat and walked over to greet Samantha, gave her a hug, and invited her to the table. "Just in time for the lunch order to arrive."

The waitress said hello to Samantha and asked if she will be joining the guys.

"Yes, I will be joining them, and I'd like a coke, please."

"Sure," the waitress said. "I'll be right back."

A few moments later, the waitress came back with Samanthas coke and an extra plate for her. Samantha thanked her. The guys had ordered a large pepperoni pizza, so there was plenty for Samantha, as well. Johnathan took the spatula and picked up a slice of pizza and put it on Samanthas plate.

Samantha started the conservation with the guys. "We have an appointment with the town historian at four. I already had a small conservation with her on the phone earlier, and I think that she can give much more insight on the Moon Bay Cottage. We can head over there as soon as we get done eating."

"That sounds good," Johnathan said.

All three of them finished eating, and Johnathan asked for the check. Samantha started to pull out her wallet from her pocketbook, and Johnathan told her to put that away, that lunch was on him. Johnathan handed the waitress the check back with $40, and the waitress asked if he needed change. He did not, and she thanked him. All three got up from the table and headed outside. Johnathan said that he had his car, but Samantha offered to drive them again.

Samantha, Johnathan, and Watts walked over to her vehicle. They all got in. Samantha backed out of the parking spot, and they were heading to meet the town historian. It took them around 35 minutes to get there, but once there Samantha parked, and the guys got out of the car. Watts and Johnathan were waiting on the outside of the car for Samantha.

Johnathan smirked and said to Watts, "Always waiting on a woman."

Watts couldn't help but laugh, and finally, Samantha got out of the car and walked around and took Johnathan's hand.

"Are we ready for this?" she asked.

"Oh yeah" Johnathan and Watts said in unison.

The three of them walked up the steps to the town hall. Watts opened the door, and as he did, an old-time bell that jingled. The town hall had beautifully shiny wooden floors, and there was a smell of an old-time wood, like the building has been there forever. They walked up to the secretary and told her that they were there to meet with Elizabeth.

"Oh, you're looking for the town historian?"

"Yes," Samantha said. "We have an appointment for four o'clock."

"Have a seat, and I will let her know that you are here. What's your name?"

"My name is Samantha."

Elizabeth came out to the waiting room and told Samantha to come on back.

"Can my boyfriend and his colleague come back as well?"

"Of course," Elizabeth said. "You all can come back."

As they were walking back, Elizabeth had mentioned that she had found a lot of information on the Moon Bay Cottage.

"That's awesome," Samantha said. "Well, we can't wait to see what you got for us!"

Elizabeth took them into a conference room that had a large executive conference table and told them to have a seat. All three of them found a chair and sat down, then Elizabeth handed out a folder that had information that she had found on the cottage. When they opened the folder, and the first page was the history of Moon Bay Cottage. That paper read,

> *Moon Bay Cottage was built in 1801. It was built by William Vanderbilt. Vanderbilt was married to a lady by the name of Margaret. Mr. Vanderbilt and Margaret Vanderbilt had two children: one by the name of Mildred and one by the name of Ryan. There was a lot of unpleasantness in the cottage. Mildred passed away at the age of 12 from the black plague. Then three years later, Ryan, who was 16 at the time,*

passed away from a farming accident. After Ryan had passed away, the Vanderbilt's fell on hard times because they both had gotten so depressed. Just a year later, in 1816, Margaret was so depressed that she would not come out of her bedroom. She would not eat or even drink. No matter what Mr. Vanderbilt did or said, he could not get Margaret to budge. She eventually passed away from malnutrition and dehydration right in their bedroom. Mr. Vanderbilt noticed that she had passed away when he came back in from working all day. Needless to say, Mr. Vanderbilt took this extremely hard, and after he buried his wife, he didn't want to continue on any longer. So, he took his 45, went into the living room, put the barrel into his mouth, and pulled the trigger. It killed him immediately, and no one in the town even knew what happened until two weeks later. None of the townspeople saw or heard Mr. Vanderbilt, and so the townspeople started to get worried. Mr. Vanderbilt was a very well-known person, so one of the towns people got ahold of the local sheriff and asked them to go to Mr. Vanderbilt's home to check in on him. Naturally, once the sheriff got there, he found Mr. Vanderbilt dead with the gun still in his hand.

Ever since the Vanderbilt's demise, the house sat empty until October 1911 when there was some so-called devil worshipers acquired the house. It has been said that the devil worshipers performed all sorts of demonic cult rit-

uals in it. They took peoples chickens from nearby houses and used them as sacrifices. One time during a sacrifice, it turned into a horror show. One of the participants during the ritual got out of line, and it was one of the guys that was performing the sacrifice's sister. He and the other cult members did not go for that, so they tied her up, stripped her, and sacrificed her by plunging a dagger into her chest. Right after, that they all left, but she was still alive, and no one helped her. After that, the townspeople got word about what had happened and took matters into their own hands. There was a mob that got together, rounded up all the cult members, took them out to the pasture to the oak tree, and hung each one of them.

"That's the information that I got on Moon Bay Cottage, so I wanted to wish you good luck on your paranormal investigation."

"Thank you so much." Samantha said. "If we have any more questions, can we contact you again?"

"Of course! Let me know if there anything else I can help you with."

Chapter Seven

Amy and Watts

The day before the high-profile investigation arrived, Watts was very excited. In fact, he was so excited that he tossed and turned just about all night. Watts had requested this Friday off, as well as the leave request for the time to go on this investigation. At around 0700 that morning, he checked the weather so he could prepare for the day. It was unusually warm for this time of year, highs in the 70s, clear skies with a slight westerly wind of four to five miles per hour, and no weather alerts issued. Practically jumping for joy, Watts got into a civilian pair of shorts and a t-shirt and headed over to the chow hall for some breakfast. When he signed in at the front, there were hardly any soldiers in line, as they were not done from physical training just yet. Watts went to the grill and ordered a cheese omelet, then went down the line and then got some potatoes, grits, and French toast with melted butter and a plate full of syrup. As he sat his tray down, he went over and got two glasses of milk. After eating breakfast Watts went back to the barracks to chill out for a while and wait for the time to go on the date.

Watts was laying in his bunk and fell back to sleep as he had a full belly from breakfast. But before he drifted off, he had set his alarm on his phone so that just in case he did fall asleep, he could be up in time for the date. After all, he did not want to miss this date because one, he had to draw up the courage to ask for this date, and second, he had not been on a date in years. He thought Amy was absolutely beautiful. As he was sleeping, he ended up having a couple of dreams. One dream was about the upcoming paranormal investigation and how he perceived everyone was going to look doing a paranormal investigation naked and busted out laughing at what he thought was funny. Luckily, his roommate was not there to hear that. The second dream Watts had was about the date he was about to go out on. He was just thinking about how he would be holding Amy's hand in the planetarium and how he so wanted to kiss her.

Eleven hundred hours came, and his phone alarm rang, and he reached over to turn it off. Watts sat up in his bunk for a minute or two, wiped his eyes to get his bearings. He jumped down and grabbed his shower stuff. He stripped naked and wrapped the towel around his waist, then headed down the hall to the showers. Watts took his time in the shower, making the water hotter and hotter to try and relax his muscles, and it also felt good on his shoulders. Ten minutes later, he turned the water off and stepped out into the changing area, but since he didn't have any clothes with him, he dried off with his towel and then wrapped the towel back around his waist and headed back to his room. Once back to his room, Watts opened his locker and pulled out a pair of khaki pants and a pull over, collared black shirt. He also grabbed a nice pair of shoes and socks and skipped the underwear, as Watts went commando ninety percent of the time. By this time, it is now 1230 in the afternoon, and Amy was supposed to be there by 1300 hours.

After Watts was dressed, he headed down to the new iron bench right outside the barracks to wait for Amy. As he was sitting there, he was playing a game on his phone while occasionally looking up to check his surroundings and watch for her. Still not seeing Amy, he went back to playing on his phone.

At 1250 hours, Amy pulled up and rolled down the driver's side window. She grinned at him. "What's a nice boy like you doing in a place like this?"

Watts laughed. "Oh, I'm just slumming it."

Amy unlocked the door and told Watts, "Hop in, cutie!"

Watts smiled at her while he put on his seat belt.

"Are you ready?" Amy asked.

"Totally ready," Watts replied. "I already got the tickets for the planetarium through the MWR office. They're VIP tickets. We also have a buffet at the planetarium right after the showing, which is space-themed, as well."

Amy was excited, as she has not had anyone in the past treat her to anything like this before. Because both Amy and Watts loved space, she was sure that she was going to love this. It made her heart skip a beat when Watts told her that. She looked at Watts, trying not to show how excited she was about him and what he had planned for them. She simply said, "That's cool."

As Watts looked at her, he could not get over how beautiful she was, and how he had waited for a girl to come along like Amy. As the two of them finally made it to the planetarium, Amy pulled into the parking lot. They drove around the parking lot looking for a spot. Watts saw a sign right by the front door that read, *Veteran's parking only*. Watts told Amy to park there

As she pulled into the Veteran's parking spot, she asked Watts if he was sure that she could park there. "I don't have Veteran's license tags on my car.

Watts told her that was ok. "If anyone questions us, I'll just show them my military ID card."

They both got out of the car and walked towards the entrance door.

Once they got to the front doors, Watts held open the door for Amy and said, "After you."

Amy was shocked that Watts was acting like a gentleman because her past experiences with dating. The guys would not treat her like that, and she had to pretty much fend for herself. So, this date was definitely starting off on the right track. Once inside, Watts and Amy looked for the information desk, and after reading a couple signs, they saw one that said *Planetarium Entrance* with an arrow. Following the signs, they went up to the counter, and the customer service rep asked if he could help them. Watts gave the gentleman the two VIP tickets, and the gentleman behind the counter gave them both a different color wrist band that other patrons did not have. The gentleman told them that their wrist bands were VIP wrist bands and that they would also allow entrance to the buffet after the show.

"Is there anything else that I can help you guys with," the gentleman asked.

"Just after the show, where do we go to eat?" Watts asked.

The customer service rep said, "There will be someone in the planetarium that will guide those that have VIP tickets. But if you go through these doors to your right, show the usher your wrist bands. He will guide you to VIP seats inside the planetarium."

When Watts and Amy walked through the doors of the planetarium, they immediately saw the usher.

After they showed him their wrist bands, he radioed into someone else and said, "I have two for VIP."

The radio crackled as the voice from the other radio said, "Send them over."

THE NAKED PARANORMAL INVESTIGATORS 55

The usher told Watts and Amy, "Walk around the center of the floor, and you will see someone over on the other side that will take you to your seats. VIP seats are special seats and have the greatest view of the dome. These seats here are general admission."

As the two of them rounded the center where the start projector was, they saw the other usher and told him that they were sent over by the other gentleman.

"Sure, I just need to check your wristbands." He checked their bands. "Excellent choice. Come this way."

Watts and Amy followed the usher, and he took them up a few steps that were roped off and showed them the to their seats. They settled in their reclining chairs.

Watts said, "These are excellent seats."

"They are super seats," Amy said. "What's the show about today?"

"The show's about the journey through our solar system."

"That sounds wonderful. I don't know why I didn't get into astronomy instead of paranormal investigations!"

"I know what we can do, Amy. We can start our own planetarium, but it can be a nudist planetarium." Watts laughed.

"You know...that's not a bad idea, Watts! We should definitely look into starting that, and then we can be business partners," Amy said, joking around and laughing.

As they were talking, one of the planetarium presenters came on over some speakers around the planetarium dome. "Ladies and Gentlemen, my name is Greg, and I'll be your presenter this afternoon. Today, we're going to take a voyage through our universe. We will go from the moon landing in 1969, to the landing of the rover on Mars, and then to the outer universe of our solar system. Please silence all cell phones, so not to interrupt the show for other guest. The show will last forty-five minutes, so sit back, relax, and enjoy the presentation."

Once finished his announcement, the planetarium went dark, and the show started off with the night sky with summer night sounds. Watts reached over and took Amy's hand to hold it and held it through the entire show.

After the show was over, Greg came back on, and over the speakers, he said, "Thank you for visiting us today. We hope you enjoyed the show. The exit is to your left, but if you have a VIP pass, just show your VIP wristbands to the usher, and he will direct you to the next section."

As everyone was leaving, Watts and Amy showed the usher their VIP wrist bands, and the usher directed them through a different door. "Just go through these doors, then you'll either take the elevator or the stairs down one floor marked VIP area. Go through the double black doors. Once there, someone else will guide you to your next destination."

Amy and Watts walked to their next destination within the planetarium. Watts would not let Amy's hand go and held it the entire time. They entered into the buffet area and were in awe as the buffet area was just like the regular planetarium, except instead of having chairs around the center of the projector, it had tables around with six chairs at each table. On the back wall, there were tables set up with chafing dishes for the food. The room had a dome ceiling for the projection of stars. The usher directed Amy and Watts to their assigned seats, and when they got to their table, Watts pulled the chair out for Amy. Amy was again surprised, never having had a man do anything for her.

Once everyone was seated, Greg walked back into the room to let everyone know that lunch would be served in 15 minutes, and that there would be a planetarium show as well during lunch. The menu had changed from the original menu. Now, there will be prime rib, mashed potatoes and gravy, corn, and green beans. After lunch, there would be different deserts, and they had Coke products and iced sweet and unsweet tea.

"For the planetarium show, it will just be a silent show with no narration. But I can put the sound on if everyone would like the story. We can take a vote. By the raise of your hand, who would like to have the narration?" Only five people raised their hand. "Who would like a silent show during lunch?" Ten people raised their hand. "Ok, so it's a silent show," Greg said.

The catering service began filling the chaffing dishes with the food, and once they were done, the catering supervisor told Greg that they were ready to serve.

Greg told the group, "Lunch is now served; please go and help yourself."

Watts and Amy went up in line and got their lunch and drinks. Once back at the table, and everyone started eating, the lights went dim, and the show started. The show started out with a Saturn V rocket taking off which was Apollo 13 taking more astronauts to the moon again.

As everyone was still eating their lunch, Watts and Amy had finished. Watts was a fast eater because of the military. He then put his arm around Amy and lightly rubbed her shoulder. When everyone else was finished eating, Greg invited everyone for seconds, as there was plenty left over. People went up, and the caterers served them seconds. They took the leftover food back, cleaned the serving tables off, and brought out desserts. For dessert, they brought out some New York style cherry cheesecake, chocolate cake with vanilla icing and an edible moon picture, chocolate chip cookies and sugar cookies with a solar system edible design. Fifty minutes later, the show ended. When dessert hour was over, Greg, had thanked everyone for coming out and hoped that everyone enjoyed both shows and wished everyone safe travels home.

Watts once again took Amy's hand again as they were walking to the car.

Amy gladly held Watts hand back. "I had a wonderful time. I've never had such a wonderful time ever on a date. Thank you so much, Watts. I'm so glad that you finally asked me out on this date."

Once Amy got back on post and pulled up to Watts's barracks, she found an empty parking spot right in front of the barracks. They both got out of the car and sat on the iron bench.

Amy once again thanked Watts for a wonderful afternoon. "I've never been treated like a queen on any other date, ever."

Watts responded, "You're welcome, and it was my pleasure. Do you know how much courage I had to build up to ask you out? That was one of the best decisions that I had ever made. I would love to go out with you again."

"I would absolutely love that, Watts," Amy told him.

"But for now, it's now five pm, 1700 hours military time, so we should try and get some rest tonight. We have the big investigation tomorrow, and we're going to be up really late. And we definitely don't know what we are going to run into."

"That sounds good to me. Do you want me to pick you up tomorrow as well?"

"I'm supposed to ride with Samantha and Johnathan tomorrow, but I can let them know that I will ride with you. As long as you're sure that you don't mind picking me up." He paused. "Although Samantha is going to be here anyway. I don't see why both of you have to come here. I can ride with Samantha and Johnathan tomorrow to the investigation. But if you want—and if you're ok with this idea—I can stay with you after the investigation."

"I would love that. We can go over to my house and watch a movie or something."

"That sounds wonderful," Watts said. "I can't wait. I hope that I can sleep this evening, unlike last night where I tossed and turned the whole time."

"You need to figure this out about sleeping because we're going to have a long day and night tomorrow. I would maybe take something that can help you sleep through the night but that won't make you all groggy in the morning when you wake up."

"I don't have anything here to help me, so I'll go see if they have anything at the PX. I'm sure they have some type of over-the-counter sleep aid that I can get. They don't have a pharmacy, but they do have a section with like Tylenol and pain relivers and such, so they may have something. even if they just have Benadryl," Watts said.

"Benadryl works and does make you drowsy, so even if you get that, that should be good enough. It'll also help you if you happen to get itchy from like mosquitos or what not. Do you need a ride up to the PX?"

"Sure. If you are ok with driving me."

"Well, I wouldn't have asked if I wasn't ok with driving you, silly." She nudged him and smiled.

As they both got back into Amy's car, she drove Watts to the PX. Amy was able to go in with Watts as she was with a military guy. Watts went to the medication aisle, found the Benadryl, and headed to the checkout. At the checkout, Watts handed the cashier his military Id card, then the cashier scanned it and handed it back to him. She scanned the Benadryl, and it rang up $12.99. Watts handed the cashier his debit card and paid for his purchase. Once he got his debit card back, he and Amy headed back to the barracks. As they drove, Amy asked if the purchase should have been more because of tax. Watts told her that there was no tax on anything bought from the PX.

Back to the barracks, Amy was lucky to get her same parking spot that she had when they left.

Watts said, "How lucky can you get, getting the same spot back?"

Amy said, "I know...that never happens with me."

"That kind of stuff never happen to me, either, when I was still at home before I joined the Army." Watts looked at Amy and put his arm around her again.

Amy did not mind that at all. "I really had a wonderful time as well. And I'm looking forward to tomorrow's investigation of Moon Bay Cottage. I've been looking forward to this for the last month."

"Samantha said that we are going to investigate naked. Is that true?"

"Yes, that is true, Watts. We are nudist paranormal investigators. The entire team always investigates naked, as long as the temperature is right. Of course, we don't investigate naked during winter if there's a location that doesn't have any heat, but if the location does have heat, then yes."

"Cool I so cannot wait, so we better call it a night. Or call it a day, I mean! Just so we can get enough rest for tomorrow."

"I agree," Amy said. "I'll see you tomorrow when you Johnathan and Samantha get there. The team will probably get there before you guys do, but I can't wait to see you again tomorrow."

Watts got up and gave her a hug. "Be very careful going home, and I'll see you tomorrow."

As Amy drove away, Watts waved at her and waited until she was out of sight, then went up to his barracks room. He took a Benadryl and went to sleep for the night.

Chapter Eight

Investigation of Moon Bay Cottage

The day finally arrived for the investigation of Moon Bay Cottage. The entire paranormal team was extremely excited, as were Johnathan and Watts.

Early that morning, Samantha called Johnathan to finish up go over the finalized plans. Samantha wanted to make sure that Johnathan and Watts were still going to go with them. Johnathan assured Samantha that he and Watts was certainly going to go.

"Cool! I will pick you two up at 1100 hours." Since Samantha was hanging out with Johnathan, she was starting to become an expert at military time.

"I'll be ready when she gets there." After Johnathan hung up the phone from talking to Samantha, he immediately went up to Watts's barracks room and knocked on the door. "We're going to be picked up at 1100 hours, so get ready. We can run up to the PX and grab some things if you want to take anything."

Watts and Johnathan went downstairs, and once outside, they started to head to the car but then Johnathan asked, "Want to just walk to the PX?"

"Sure, we can walk," Watts said. "After all, that will get me ready for all that walking we'll be doing tonight."

Johnathan looked at Watts. "What are you talking about, turd? You're in great shape."

Watts started to laugh. "Thats the very first time you called me something."

"You know I was only joking, right?"

"Yeah, I know," Watts said.

As they continued to walk down to the PX, Johnathan decided that he was hungry. "Let's stop at Burger King and get some breakfast."

"Sounds good," Watts said. "I haven't had Burger King in a long time. That definitely sounds yummy, and I'm sure it'll beat good ole Army chow for a change."

When the two of entered Burger King, they both stopped and looked at the menu.

"Do you know what you would like, Watts?" Johnathan asked.

"Yup, I sure do. I am going to get a bacon, egg, and cheese biscuit sandwich with some hash browns and an orange juice.

"That sure sounds good. I think I'll get the same thing."

After Johnathan and Watts ordered and got their food, Watts grabbed the tray, and they found seats in the dining room.

"Oh, shoot! Forgot the ketchup," said Watts.

"I'll get it for us."

"Thanks, Staff Seargeant."

After the two of them ate, they continued on to the PX. They shopped and getting a few things that they both thought that they needed for the night. They started heading back to the barracks. While walking back, they passed right by the Burger King again.

Watts wanted to be a smarty pants. "Well, that looks so familiar."

"Sure does," Johnathan said.

Johnathan started asking Watts more questions about his growing up while they walked. Before they knew it, they were back at the barracks.

Watts said, "Wow, that seemed pretty quick. We got back so fast. So, all we need to do now is wait till eleven for Samantha to pick us up. What time is it now? I forgot my watch and left it in my room."

Johnathan looked at his watch. "It's 1030 hours."

"That late already? I'll be right back, Sarge. I'm going to run up to my room and grab my watch." Watts went up to his room to get his watch, and then he needed to use the bathroom while he was there.

Johnathan was still downstairs waiting for Watts to come back, and several more minutes had passed. Finally, Watts came back out.

"What took you so long, Watts?"

"I just had to use the bathroom."

"Oh, ok," Johnathan said.

The guys sat on the famous iron bench again, waiting for Samantha. It seemed that they were the only two that ever used it. As they sat there and was chit chatting, Samantha pulled up and was playing some MC Hammer on the radio.

"Hey guys," she said. "It's the big day. I'm super excited."

"We are, too," Johnathan said. "I've never been on a paranormal investigation before, and I'm so looking forward to this."

"Well, I've been wanting to investigate this place for a couple years, but we could never get the permission to do so. It was my researcher that was able to pull some strings to get us in for tonight. I was absolutely ecstatic when she told me that we're able to finally investigate this place. When we finally get there, that's when reality will sink in as it still seems like a dream."

Once they were on their way and off post, Watts told Johnathan and Samantha that he plans to stay with Amy the night after the investigation.

"Really?" Samantha said.

"Yes. Amy and I discussed it yesterday when we went out on our date."

"Oh, snappy," Johnathan said. "Sounds like you're going to have a very good weekend.

Samantha sat quietly for a minute, then caught his eye in the rear-view mirror. "Look. Amy has been treated really bad buy men in her past. Please don't hurt her again."

"You have no worries, Samantha. I would never think about that doing that."

Samantha then changed the subject and started talking about what the plans of the night. "The entire team has gone and got our vans. We're supposed to meet at a park and ride. Then, we're all going to hop in our company vans and ride together. One van has all of our investigating equipment, which includes our cameras, stands, electronic voice recorders, cameras, and what not. The other van is our command center that's set up like an office in the back and has mounted monitors that we use to watch the cameras."

Watts said, "This is like professional investigation."

"We are professionals, Watts," Samantha said. "We're not amateurs at this. We've been doing this for years and years."

Watts apologized. "I didn't mean anything with that. I was just impressed."

"It's ok, Watts. I didn't take it personally. I was just telling you that we've been doing this for a long time."

After an hour and a half of driving, Samantha, Watts and Johnathan arrived at the park and ride. When they pulled into the parking lot, she immediately saw her investigation vans way over at the end of the lot. The vans had a sign on the sides that read *Pikes Peak Naked Paranormal Investigations* with a web address and a phone number. Samantha pulled up next to the vans and parked. One van was completely black as that van was the command center, and the other van was blue but was longer and had multiple rows of seats. This van also had plenty of room in the very back that was packed up with camera cases and recording equipment. They all got out of Samanthas SUV and got into the passenger van.

As they got in, Tom, who was driving the passenger van, and asked, "Are you all were ready.?"

"We are totally ready," Samantha told Tom. "So, let's hit it!"

Tom pulled out and the command center van, that was driven by Ryker and Grayson, immediately followed right behind.

"It'll be about another hour drive before we get to our destination. If anyone would like to lay back and take a nap until we get there, go right ahead," Tom informed them.

No one seemed to take advantage of that except for Watts. He fell asleep almost immediately.

Tom said, "Wow! How can he fall asleep so fast?"

Johnathan said, "He's a soldier; he can sleep anywhere, at any time. We soldiers take advantage of any possibility to sleep that we can get."

After driving for thirty-five minutes, Tom started to see digital signs that read *Moon Bay Cottage: 6 miles, 25 minutes*. "We are really close," he told everyone that was riding in the van.

Johnathan asked someone to wake Watts up so he could be bright eyed and bushy tailed when they arrived at the location.

Amy gently shook Watts. "Wake up."

Watts opened his eyes. "I'm awake."

"Good. We have twenty to twenty-five minutes before we get there."

"Awesome," said Watts. "I'm so excited for this."

Everyone in the van got completely quiet for some strange reason, and no one knew why. Finally, Tom saw a sign on the side of the road that was nearly covered up with vegetation with an arrow pointing to the right. The street itself was nearly covered with trees and brush as well. After making a right hand turn down the street, which was more like a dirt road, everyone looked at each other.

"Wow, this road is spooky," Tom said.

It was only around five in the evening, and because the dirt road was through the woods, it seemed darker than what it actually was. Still driving along, they eventually came to a clearing and right in front of them was Moon Bay Cottage.

"Oh, crap," Samantha said. "This place doesn't look like a cottage at all."

It was a run down, two-story, five-bedroom, three-bath house. It had an attic and a basement, as well. Right in front to the house and slightly to the left was a quarter of a mile pond with a raggedy pier.

"Ok. Everyone, let's get out and go over what we're all going to do this evening. Ryker and Grayson, I would like you to set up command center right over there next to the pond. Go ahead and pull the command vehicle over there now so when we set up, we'll be ready to rock and roll. Everyone else, let's start unloading all of our equipment."

By this time, it was getting darker, and the moon was rising over the pond.

"This is going to be a great night for a paranormal investigation," River said. "It is going to be perfect."

Samantha asked, "Does anyone know what the weather is going to be tonight?"

Julia took out her phone and pulled the weather app up. "My weather app says that it's supposed to be clear with a high of 68."

"That is a perfect temperature for investigating naked."

Grayson came back over with the rest of the group, with Ryker following behind. "Is there anything you need us to do before we go back to the command center, Samantha?"

"Sure, let's get all of our static cameras set up. Once they're set, you two can go back and let us know what angles you would like us to set. Ok everyone, grab a walkie, and we'll be on channel two this evening."

Once everyone entered the house, there was an immediate feeling of a negative presence that everyone felt. Samantha said, "Shake the feeling off, everyone. We have a job to do."

Samantha was directing everyone where to place the static cameras, and once the cameras were placed, she instructed Ryker and Grayson to head back out to the command center. The command center had a built-in power station that all the equipment could be plugged into, so Ryker and Grayson started plugging in all the equipment, as well as connecting it to the two monitors. Ryker took the walkie talkie and did a radio check.

"Radio Check over," Samantha answered first, loud and clear, then Tom and then everyone followed suit.

"Copy that," Ryker said back over the radio.

"Ryker, start letting us know how you want these static cameras."

"Copy that. The first camera. I want you to point it directly down the hall. Ok...now tilt up slightly...perfect! Now, push in just a hair...stop, perfect. Camera two, I'd like down in the basement on the back wall pointing to the stairs please. Ok, now just tilt up...stop. That's perfect for camera two. Camera three I would like up in the attic."

"Ok, where at in the attic?" Tom asked.

"Put the camera over on the left side wall. I'd like that to point towards the window since there are claims of apparitions in that window. Perfect, Tom. No adjusting needed on camera three."

"Awesome," Tom said.

"Is there any one with camera four?" Ryker said over the walkie.

"River here. I'm right with camera four."

"Good. River, I'd like camera four set up in the living room, pointed directly up the stairs leading to the upstairs bedrooms."

"Copy that." River took the tripod and camera and placed it at the bottom of the stairs facing upwards.

Ryker came back on the walkie "Ok, River. I need you to tilt the camera down slightly...keep going, keep going...and stop. That looks good, River. Thank you."

Samantha came back on the walkie and told everyone to meet out at the command center.

Once everyone got out to the command center, Samantha wanted to have a briefing with everyone. Just about everyone got out to the command center at the same time.

Grayson asked Samantha, "Do you want us to step down from the command center?"

"Yes, please." Samantha started the briefing off. "Welcome to Moon Bay Cottage, everyone. This is what we been waiting for, and it's been two years in the making. As you all know, we have some special guest with us this evening. Welcome, Johnathan and Watts."

"Thank you, and it's a pleasure to be here as we been looking forward to this. I know we haven't been waiting for two years like you guys. It's been just a couple weeks. We are still honored to be here investigating with all of you guys."

"Thank you, Johnathan," Samantha said. "So tonight, we'll be in pairs. No one is to be alone unless Ryker, Grayson, or I give you specific permission or if one of us tell you to go alone to try and bring out the spirits. Also, Johnathan and Watts have never been on a paranormal investigation. They don't know how this equipment works, so someone will need to be with them all the time. If there's an emergency, please call over the walkie. Let us know where exactly you are located and what the emergency is, and we will come to you. If you see or hear anything, let us know over the walkie immediately, as it may not be a ghost but could be one of us making that noise. If it something unexplained, let's try and debunk it, as it could just be something like the house still settling or the wind. As usual, this is a nude investigation, so once this meeting is over, we will get naked and do our thing. Are we ready to do this? Everyone put in their hand and on the count of three, yell Pikes Peak."

"One, two, three...Pikes Peak!" Everyone yelled out and raised their hand in the air.

Once the meeting was over, Tom went to the passenger van and grabbed bags and a storage tote, then brought it over to the command center. "Ok, everyone, here are bags for your clothes and a permanent marker. As usual, please put your name on the clear bag and put your clothes in there. Place the bag inside the tote. You may go completely naked, or you can go as comfortable as you like, or you can go with just shoes on. It's your personal preference."

Almost immediately everyone said that they were going to go investigate completely naked.

"That is perfectly fine," Tom said. "But be mindful of where you are walking because of your bare feet. Going through earlier, I didn't see any hazards, but I wasn't looking for hazards, either."

"It does seem safe enough" Samantha said. "It'll also be less contamination on our audio equipment."

Everyone got undressed and did what Tom had asked: they placed their clothes in the plastic bag and placed the plastic bag in the tote.

Once everyone was naked, Samantha gave everyone a strap with a clip on it. "Here, everyone. Use this strap so you can carry your walkie around, and that way, you won't have to worry about carrying it along with your investigative equipment."

Watts said, "This is so cool and so convenient at the same time."

"Are there any more questions?" Samantha asked.

"Yes," Amy said. "What are the teams going to be tonight?"

"Good question," Samantha said. "So here is the breakdown. "It's going to be Johnathan and I, Amy and Watts, Julia and River, and of course, Ryker and Grayson. Tom, you can be a floater and join any team whenever you wish. I'd suggest that you spend some time with each team tonight."

"Sounds good," Tom said

"So, let's do this!" Samantha said.

As they entered the door, each and every one of them had the same feeling as they all did earlier, but this time, it seemed to be more prevalent. It was not surprising because it was eight p.m. and totally dark with a very bright moon up in the sky. The pond even had an eerie presence to it as there was a foggy mist coming off the water from the slightly cooler evening air.

Inside the house, Samantha said, "Amy and Watts, start down in the basement. Johnathan and I will start in the attic. Julia and River, you guys can start right here in the main part of the house, to include the upstairs bedrooms."

As Samantha and Johnathan were heading up the stairs to the attic, they thought they heard a low growl.

Johnathan asked Samantha, "Did you hear that?"

"Yes, I did. Let's do an EVP session when we get up there, and we should let everyone know that we thought we heard a growl." Samantha handed the walkie to Johnathan. "Please let everyone know what we heard. Also, when you tell them, ask if anyone else had heard it."

Johnathan took the walkie and pushed the side button. "Samantha and I thought we heard a low growl heading up to the attic. Anyone else hear that?"

The other teams came over the walkie and said no.

Samantha said, "Let them know that we are going to do an EVP session, so they know to try and keep the noise down."

Johnathan announced over the walkie, "Samantha and I are going to do an EVP session."

Samantha took the electronic voice recorder and turned it on. "Johnathan, this is how we do an EVP."

Once Samantha was ready, she started asking questions. "Is there anyone here with us?" She waited for about 30 seconds, then asked another question. "If you are here with us, what is your name?" After another 30 seconds, she asked Johnathan, "Do you want to try and ask a couple questions?

"Sure." Johnathan asked, "Did you die in this house?" After thirty seconds, he asked, "How did you die?" Then, he waited another thirty seconds.

Samantha asked Johnathan, "You think we should play it back and see if we got anything?"

Being excited, Johnathan said, "Yes let's do it!"

Samantha rewound the recorder, then hit the play button. The first question that Samantha asked, there was no response. On her second question, there was a voice that came on and said, "Get out."

"Whoa! Did you hear that, Johnathan? Let's listen to it again." Samantha rewound the digital voice recorder back a few seconds. Then, she hit the play button again. After hearing Samantha ask the entity's name, almost immediately, the same voice came back on and said again, "Get out."

"Wow," said Johnathan. "Let's see if I have any response to my questions."

Samantha let the voice recorder play, then they heard Johnathan ask, *did you die in this house?* Following that question from Johnathan, they heard the same low growl that they heard heading up to the attic.

"Whoa. That sounded like it was an evil spirit. Let's switch with another team and see if they can get the same response up here." Samantha shivered.

She took the walkie back from Johnathan and went on. "We are going to switch places. Amy and Watts, why don't you guys come up to the attic? Julia and River, you guys go down to the basement. Johnathan and I will do the main house. As we pass each other, I do want to advise you guys of something."

When Samantha and Johnathan passed Amy and Watts, Samantha informed them that they did get an EVP while up in the attic.

"Really?" Amy said.

"Yes, and it sounded demonic. We'll have Ryker and Grayson evaluate it in a couple minutes. Why don't you guys grab a handheld mapping camera and take it up with you."

"Copy that," Amy said. "Watts, can go outside and grab one of the handheld mapping cameras?"

"Hold on a minute," Watts said. "Aren't we supposed to stay together unless given permission?"

"You're absolutely right," Amy said. "I forgot all about that. I'm sorry, I will go with you."

As they started to head out the door to get the mapping camera, there was a dark shadow that passed right in front of the door.

Amy looked at Watts. "Did you see what I saw?" It moved extremely quickly, and they both only had a glimpse of it.

"I did," Watts said. "Scared me...I was not expecting that."

Amy called over the walkie and told everyone what her and Watts just witnessed.

"That's great," Ryker said. "Unfortunately, we don't have a static camera facing the door to get documented proof of the shadow figure."

When Amy and Watts got outside to the equipment, Watts looked up into the night sky and had noticed that the moon was partially covered by clouds. "Look. Is it supposed to rain or storm tonight?"

Amy told him, "No. It's supposed to be clear and mild temperatures according to the weather report. It's been the warmest, dryest fall on record."

"Well, it looks like the weather report was wrong."

She looked up into the sky as well and saw that the moon had been partially covered by clouds. She immediately thought about letting the team know. When Amy took her walkie out to let everyone know, she felt a rain drop on top of her head. Although it was only partially cloudy, she still felt a rain drop, but only one drop. Amy then told everyone over the walkie, "It's starting to get cloudy. I just felt a raindrop."

Samantha came back over the walkie and said, "I'm not too concerned about that right at the moment. Let's just keep going."

Amy and Watts got the mapping camera, and Amy thought they should take a regular handheld camera with them as well. Watts grabbed the regular handheld the camera and headed back into the house and up to the attic. Once the two of them got up into the attic, Amy showed Watts how to use the handheld video camera while she used the thermal imaging camera.

As Watts was playing around with the camera that he had, he saw that he had caught an apparition on his camera. "Look! I got something on video...how do you play this back?"

"We can take it out to the command center, and they can review it with us."

As they were discussing that, Grayson came over the walkie telling Amy and Watts that they were seeing something on static camera. "It appears that we see a figure standing in front of the window, and it looks like it's wearing clothing from the eighteen hundreds.

As Amy and Watts looked at the window, Amy spoke back through the walkie. "We don't see anything with our naked eye, no pun intended."

As they investigated and moved through the cottage, there looked to be a set of glowing eyes over by one of the windows. Watts whispered, "Amy, do you see that? It definitely looks like we are being watched."

"Come on. Let's go see what that may be."

Upon checking and researching what the eyes could be, Watts came to a conclusion that what they were actually seeing was a reflection from the night vision cameras in the windows. Seeing the eyes was debunked. As Amy and Watts continued to move about the cottage, they came to the top of the stairs that leads to the basement. As they both stood there, pointing their cameras towards the bottom of the steps, they caught another set of eyes. This time, it was not a reflection but an actual set of pure white eyes looking up at them. Upon seeing this, the adrenalin rushed through them. They were quick to jump into action and go down into the basement. Amy immediately called over the walkie to Samantha about what they had caught. Amy told Samantha that her and Watts were going to go down into the basement to investigate further. They searched the basement, but they found nothing further at that time.

Amy informed Ryker and Grayson about what they had caught on their handheld thermal imaging camera.

Ryker said, "Cool deal. Why don't you guys bring it out to us, and we can review the footage."

"Sounds good to us," Amy said.

When they went back outside to take the video camera to Ryker and Grayson, Watts looked back up in the sky, and the clouds had totally gone away. "Hum...ok. It must have just a cloud passing by."

Once they were back at the command station, Ryker asked Amy and Watts to return to the house and take the electronic voice recorder in with them and do an EVP session. He handed Watts the EVP recorder. He and Amy headed back inside.

Ryker said over the walkie to all the teams, "Samantha, is it was ok for Amy and Watts to do an EVP session in the basement?"

Samantha agreed and said that was a great idea. So, Amy and Watts switched with the team that was in the basement.

Once down in the basement, Amy started the EVP session by asking, "Is there anyone down here in the basement with us?" Then, using the standard protocol for the paranormal group, she waited 30 seconds. After 30 seconds were up, she asked another question. "How did you die in this house?" Once again, she paused.

Watts asked a question, "Are you ok with us being here investigating?" Then he waited 30 more seconds. "Do you want us to tell your story?" Right after that last question Watts asked, he had a burning sensation on the back side of his back. "Ouch!" he said loudly.

"What's wrong?" Amy asked him.

"I have this burning down the right side of my back."

"Let me look." Samantha said.

Watts stood up and turned around. There were three long scratches going down his back.

Amy was worried. "That's not good." She immediately got on the walkie and told everyone that Watts was attacked by an unseen force and had marks on his back.

Samantha came back on and told everyone to meet her at the command center. Everyone went outside and met at the back of the command center. She then asked Watts to turn around so she could see what had happened. There were three scratches down the side of his back and were starting to bleed.

Samantha told Watts, "There is definitely evil in this house. I'm not going to call it a cottage anymore because this is nowhere near being a cottage. Anything in threes is a mockery of the Holy Spirit, and this is definitely a sign of an evil presence. Grayson, can you get me the first aid kit so I can take care of these scratches for Watt?" She got out some alcohol pad wipes and wiped down Watts's wounds.

"I'll be fine," Watts said. "But there's something in this house that does not want us here. We even asked if it wanted us to get its story out to the public to clear its bad name and make it good. And that is when I got scratched."

It was then close to three a.m. which was also known as the witching hour. "Not saying that all bad things happen around this time, but it does seem to increase around this time," Samantha told everyone. "Let's finish up this investigation and get some rest. Tomorrow, we can review all the data we collected. We can go for another hour or two and then call it a night. Let's just send one team in at a time for the rest of the night. Amy and Watts, since you guys just had an encounter, I want you guys to stay out here. Julia and River, I want you guys to go back down into the basement and do another EVP session."

"Ok," River said, so they headed back into the house and towards the basement. Halfway down into the basement, the air got extremely cold. It was cold enough that they both could see their breath every time they breathed. Julia got on the walkie and informed Samantha that the air was extremely cold. Even though they both were naked, the air did not seem to bother them while naked but only when they exhaled.

Once they both reached the basement, they walked past the static camera, and both Ryker and Grayson could see them on the monitors walking by. Ryker came on over the walkie. "Julia and River, I can see you guys on the monitor now."

"Copy that," River replied. "We're going to start our EVP session now."

Julia started asking questions first. "We know you are down here as you attacked one of our team members. Who are you?" Once again, keeping with the protocol, she waited at least 30 seconds. Then asked another question. "We told you that we could tell your story and clear up your name if it needed to be cleared up. Would you like us to tell your story?" Another 30 seconds went by. "Do you have family still living that we can inform that you are doing well?"

There was a wooden box that was sitting on the shelf in the corner, and with that question, it went flying across the room. It made such a loud noise that it scared both Julia and River, and they both jumped.

Ryker came on the walkie. "Are you ok? I saw the box flying past the camera."

"We are fine," Julia said.

As Julia was speaking, Grayson caught what appeared to be a demonic entity on the camera. "Julia and River, you guys need to get out of that basement, now!" Grayson was panicked over seeing it, and both Julia and River hurried and scattered back upstairs.

Julia asked, "What was wrong? You scared us!"

"There was a demonic entity on camera, and I didn't want you guys down there anymore."

Samantha came on over the walkie and told everyone to wrap up. "We can get some rest and go over everything tomorrow."

As they all went back into the house, the entire house was freezing cold.

Samantha said, "Ok, let's hurry up and get all this equipment packed up and get out of here. The rumors seem to be true."

It only took twenty minutes to get everything packed, up get dressed, and get back on the road. Instead of them driving all the way back to the park and ride, they all decided to stop at a motel for the night. Once they went there, they asked for adjoining rooms. The front office clerk was able to accommodate them as the motel was pretty empty that night. Once settled in the rooms, everyone fell asleep because it was a long day and night.

Chapter Nine

Moon Bay Cottage Evidence Review

It was the day after the famous paranormal investigation of Moon Bay Cottage. Tom was the very first one awake and out of bed. When he woke up, he sat up on the side of the bed trying not to disturb Julia, who shared the bed with him. Then, he looked over to the small and very uncomfortable couch that was in the section of the motel room as you walk into the room and saw Ryker sleeping on it. Even though this was a motel, it was very fancy and very clean. This room reminded him of a fancy hotel room. Then Tom stood up and walked over to the windows and flung open the curtains, and as he did, the sun shone through the windows. He told himself that he needed a shower, and he got naked right in front of the windows, not caring one bit if anyone saw him walking into the bathroom. As he went into the bathroom, he kept the door open because everyone here seen him naked many times except for Johnathan and Watts. But they even saw him naked last night for the first time. When Tom turned the water spicket on, it made a squeaking noise, and that woke Ryker up. When Ryker opened his eyes, he was facing the bathroom and had seen Tom standing there naked trying to get the water temperature right, not too hot and not too cold.

Ryker sat up on the couch trying to get the stiffness out from sleeping on the couch all night. "Good morning, Tom."

Tom said, "Good morning. I'm going to take a quick shower, and then I am going to wake everyone up to get ready for the day. We have a lot of data that we have to go over today from last night's investigation."

"Sounds good," Ryker said. "Do you want me to go wake everyone up?"

"That would be awesome," Tom said as he stepped into the shower and closed the shower door.

Ryker got up, and the first person that he went to was Julia because she was the closest. "Julia, you need to wake up. It's that time."

Julia made a moaning sound. "Why can't I just have another half hour."

"Nope, you need to wake up. I need to go wake everyone else, so get up." Ryker then went through the adjoining room door and walked into the room. That room had two queen beds, so he went to the windows first and opened the curtains and blinds. The first bed Johnathan and Samantha were sleeping in, so Ryker walked over to the first bed and decided to pull the covers and sheet down off of them. When he did that, he was kind of shocked when he seen both of them were sleeping naked. He shook on Samantha. "Wakey, wakey."

Johnathan woke up as well. "Good morning, Ryker."

Ryker said, "Good morning, Johnathan. Who is in that bed?"

"That would be Watts and Amy."

Ryker turned around and did the same thing with the sheets and covers that he had done with Samantha and Johnathan. He grabbed the corner and threw the sheet and covers down towards the bottom of the bed. Ryker was not surprised this time as he was expecting Watts and Amy to be naked as well. He was right, but this time he shook Watts to wake him up as Watts was sleeping on that particular side.

Ryker asked Samantha, "Where is everyone else was?" They were all supposed to have adjoining rooms.

"The only adjoining rooms we have are our two rooms. River and Grayson are in room 122, right next to your room to the right."

"Ok," he said, and left the room and walked down two rooms to room 122 and banged on the door.

River seemed to jump right out of her own skin when Ryker banged on the door. "Who is banging on the door like that?" she yelled.

"It's Ryker, and it's time to get up."

"Is everyone awake?"

Ryker yelled, "Yes, we're awake. You need to stop yelling. You're going to wake up other people that are still sleeping around here. We're going to meet in Samanthas room, so get ready and meet us all there."

When Ryker got back to his room, and by this time, Tom was done with his shower and was dressed again. "Let's head over to Samanthas room."

As the entire team met up in Samantha's room, she was checking her phone for any new messages or possibility of any missed calls that may have to do with booking more clients for more investigations. Seeing no calls or text messages, she told everyone, "We are going to mount. First thing we are going to do is stop and get breakfast."

The same team members got back into the vans that they came down in. Ryker and Grayson mounted up in the command center van, and the rest of them mounted up in the passenger van. Tom asked where everyone wanted to go for breakfast and nearly everyone said that they didn't care.

"You all sound just like my wife. I saw a diner on the way down here, so we'll go there."

Samantha got on the CB radio and told Ryker and Grayson that they were going to stop at the Pikes Peak Diner. Grayson came back over the CB radio and acknowledged it by saying 10-4.

After breakfast, the team loaded back up in the vans and headed out and headed towards home. On the way home, they were looking for a small hall to rent to set up so that they could go through all the evidence. After driving for an hour, they were going through a small town that was located in the mountain region of Pikes Peak. They had seen a sign that read *hall rentals, by the hour or by the day*. It was located at the back of the local VFW post. The team decided to stop in and talk to the post commander about how much the hall rental would be.

"The price for the day is $175. For an hour, it would be $80, and for the week, it would be $500." The post commander asked if anyone there was a veteran.

Johnathan and Watts both said that we are both serving in the Army now.

The commander said, "There's also a military discount. The discount will be 20 percent off whatever agreement that you sign. I''ll leave you folks alone so you can decide."

"That is so awesome. What do you think, Samantha?"

"Let's rent this hall. All we will need it for is the day, but we can rent for another day if needed. We will also need a private rental because we will be naked, we are nudist. That way, no one else will come in while we are reviewing the evidence collected and be in shock."

Johnathan went to get the commander of the VFW and told him that they wanted to rent the little hall out.

The post commander came back with his clipboard and the contract, and Johnathan and Samantha sat down with him at a little, round table that was over in the right corner to go over the contract.

The post commander asked, "How long you want the hall for?"

Johnathan said, "We would like it for one day, but would like to have the second day on standby just, in case that we need it."

"Great," the commander said. "So, here's what I'll do. I'll only charge you for one day but will have the contract for two days. That way if you need the second day, it will be reserved."

"Perfect," Samantha said. "But do we need to pay for the second day up front?"

"No, I'll only charge you for the first day, but the second day will just be reserved, and we will straighten up then."

"That's perfect," Samantha said. "We want the hall for tomorrow and stand by for Tuesday."

"Yes, I will start the contract for Monday, November 2, and I will take the payment for the hall today."

Johnathan told the commander, "I'll pay for Monday, and that way if we need the hall Tuesday, you will have my card on file if we need another day."

After signing the contract, the team headed out to the small hotel that was right there in town, signed in, and got to their rooms. Each and every room had a beautiful view of Pikes Peak.

After getting a good night's rest, the team woke up pretty early to get a good start on getting tables and all the equipment that was needed for the evidence review. After checking out of the hotel, they immediately went to the VFW hall, which was just three blocks away. When they pulled around the back where the hall was, the post commander was already there to meet them and give them a code to get in. After receiving the code, the post commander left, and the team went into the hall to set up. There were tables already set up so that was one thing that the paranormal team did not have to worry about. All they had to do was rearrange the tables to be over by a power source to be able to plug in their equipment. After moving the tables and setting up the equipment, it was time to start the review. Once the entire team was set, Samantha hung a *DO NOT DISTURB* sign on the outside door, as well as on the door that led into the VFW dining room and bar area. Once the signs were placed on the doors, the entire team got undressed and started the evidence review.

Ryker and Grayson, since they were the command center team, took the video evidence. Tom and River took the audio review since Tom was the technical person. Then Samantha, Johnathan, Watts, and Amy were reviewing the electronic voice recorders. There were hours of evidence that had to be reviewed from this investigation. While Ryker and Grayson were slowly going through all the video evidence, an hour into looking at the monitors they saw a shadow figure. Rewinding the video to watch it again, there was no doubt a shadow figure that was standing right there in the main hallway, looking right at the camera. It stared not just the camera but also at Samantha and Johnathan as they were changing locations. This shadow figure was very dark with red glowing eyes. It was very evil looking, so Ryker asked Samantha to come over to take a look. Samantha and Johnathan both went over to where Ryker was sitting. He rewound the video for the second time and hit play again. Ryker told Samantha to watch this area right here and pointed at the back of the hallway. Fifteen seconds into the video, the shadow figure appeared with the red eyes. Samantha and Johnathan were both stunned.

"That's one evil presence." Samantha said, and both Ryker and Grayson agreed. "Anything else?"

"Not right at the moment. We'll continue with reviewing, and if we find anything else, we'll definitely let you know."

Immediately after Samantha saw one piece of the video evidence, Tom called her over. "Hey, listen to this."

He gave her the headphones and as he replayed the audio, there was a deep, low voice that said, "Die."

"Wow, that voice did not seem to be of any of the ones that had passed away in this house. I am wondering if there is something else going on here that we may not have been able to find out."

"That is very possible," Tom said.

As they continued to review the evidence that was gathered during the investigation, Ryker noticed that one of the cameras had picked up another entity. This time, the entity appeared to be peeking from one of the bedrooms down the hallway. This entity did not seem to have a demonic appearance but looked like a man in some type of period clothing and was wearing a hat from the 1800s. It was very distinctive, and the details were clear. Ryker was really amazed at how much detail that could be seen with this anomaly. When Ryker came across this video footage, he also had Grayson take a look at the footage. Grayson also could not believe on how clear and defined the footage was. He also knew that he was possibly seeing William Vanderbilt. Grayson came up with an idea to have the team that was going through the voice recordings sync their footage to the same time.

When the review of the voice recording was played back you could hear Samantha ask, "Mr. Vanderbilt, are you here with us?" After few seconds had passed, and they heard a faint voice say "Yes." Right after that, a young girl's voice said, "Daddy." Everyone was so excited.

"Wait, let me play that back." They replayed the conversations.

After hearing it again, everyone was whooping and hollering, excited about it.

Samantha yelled at the entire team. "Quiet down! If there is anything else that was on the recorder, I need to be able to hear it."

Sure enough, right after they heard the little girl say, "Daddy," they heard her say, "I'm scared."

"What?" everyone said at the same time.

Samantha wondered what the little girl was sacred of. After a minute of listening to the audio, this very deep almost like a growl voice said, "Get out!"

That was when they all knew what the little girl was scared of.

After reviewing all the evidence that was collected the night before, it was two in the afternoon. The paranormal team thought that they had enough evidence to take back to the caretaker of Moon Bay Cottage, so they packed up their equipment and headed home. After they got home, Samantha decided that she would have everyone stay at her house so that she would have company and also have help transfer the evidence to a thumb drive so she could present it to her client. After an hour of transferring the data, it was 5:30 p.m. and everyone was starting to get hungry. Johnathan mentioned that they should all get something to eat, so Samantha ordered pizza for everyone. Two large pepperoni, two large cheese, and two large meat lovers' pizza and two, two-liter bottles of soda for delivery from G's Pizza and Subs. After giving the girl her card information and the address, they all sat around talking about the investigation and how they caught all the evidence. Forty-five minutes later, the pizza showed up, and it was about time because they were all starving. Samantha suggested they eat because she had a ten-person hot tub out back they could all get in and have a soak and continue discussion about the investigation.

"We all have to get in naked because just as if you were at a nudist resort, I don't allow clothing in my hot tub or pool."

Ryker laughed. "Well, we don't have bathing suits with us anyway."

"This is true," Samantha said.

After eating dinner, Samantha cleaned up with the help of Ryker and Johnathan. She went into the linen closet, got towels for everyone, and told everyone to come with her. They all headed out to the back yard where the hot tub and pool was. Since yesterday, the weather has gotten much colder, and the pool itself had already been closed down for the season. It was a fabulous yard with a big privacy fence, the inground pool, and an amazing huge hot tub. The hot tub was under a beautiful wooden canopy with a fire pit right next to it.

"Ok, everyone...get naked, and hop in!"

At that time, everyone got naked and joined Samantha in her hot tub that was 101 degrees. Once everyone got settled in, she activated the jets. Just about everyone breathed a sigh of relief, as the jets felt amazing on everyone's backs. Samantha then started up the same conservation that they all were having in the house, and that was from their awesome paranormal investigation from the other night.

While in the hot tub, both Johnathan and Watts were discussing their careers in the US Army. Johnathan had ten years in, and Watts only signed up for a two-year trial period that his recruiter had heard of as a new enlistment opportunity. Since they investigated at Moon Bay Cottage, they both came to an agreement that this is what they wanted to do and decided to walk away from their military career. Johnathan had discussed another opportunity with Watts. Instead of just walking away from the Army all together, they could enlist in the National Guard, and they had Artillery National Guard units around Colorado. That would definitely give them more time to invest in the paranormal team.

After being in the hot tub for over an hour, everyone was pruning up. Samantha made a suggestion that maybe they could get a fire going in the fire pit.

Johnathan was ecstatic about that idea. "Ok, I'll need a couple of you guys to stack some wood in the fire pit, and make sure that it's in a pyramid at first. That's the best way to start a fire when it is just starting out."

A couple of the guys got the wood situated, and Samantha gave the matches to Johanthan. "Here you go, soldier. Let's see some of those skills."

After a few tries, Johnathan finally got the fire started. Everyone sat around the fire pit just chatting away until it became like two in the morning.

"I think we need to call it a night," Ryker said. "I'm heading to bed."

Right after that, everyone else followed.

Chapter Ten

Military Seperation

The following Monday after Johnathan and Watts had the talk about leaving active duty and possibly enlisting in the National Guard, Johnathan took Watts and headed to the commander's office to have a talk with him. As they entered his office, both of them came to attention and saluted the captain.

"Sir, Staff Sergeant Smith and Private Watts reporting, Sir."

Once the captain gave his salute, both Johnathan and Watts dropped their salute.

"First thing, at ease soldiers, and have a seat. What can I help you soldiers with?" the captain said.

"Sir, Watts and I are coming to let you know that we both came to a decision that we are both going to End of Time Service from active duty and enlist in the National Guard."

"I see," said the captain. "What made you two decided to do that?"

"Well, Ssir," Johnathan said. "We have some other obligations outside of active duty that we need to attend to. I love my job here, Sir, but I just don't have the time anymore. I think it would just be better if I go ahead and step away. I decided on the National Guard so that way I can still do what I love in the Army as well as what I love to do as a civilian."

The captain looked at Watts and asked him the same question. "What made you decide on this decision? Smith didn't talk you into this decision, did he?"

"No, Sir. In fact, I went to Staff Sergeant Smith about it since he is my section chief," Watts responded.

"I see. And when is your ETS date, Private?"

"My ETS date is December 1, Sir."

"And when is your ETS date, Staff Sergeant?" the captain asked.

"My ETS date also in December, Sir. It's a coincidence that we both have the same ETS month. But my ETS date is December 5."

"I see," the captain said. "Are you sure that you guys want to leave active duty and go into the National Guard?"

"Yes, Sir, Watts said.

"Yes, Sir," Johnathan said.

"Very well, Staff Sergeant. Let me work a few things and get some information from upper command because I have heard some things, and I want to check and see if it is official yet. You guys come back to see me at 1400 hours, and I'll let you know more information about what we can do."

Johnathan and Watts headed to the motor pool to perform maintenance on the Howitzers.

At noon, Johnathan told his section to go to chow and informed them that he and Watts had to go see the battery commander at 1400 hours. He directed them to return to the motor pool right after chow. The entire section headed to the chow hall, and they all sat together. Johnathan told Watts on Saturday not to mention anything to anyone in the section about what their plans were and that he would brief the section when it got closer. Watts agreed.

After chow, Johnathan reminded the section to head on back down to the motor pool while he and Watts went to talk with the battery commander again like they were instructed to do. Once back in the commander's office, the clerk told them that the commander had stepped out for a few minutes and to have a seat. Five minutes had passed, and then ten minutes had passed, then fifteen minutes, and then twenty minutes. After the twenty-minute mark passed, the commander finally came back to the office.

"Just like the Army," Johnathan mumbled. "Hurry up and wait is the motto around here."

The commander heard Johnathan say something but could not quite make out what he actually said, "What's that, Staff Sergeant?"

"I didn't say anything, Sir."

The captain clearly didn't believe him, but decided to let it go. "I'll be ready shortly, so stand fast for a minute. I'll call you two back in a bit."

Once again, Johnathan and Watts waited.

Three minutes later, the commander called both of them back to his office. Johnathan and Watts rendered a salute. "Staff Sergeant Smith and Private Watts reporting as ordered, Sir."

The commander rendered his salute, and once that happened, both soldiers dropped their salute.

"Have a seat, guys."

Once they were sitting, the commander opened up the meeting. "I was just talking to the colonel, and he informed me that the Army just came out with a new early termination program. I checked your records. You both are eligible for this program. The early termination program has several types of discharge: Honorable, Other than

Honorable, and Dishonorable. Both of you fall under the Honorable discharge since either of you have gotten into any trouble. You both said that you are scheduled to ETS in December, so I can go ahead and process your discharges to be effective November 14. and then you are able to go ahead and get out about a month early. The reenlistment code on your discharge will be the code so you can reenlist, whether you'd like to come back to active duty or reenlist in the Reserves or the National Guard. While I am processing your discharge paperwork, here are some clearing forms that you two need to go around and get signed off. This includes the PX to make sure that you do not owe anything with them and the Commissary, as well as with the unit's sergeant major and first sergeant. Staff Sergeant Smith, I would recommend that you brief your section on what is going on because you guys only have two weeks to get all this done."

"Copy that, sir. I'll brief them today after close of business formation."

When the meeting with the commander, came to an end, the soldiers stood to attention and rendered a salute. The commander saluted back and said they were dismissed.

It was 1530 hours when the meeting with the commander was finished, and final formation for the day was at 1600 hours. Johnathan and Watts headed down to the motor pool to check on the section to see how they were doing and what was done. Once they arrived at the motor pool, the section was just wrapping up for the day. The other sections were wrapping up, too, so everyone could make the 1600 formation. Once everything was put away and the howitzers were locked and secured, Johnathan had a formation of the battery and marched the entire battery up to the orderly room parking lot for formation.

The First Sergeant came out and put out the information that he needed share, the orderly room clerk had mail call, and then everyone was dismissed for the day. Johnathan made his section stand fast so that he could brief his section his and Watts' departure. The section was in shock and disappointed at the same time.

"How are we going to do this without you, Sergeant? We make a great team, and we don't know if we can do this with a new section chief," one of the other privates said.

Johnathan said, "You are the best section that I ever had. I have all the confidence in the world that you will go on and succeed. Just keep doing your job to the best that you can, and you will move up. Please do not be sad for us, as we will still be living in the Pikes Peak region. You are all more than welcome to come visit me anytime you want. I have all of you guys' phone numbers, and I will call and invite everyone of you over for a barbecue."

The next two weeks went by fast, and it was time for Johnathan and Watts to leave. That day, the battery threw a going away party for the two of them, but the entire unit was there. They had food, drinks, and a cake that was in a shape of a howitzer that they had made from a bakery that was in town and known for fancy cakes. After the party, Johnathan and Watts shook hands and gave everyone hugs and left to go and enlist in the National Guard right away so that they could keep the same rank that they currently had. Once enlisted in the National Guard, the guys went to their new unit to get a Drill Schedule and then went to do their new job as ghost hunters.

Chapter Eleven

Amy and Watts New Nudist Club

Six months had passed since the entire paranormal team had investigated Moon Bay Cottage. Since then, they had been very busy. However, everything had been quiet in the paranormal realm of things recently. The entire team was happy for the break they were having. Johnathan and Samantha had continued to date each other, even though Johnathan had to go away for a few weeks for training in California. Amy and Watts also continued to see each other, and because Watts was in Johnathan's artillery section, he also had training in California. While on this six-month break, there had been some new relationships formed within the paranormal team. Tom had started dating Julia, River started dating Ryker, but Grayson was left out in the cold for relationships. But that did not last long as River had a friend, and she had set her friend and Grayson up on a blind date. When they both arrived for date night, they immediately hit it off with each other. Now, Grayson did not feel like the outsider of not having someone special in his life.

Amy and Watts had decided to go where their first date was at: the planetarium. Watts had ordered the same program tickets as their first date, that included the buffet right after the show downstairs. When they arrived at the planetarium, there was a huge sign in the lobby window that read FOR SALE BY OWNER. Immediately, Watts knew that this was his chance to make his dream come true and have a nude planetarium for the local nudist and any visiting nudist. Upon entering the planetarium, he had asked the lady at the check in counter to speak to the owner.

The lady said, "The owner isn't here at the moment, but is there something that I can help you with?"

Watts said, "I saw the sign in the front window about the planetarium being for sale. I wanted to ask about buying it."

Amy looked at him in shocked as she forgot that the last time they were there, and he had said something about buying something like that and turn it into a nudist venue. "Are you really looking into buying this place?"

"Absolutely!" he said.

She could not believe it. "Really?"

"For sure for sure," Watts said. "I mentioned this to you last time we were here."

"I know. I totally forgot, but I didn't know you were serious about that. I thought that you were just joking around."

"Not at all," Watts had said. "I was dead serious. And now this is my perfect opportunity to buy this place and turn it into a nudist planetarium."

Amy and Watts stood over to the side of the counter waiting for the current owner to come out, and after about 15 minutes, the owner came out to greet them. When he came out, he asked the customer service rep that was sitting at the counter where the two of them were. She motioned over to the side where Amy and Watts were standing.

As the owner walked over to Amy and Watts, he extended his hand for a handshake. "My name was Scott. Who do I have the pleasure of speaking to?"

Amy and Watts held out their hands for the handshake. "My name is Watts, and this is Amy."

"Nice to meet you," Scott had said. "Please follow me to my office."

Once in the office, Scott sat behind his executive desk and told Amy and Watts to have a seat. They noticed there was a very nice, very expensive black leather sofa behind them. Above the sofa was a huge picture of Saturn hanging on the wall. This picture looked like it was a professional picture that was actually taken and not one of those cheesy pictures that you would buy off of the internet. As the both of them sat down on the sofa, they noticed the sofa was very firm but soft and comfortable at the same time.

Scott shuffled some papers around and then asked Amy and Watts, "What can I do for you today?"

Watts was the first to speak. He explained that on his very first date with Amy they had come to this planetarium and had mentioned that he would love to buy this place. And then, six months later, they came back and noticed the *For Sale* sign in the window as they entered. "So, this is the perfect opportunity. I would like to know what you are asking for it, and we can go from there."

Scott was so impressed about their love story that he told them that he would definitely work with them about buying the planetarium. Scott also mentioned that their love story was so sweet, and how wonderful it was to spend their very first date in space, technically speaking.

"Aww, thank you, Scott. That's so nice of you. So, what is the asking price for the planetarium?"

Scott looked at them both and responded with a half of a million.

"That a lot of money," Amy responded.

"Yeah, I know. There were a lot of expenses I incurred while owning this place, and I'm trying to get out of that debt."

"I can certainly understand that" Watts said. "Can we negotiate a price of $300,000? That's only because we would like to put some money into renovating the place. We are still going to keep it as a planetarium, but we're going to sink a lot more money into the renovations."

"That's not going to work," Scott said. "I need to get out of this debt that I put myself into."

Watts then asked Scott about his debt and what he needed to bring everything current.

"Well," Scott said. "I'm in debt for $225,000. After I sell this planetarium and pay off all my debt, I will have a little left over to live off of."

"I see," Watts said, then came back with a counteroffer. "How about we give you $100,000 for the planetarium, and we'll pay off your debt as well. Then, we will give you another $50,000 to live off of?"

"That offer was getting closer to something I can work with. Let me think about that offer. Can I get back to you tomorrow?"

"Sure," Watts said. "Here is my card and number. Just call or text me if you decide to accept that offer."

Amy and Watts were escorted out of the office and headed over to Amy's house for the night. Both of them were quiet on the way home.

"How are we going to be able to afford this? I have some money in savings, but not nearly enough." Amy frowned.

"Don't worry. I came into a pretty decent inheritance right after I left the Army full time. I've been looking for an investment. I heard property is usually a good way to do that."

Once they got back to Amy's house, she cooked up some spaghetti and meatballs for dinner. While Amy was cooking the spaghetti, Watts threw some garlic bread in the oven. After dinner and all cleaned up, they both took a shower and headed to bed for the night. Being nudist, they both went to bed naked, and Amy told Watts that he could share her bed with her.

The next morning as the sun was coming up and shining through the bedroom window. Amy was the first one up and out of bed. She stumbled to the kitchen to start cooking some breakfast for the both of them. Still naked, she did throw on an apron just to keep grease from splattering on her. She got the eggs and bacon out of the refrigerator, took out bread for toast, and once all that was done, she poured herself a small glass of orange juice. She then got out her frying pan and a bowl to scramble the eggs in. Placing the frying pan on the stove, she turned the flame on to a medium setting. It only took a minute for the bacon to start sizzling. Upon the bacon starting to cook, Watts smelled the bacon cooking and woke him up. Being a bacon lover, he decided to get out of bed and walk into the kitchen.

"Good morning, sleepy head," Amy said.

"Good morning," Watts replied. "I absolutely love bacon. That smells delicious."

"That's good," Amy had said. "So, how do you like your eggs cooked?"

"I'll take my eggs any way that you want to cook them."

"I was just going to do scrambled, if that's ok with you."

"That is perfect," Watts said.

"Would you like some orange juice?"

"Sure, I'll take some. Do you have milk? I like milk with breakfast."

"Yes, I have milk that you can have." She took two glasses from the cupboard.

Once breakfast was done cooking, Amy pushed the toaster button down. Once that was done, she buttered the toast and placed that on the table as well.

"Breakfast is delicious, Amy. Thank you so much."

Before they were done eating breakfast, Watts's phone buzzed with a text message. He did not recognize the number, but the message read, *this is Scott from the planetarium. I have a counteroffer for you. Can you call me as soon as you get the chance? Thank you.*

Watts told Amy that was Scott from the planetarium. "He said that he had a counteroffer for us and wants me to call him as soon as I get the chance to."

"Wow! It's early, so he must be wanting to get rid of the planetarium really quick."

"Yep. I'll call him as soon as we get cleaned up from breakfast."

After about another 20 minutes, they both had got done eating breakfast and got all the dishes put into the dishwasher. Once that was done, Amy and Watts went into the living room and sat next to each other on the sofa. Amy's sofa was not nearly as comfortable as the sofa that was in the owner of the planetarium's office, but it was still a very nice.

"Ok," Watts said. "Are you ready to call Scott back?"

"Yeah. Let's go ahead and see what he has to say."

Watts tapped on the information tab that was on the text message, and it displayed the phone number that the text message was sent from.

Scott picked up on the third ring. "Hello?"

"Hey, Scott, this is Watts. I received your message, but Amy and I were in the middle of eating breakfast, so we are just now getting around to calling you back. You said that you had a counteroffer for us?"

"Yes. I was up pretty much all night last night and thought about this to no end. I have an offer for you. How about this. How about if I sign the planetarium over to you, but then you can take over everything and just pay me $50,000 to live off of. How does that sound?"

"Am I hearing you correctly? You just want to sign the planetarium over to us, and all we need to do is just give you $50,000?" Watts looked at Amy in disbelief.

"That is correct, Watts. I loved the story that you had told me about you and Amy coming to my planetarium on your very first date."

"Hold on, Scott. Let me put the phone on speaker so Amy can hear this also. Ok, the phone is now on speaker, and Amy is here with me. Can you repeat what you just told me?"

"Sure. Hi, Amy."

"Hi, Scott," Amy said back.

"I'd like to just sign the planetarium over to you and Watts. All I need is the $50,000 to live off of. But there's only one catch: you have to keep it as a planetarium."

"Oh, we don't have any plans not to keep it as a planetarium. Can we call you back in an hour with our decision?"

"That would be fine, Watts. I'll be here waiting."

After Watts hung up the phone, he and Amy were dancing around in her living room all excited.

"Ok, let's calm down and talk about this. That sounds like a deal that we can't refuse. We were going to keep it as a planetarium, anyway.

The only difference is that we were going to turn it into a nudist planetarium."

"Can I as you a question, Watts? If we buy this planetarium, can we still do our naked ghost investigations?"

"I don't see why not, Amy. We can always hire people to run and operate the planetarium while do ghostly investigations. I still love to do ghost investigations. Well, it has been 45 minutes, and we told Scott that we'd call him back within an hour to give him our decision. Are we ready for this? Once we agree to this, there's no turning back."

"I am so ready! Let's do this."

Watts picked up his phone, dialed Scott's number, and immediately put the phone on speaker. Once again, the phone rang three times, and then Scott answered.

"Hey, Scott. Amy and I are going to accept your offer. We would like to come in today and sign all the paperwork that's needed. We'll stop by the bank and get you a cashier's check for the money."

"Sounds good, Watts. I'll see you really soon. My lawyer will have the paperwork ready by lunchtime. I'll be at the office the rest of day waiting for you."

After Amy and Watts got dressed, they headed out to Watts's bank to get a cashier's check. He had a slightly difficult time getting that much because the bank teller wanted to know what the money was for.

"Keeping it personal," Watts told the bank teller. It was none of her business. It was his money, and it was up to him to use it for whatever he wanted.

After a few rounds of going back and forth with each other, the branch manager overheard their conversation and came over to see what was happening. "Can I help you, sir?"

Watts tried to contain his frustration. "All I wanted was to get this cashier's check, which is my own money. Ms. Laura here is being nosy and wanted to know what the money was for. It's none of her business."

"Is this true, Laura?"

She admitted it was, looking sheepishly at the floor.

"Laura, just print his check and give it to him. It truly is none of your business on what he uses it for. All this could have been avoided if you would have only done this in the first place. Here you go, sir. Have a nice day."

"Thank you," Watts said.

Once Watts had his cashier's check, he and Amy headed out to the car to head down to the planetarium. Once at the parking lot at the planetarium, they found a parking spot and headed into the planetarium. As they both were walking, Amy noticed that the space next to the planetarium was up for rent or sale as well.

"Hey, Watts. Look, do you think we can check this as well? We can turn it into the paranormal headquarters."

"I certainly don't see why not, Amy. Let's go in and get the planetarium taken care of, and then we can inquire about that space."

Once inside the planetarium, they walked up to the information desk and told the lady sitting behind the desk that they were there to see Scott.

"Sure. Let me call him." The lady picked up her desk phone and hit a button and immediately spoke into the receiver. "Sir, there are a couple of people here that are asking to see you." She looked at Amy and Watts and asked them their name, and they told her. "Thank you, sir."

She hung the phone and told Amy and Watts that he would be right up. Within five minutes, Scott came up and greeted them and asked them to come on back to the office. Once back in the office, they all sat around the executive conference table. Scott grabbed an envelope off of his desk.

"Before we get started, I do have my attorney joining us. He's bringing the paperwork."

On cue, the lawyer walked in, and everyone stood up and greeted him and shook his hand.

"Ok. Let's get this show started."

The lawyer took the contract out of his briefcase and presented it to Scott. After the papers were read and signed, he gave them to Watts to review and showed him where to sign. Ten minutes later and signing what seemed to be like 40 papers, the deal was done.

The lawyer double checked everything was done correctly. "The planetarium is now in the hands of the new owner, Watts and Amy."

"One more thing that has to be done now," Watts said. "Here's a cashier's check for $50,000. All made out and ready for you. You just need to deposit it in your bank account."

"Thank you so much," Scott told them.

"Thank you, Scott. We're extremely very happy about this. I do have a question before we all adjourn this meeting. When Amy and I were walking in today, we noticed that the lot right next to the planetarium was up for lease or sale. Do you know who is in charge of that property?"

"Actually, I own that as well. That's one reason I wanted to sell the planetarium and get out of debt. I decided to go ahead and sell the property next to the planetarium as well just a day or two ago."

"That is awesome," Amy said. "We would be interested in buying that property, as well."

"Yes, I'll sell that property to you guys. I'm asking $100,00 for that location."

"I think we can make that work. We'll take it," Watts said. "Draw up the paperwork, and we'll come next week and sign what is needed to acquire that location, too."

"We will have the paperwork ready for you." The lawyer slid the contract into his case.

"The sooner we do this, the sooner Amy and I can start renovating the planetarium the way we would like to have it."

Scott, Amy, Watts and the lawyer all shook hands, and Scott congratulated them. Right after signing and acquiring the planetarium, Amy and Watts went out in the lobby, waiting for Scott and his lawyer to come out. Scott made an announcement over the speaker system for the entire staff to meet in the lobby. The planetarium was not open to the public that day so that Scott could get the planetarium sold to Amy and Watts. After Scott made the announcement over the intercom system, he then headed out into the lobby. The staff had already started arriving.

Scott said, "I have an announcement. I would like everyone to head into the projection room." After everyone was in the projection room, Scott put on a microphone and gave Watts a microphone as well.

Once the staff was settled in their seats, Scott turned on the microphone. There was a slight crackling over the speakers for a second, but it stopped almost immediately. "Thank you all for coming. I have a few announcements. First and foremost, I want to take this opportunity to thank all of you for being a great staff. Next, I want to let everyone know that today is my final day as owner of this great planetarium. As you know, it has been up for sale, and I just sold the planetarium to Mr. Watts and Amy. They are now the new owners, so you will report directly to them. Now, I want to turn the floor over to Mr. Watts."

Watts had the floor. "I'm honored to have acquired this beautiful planetarium. Amy and I came here for our very first date several months ago. Even then, we were very interested in buying the place. If anyone's worried about losing their jobs, that's not going to happen. In fact, Amy and I are going to try to give everyone a raise if you decide that you would still like to work for us. On that note, we're going to do a little remodeling, but we'll stay open during the renovation. Also, Amy and I are paranormal investigators, and we're going to purchase the building right next door. Once we acquire that building, we're going to turn that into our paranormal headquarters. If any one of you want to join the paranormal team, please come and talk to Amy and me.

"One thing that I do want to mention is that we are going to turn this planetarium into a nudist planetarium. We are going to start having nudist-friendly shows. I know that you may be very concerned or even scared about that, but I assure you that the staff does not have to be naked. We're going to place a warning sign up in the front, as well as all around the planetarium. It will read, *WARNING BEYOND THIS POINT YOU MAY ENCOUNTER NUDITY.* As of right now, we are not going to go to nude showings right away. We want to make sure that we inform the community and get the required permits. Once all that is done, then we'll go to a nudist planetarium. We'll build a new star projection room just for those that do not want to be nude. If anyone has any questions or concerns or even just want to talk to us, Amy and I have an open-door policy, so please come see us. The last thing Amy and I want is for any of you ladies and gentlemen to be uncomfortable or embarrassed or anything. Talk to us first before you make any decision. Amy and I will work with all of you. With all that being said, I'd like to invite Mr. Scott back to the floor for any additional comments or to answer any questions from all of you."

"At this time, I don't have anything else."

"Thank you, Mr. Scott. Amy and I would like to let you know that you are welcome back anytime you would like to come, free of charge."

"Thank you, Mr. Watts. I'll definitely take you up on that offer."

"Ok, folks. I have nothing else to put out at this time, so all of you are dismissed. Before you leave, Amy and I will be having a luncheon in the conference room a little later. So please, come by and have some food and drinks on us."

Chapter Twelve

The Naked Paranormal Headquarters

A week had passed since Amy and Watts purchased the planetarium. Scott had called Watts to come and sign for the purchase of the building next to the planetarium. When they arrived at the empty location, Watts just wanted to take a quick walk through the building since either him or Amy had walked through to look at the building before offering to buy it. Scott agreed to let them walk through and to point out the amenities that were already in the building. As they walked through, Scott pointed out the front desk for visitors to sign in. The front desk was absolutely beautiful with a granite countertop and oak for the desk itself that looked to be well kept. Down the hallway, Scott pointed out the main office. The main office was huge. It had a conference table with six leather chairs. Over in the left corner was an executive desk that was also made out of oak and had a mirror shine and not a scratch on it. Moving on through the building, there was another office to the left. It was not as big as the main office but still a decent size office. Once again there was a well-kept oak desk. Watts asked Scott if all the offices had the oak desk, and his assured them they did. Continuing on towards the back, there was another room that was big and had TV monitors hung on the wall. In front of the TVs, there were two huge desk that had computer connections running up through the cable access holes. Further back in the building were two more small offices and the bathroom. The bathroom was big for an office space even had a corner shower. The shower was a one-person stall with a glass door with dolphins etched into the glass. The sink was a designer sink with water that ran out like a waterfall over blue gemstones.

Watts and Amy immediately fell in love with the office space. It was exactly what they needed for a paranormal investigation headquarters. Watts told Scott that he was ready to sign the contract to purchase the location. All three of them went into the main office and sat around the conference table. Scott handed all the papers over to Watts and Amy. Each of them read through the paperwork and signed and initialed each and every one of the papers that needed signed. After all the paperwork was sign, Scott reached out his hand for a handshake and congratulated Amy and Watts for their new office.

"Thank you, Scott. And once again, my offer stands for you to visit the planetarium at any time free of charge. Now that we bought this location for our paranormal headquarters, you're more than welcome to come out to do some paranormal investigations with us. However, please know we're nude paranormal investigators." Watts looked at Scott with a grin on his face.

Scott grinned back. "I hope to do a little traveling now that these are sold. I wish you luck, though."

After Scott left the building, Amy and Watts stayed behind to talk about how they were going to run both the planetarium and the paranormal location at the same time.

Amy had an idea. "Is there a way that we can just hire someone to run the planetarium? That way, we can concentrate solely on the paranormal investigations. We can go over the staffs' performance appraisals and see if we can promote someone to that position."

"That's a great idea, Amy, but let's get the paranormal headquarters up and running, and then, we can work on that. Although I do love space and the planetarium, I want to devote most of my time doing paranormal investigations. That's my passion, and I want to keep doing that."

After Amy and Watts had their talk, they started to work on the paranormal headquarters immediately. Amy went online and found some ghost pictures that she ordered and would arrive in two days, while Watts started dusting, sweeping, and mopping the furniture and floors. Amy asked Watts if they should tell the rest of the paranormal team about the location now or wait until they had everything up and running. Watts thought it was a good idea to just wait until the building was ready to be occupied before either of them mentioned anything to the team.

"Ok," Amy said. "I'm so excited, but we can wait. It won't be long getting this location up and running since almost everything we need was already there and ready to go."

After another four days of working in the paranormal headquarters building, everything was set and ready to open. Watts had ordered brand new computers and hooked them up to the TV monitors that were mounted on the wall for the video evidence review. He also ordered brand new speakers and had them mounted on the wall for the audio evidence review. Amy placed flowers on the front check-in desk and hung her ghost pictures. The pictures she found online were real photos from other paranormal teams from around the country.

Watts also ordered the same warning signs that he had ordered for the planetarium that read *WARNING YOU MAY ENCOUNTER NUDITY BEYOND THIS POINT*. They hung those signs, as well. Everything that the two of them hung up used adhesive strips so there were no nails to put holes in the wall.

Once everything was hung and ready to go, Amy asked Watts about calling Samantha to come and take a look. "I'm hoping for that she'll be impressed and like everything that we have done for the team. I mean, we spent a lot of money, so I hope that they'll be satisfied."

Amy got off the phone with Samantha, she said, "Samantha will be here in 20 minutes. I didn't say anything about the new headquarters to her because I want it to be a surprise. I told her that we'll meet her in front of the planetarium. Then, we both can tell her the news about the brand-new paranormal headquarters."

They stood right outside of the planetarium entrance on the sidewalk. Samantha drove by them and waved, then turned and found a parking spot, got out of her car, and walked up to them. Samantha gave both Amy and Watts a hug.

Amy asked, "Samantha, would you want a new headquarters for the paranormal team?"

Samantha was trying to run the entire team from her house. "I'd love to have a headquarters for the paranormal team, but I just don't have the money for one."

Watts joined in the conservation. "Samantha, don't worry. We will figure something out. Let's go for a little walk." He gave Amy a conspiratorial wink.

Amy and Watts stopped walking when they reached the entrance of the office building.

Samantha asked, "Why did you guys stop?"

At that time, Watts took out a set of keys from his pocket, picked out the key to the door, and unlocked it. Samantha looked both confused and surprised that he had a key to the door. They stepped inside.

"Come on, Samantha," Amy said.

Samantha hesitantly stepped in the doorway. Once Samantha was inside, Amy and Watts yelled, "Surprise! Samantha, this is our new paranormal headquarters!"

"What?" Samantha was in disbelief.

"We bought and turned this vacant building into a headquarters for us. Do you want a tour of the place?" Watts extended his arm for Samantha to take.

"You're joking," she said, but took Watts arm anyway.

They took Samantha around and showed her all the offices and the evidence review room She started to cry as she still could not believe what was happening.

Amy hugged her. "I hope these are tears of happiness."

Samantha nodded. "I cannot believe that you guys did all this. How much was all this?"

"What we paid for it isn't important, but what is important is that you like this. It's an investment in our future." Watts smiled.

"Yes, I am totally in love with what you guys have done. When can we move in?"

Watts said, "We can move in at any time...it's all ready to go."

"There's so much I need to pack up. I need to tell the rest of the team and get them to pack all their equipment up and move in here."

"Look," Watts said. "I even have the permits from the jurisdiction to even be naked if we wanted to."

"That is amazing," Samantha said. "I can't wait to get started. We have advertising to do, including printing flyers, business cards, and everything else. And I think we may need to update the company name."

Once Samantha told the paranormal team about the new headquarters, Amy and Watts wanted for the entire team to meet them at the building. He needed to give the entire team keys and the alarm code to the building. The team arrived at the location, but before anything was given out, Amy, Watts, and Samantha gave the team a tour of the new headquarters. Each and every one of the paranormal team was so excited and could not wait to get started having more paranormal investigations. The problem was not with investigations but getting clients to hire for the investigations. With this new building, it would give them a fresh new start, extra motivation, and a more professional appearance. As the paranormal team moved in, everyone got settled in the new offices. Samantha and Johnathan took the main office as Samantha was the CEO of the paranormal team. Amy and Watts took the second biggest office as they actually bought the building for everyone. Ryker and Grayson took the evidence review room, while Tom took the very back office. Julia and River were at the front desk.

Since Tom was the Tech Ops person, Samantha tasked him to create flyers to pass out throughout the surrounding neighborhoods. He was asked to develop a new website so people could find them if they needed a highly trained paranormal team to investigate activity. Tom was also tasked with making business cards for each of the team members and one for the entire team. The flyers were the first to be designed, and about 5,000 were printed. They were very colorful and very detailed. The flyer stated that the team was very professional and were skilled even though they do investigations totally naked. Next up for design was the website. The website included the experience that everyone had, and it included a naked picture of the team all together, along with contact information and customer reviews. The next thing that Tom designed and had printed were all the business cards for the team. He designed each team member a business card with *Pikes Peak Naked Paranormal Investigations.* He put the same thing on each business card except for the team member's name. Then, he added the office phone number along with each team members' business cell phone number. Tom bought each team member a personal business card holder and a multi-business card holder for the front reception desk. There was a flyer holder for the front desk as well. Once all the advertising material was printed and distributed, it was time to get the paranormal investigators out there in the public eye and get some clients. Amy and Watts paid for the signage on the building front and also on the sign as customers entered the parking lot. All that was left was to bring in clients and get back to investigating the paranormal.

Chapter Thirteen

The Naked Planetarium Club

Now that Amy and Watts bought the planetarium and the building right next to it, they needed to figure out who to hire to run the planetarium. They both wanted to concentrate on paranormal investigations as they both loved to do that. They would eventually visit the planetarium every now and then, just to relax and enjoy themselves and check up on the staff. Amy and Watts told Samantha that they were going over to the planetarium to look over the staff's appraisals.

"Look over their appraisals?" Samantha asked.

"Yes. Not only own this building, but we also own the planetarium. We bought the planetarium a week before we bought this building, but we want to concentrate on doing paranormal investigations."

"I see," Samantha said. "Good luck with your new staff."

Amy and Watts walked over to the planetarium, and the front desk associate greeted them. "Good afternoon, Ms. Amy and Mr. Watts."

THE NAKED PARANORMAL INVESTIGATORS 115

"Good afternoon to you as well, Jennifer. How are things going with you?"

"I'm doing great, sir. Thanks for asking."

"Amy and I are going to the office, so if you need anything, please let us know." Watts turned to walk away.

"I sure will, sir, and thank you. Before you go, is there anything that you need?"

"No," Amy said. "I think we are good...thank you for asking."

Amy and Watts walked back to the office and sat at the desk. Amy started to pull all the files of the employees out to go over and review the appraisals. The first one that Amy wanted to review was Jennifer's. When they opened her file, they immediately saw her last appraisal. She pulled it out and started reading through it. Everything in that appraisal was marked outstanding. The comments, too, were excellent. Looking back at the dates, it looked like Jennifer had been working for the planetarium for the last ten years. Every one of her appraisals had the highest marks.

"This appraisal for Jennifer is absolutely amazing. But let's see what the other appraisals are like."

Watts started going through the files and found all the other appraisals. As they continued to look through the entire staff's files, not one other staff member had any reviews like Jennifer's.

"Well, Watts. I know who I would like to promote to senior director of the planetarium."

"I totally agree with that decision. I still think we need to give all the staff a pay raise because none of the appraisals were bad. It's just that Jennifer's stood out with the outstanding marks. Amy, would you like to call her back to the office, and we can talk to her about the promotion?"

Amy called over the intercom for Jennifer to come back to the office. Once she got back to the office, both Watts asked Jennifer to have a seat because they needed to have a talk with her.

The very first thought that Jennifer had was that she did something wrong and that she was going to get in trouble, maybe even fired from her job. Her heartbeat was pounding in her chest. "Is something wrong?"

"Jennifer, we brought you back here to ask you something. You aren't in trouble by any means, so get that out of your mind. As you know, Amy and I have purchased this planetarium. Our goal is to turn it into a nudist destination. We are also nude paranormal investigators, so we both decided that we wanted to continue with that. We're looking to hire or promote someone to run the planetarium. Amy and I have gone through all the employee files, and yours stood out the most to us."

Then, Amy took over the meeting. "What Watts and I would like to do is promote you to senior operations manager. With this promotion also comes a pay raise. It would be official starting on Monday next week. We would like to know what your thoughts are, and if you would be interested in the position. Please take time to reflect on the offer. But there are some requirements with the position. First and foremost, this is going to be a nudist retreat, so the rules will be that anyone that enters the projection room must be completely naked. Everyone must have a towel to sit on their chair. If they don't have towels, we'll have the guest sign out a towel. They must return the towel when the show is over or when they are ready to leave for the day. Second, the common area nudity is clothing optional. Guest can choose to be naked or not there. With our experience, most nudist will be naked whenever possible. Third, the staff has the option to be naked as well. All staff that work the projection room must be naked.

We have lockers in the entrance lobby, as well as some right before you enter the projection room. I'm sure you know that. So what do you think? Are you up for the task, or do you need time to think and maybe discuss this with someone?"

"Ms. Amy and Mr. Watts. I'd like to accept the position," Jennifer replied.

Watts immediately responded to Jennifer. "That's so wonderful. How much do you make now?"

"Sir, I make $20 an hour now."

"I see. How much would you like to make on this position?"

"Sir, I'd like to make at least $22 dollars an hour."

Watts put his hand up to his chin and sighed. "Well, Jennifer, if you want $22 an hour, how about we make it $25 an hour?"

Jennifer's jaw dropped as she could not believe on what she was hearing. "That would be absolutely wonderful, sir. I totally accept the offer."

"Sounds good, Jennifer. I'm going to call a meeting with the entire staff and let them know the changes that will be taking place on Monday. We'll have the meeting in an hour."

Amy called out over the intercom to all the staff that there will be a mandatory meeting in the projection room in one hour.

Another hour had passed, then the entire staff started showing up to the projection room for the meeting. Amy, Watts, and Jennifer were already in the projection room waiting for everyone to show up.

Once everyone arrived, Amy started the meeting off. "Everyone, please quiet down so we can get this meeting started."

When everyone had stopped talking, Amy continued. "Welcome to the meeting. We have an important announcement. At this time, I would like to turn the floor over to Mr. Watts. You have the floor."

Watts started out by once again welcomed everyone to the meeting. "Amy and I have some exciting news. Jennifer is now the senior operations manager for the planetarium."

When that announcement was made, Amy and Watts were surprised by the staff clapping to the announcement.

"We feel that Jennifer is the best fit for this position right now. With hard work and dedication with each and every one of you, there's room for other promotions and opportunities. We can't thank everyone enough for their help so far. As you all know, Amy and I are also paranormal investigators. Even though we own this planetarium, both of us would like to concentrate on the paranormal field. You may have noticed that we also bought the building next door. That's now our paranormal headquarters. But enough of me talking. At this time, I'd like to turn the floor over to Jennifer to say a few words."

Jennifer took the microphone from Watts. "Many thanks to everyone I work with. As you all know, I've been here for a long time, and it's my privilege to accept this promotion. I've worked with many of you for quite a while now. Not only are you my coworkers, but you are also my friends. I promise each and every one of you that I'll be fair. At the same time, I'll uphold all the rules and regulations that the new management has laid out since they took ownership of the planetarium. They both gave me the privilege of this opportunity to advance myself. I'll mentor any one of you, if you decide that you'd like to advance your career as well. Ms. Amy and Mr. Watts, I thank you for this opportunity, and I won't let either of you down. I'll do my best to uphold your standards, rules, and regulations. Thank you both from the bottom of my heart."

After Jennifer gave her short speech, she handed over the microphone to Amy. "Jennifer, it's our privilege to be able to promote you to this position. We have the utmost confidence in you in your ability to lead and run the business. We wouldn't have promoted you to this position if there was any doubt in either of our minds."

Amy then looked at all the employees. "As a token of gratitude, we had lunch delivered. It will be served in the main lobby. So, come join us in the celebration of Jennifer's promotion. Let's get to know each other."

At the luncheon, Amy and Watts had both Italian and American cold cut subs along with wraps. Additionally, there was macaroni salad, potato salad, drinks, and dessert. They also had gotten a whole sheet cake with colorful flowers and an edible image of the solar system. It had *Congratulations, Jennifer* written in black icing. How they were able to get all that within an hours' time period was amazing, but there was a great team at their favorite restaurant.

As everyone was chowing down on their lunch, Watts wanted to make another announcement. "Attention everyone, attention. Now that Amy and I have someone in the senior management position, we're going to start back with our paranormal investigations. On Monday, we'll open the planetarium back up to the public. Just remember that this is now a nudist planetarium. All guest and staff are required to be naked inside the projection room. Here in the lobby, it will clothing optional for everyone. If any one of you don't want to be naked, please talk with Jennifer so she can arrange another position for you. No one here is going to get fired for not wanting to get naked. This is what social nudity is all about: acceptance and embracing body positivity...not sex. Just by a show of hands, who here doesn't want to be naked no matter what?"

With that question, only two team members raised their hand.

"Ok, guys, please get with Jennifer as soon as possible so she can arrange different positions for the both of you."

"Jennifer, if you need help with anything or have any issues, please let us know. We can guide you through whatever it is that you need help with. For the two that raised their hand and are nervous about getting naked, you can probably put them at the welcome desk, as that position is now vacant. They can check our guest in. They'll need to get used to seeing our guest naked. They'll also have to get used to entire families being naked, as well as individuals. Amy and I have a contract with an armed security guard company that is going to start on Monday so that this is a safe place. The security guards are not to be naked, as they're here to protect all our guest. There will be guards stationed in the main entrance, as well as in the projection room. We want to keep everyone, including the staff, safe. If you see that more guards are needed, you have the authority to reach out to the security company and request more. Amy and I will put you down as an authorized person on the contract."

Chapter Fourteen

New Contracts

Amy and Watts had a Senior Operations Supervisor for the planetarium, so they could concentrate on paranormal investigations. As the entire paranormal team was sitting in the office looking up other places that they could possibility investigate, a young couple walked in. They both looked like that they were in their early to mid-twenties. Julia was sitting at the front reception desk and gave them a friendly greeting.

The couple greeted her back. "My name is Mike, and this is my wife, Destiny. We'd like to talk with someone about some activity that has been going on at our home. We're kind of nervous to be talking about the activity, but it's picked up within the last month."

"Hello, Mike and Destiny. My name is Julia, and welcome. We are glad you came...there's nothing to be ashamed. This is why we are here! Have a seat, and someone will be right with you."

As Mike and Destiny took a seat in the waiting area, Julia called back and told Samantha. "Ms. Samantha, there's a couple here who want to speak to someone about activity that has been going on in their home."

"One of us will be right out for them. Thank you."

A few minutes later, Samantha came out to the waiting room and called them back. "Hello. My name is Samantha. Nice to meet you. Come on back to my office."

Mike and Destiny followed Samantha back.

Once the couple were in Samantha and Johnathan's office, Samantha invited them to have a seat at her desk. "This is Johnathan, my partner. Johnathan, this is Mike and Destiny."

"Hello," Johnathan said as they had a seat the desk.

Samantha took out a packet of papers that were for a contract and information. "So, Mike and Destiny, tell me what's been going on."

Mike started the conversation. "Well, we're really nervous about saying anything about what has been going on...we don't want people thinking that we're crazy or anything."

Samantha reassured them. "That's why we are here. We're professionals. We have all top-notch equipment. Just because we all here are nudist doesn't mean we are not serious about our investigations."

"Ok," Destiny said. "Well, to start, we have always had some type of activity happening in our house ever since we bought it a year ago. It's just been getting worse."

Samantha leaned forward in her chair. "Tell me what's been happening."

"Well, we've been hearing a lot of footsteps in our hallway when it's only us two home. We have a cat, and we know for sure that she's not making the noise because she sleeps with us on the bed. She seems to be spooked when this happens. We also hear noises coming from our bedroom closet. When I'm taking a shower, I get this eerie feeling that someone is watching me. I pull the shower curtain back, and no one's there, but then I notice that my towels that I had laid on the bathroom sink are on the floor."

Mike continued. "When I'm in my garage...after I use one of my power tools and turn it off, the same tool powers back on when I walk away from it. I thought that I saw a shadow figure in the corner of the garage, and it doesn't seem to be friendly in any way."

"I see," Samantha said. "Anything else?"

"Yes," Mike said. "When I go up the few steps that lead into the house, it seems like something either pushes me or trips me, and I stumble in through the door to the house. I have also been scratched on my shoulders."

"This is definitely something that we need to investigate." Samantha pulled out some papers and handed them across the desk. "These papers are to let new clients know what we do. Let's go over a couple things. If you look at the first page, this explains what we are. We're nudist, and we do our investigations naked. The first page explains how we came about this aspect of our company. The second page explains what we actually do, if you have not ever dealt with any paranormal investigators before. The third page explains about all the equipment that we use, and all of our equipment is professional equipment. So, this should ease any concerns about our credibility. Some people assume that just because we investigate naked all the time that we aren't professional. That couldn't be further from the truth. Are you still interested in us investigating your house?"

"Yes, we're totally ready for you guys to check everything out for us. Do we need to find a place to stay when you do this or can we stay there?" Mike said as Destiny read over the paperwork, then placed it on the desk.

"That's totally up to you. It's your house...just remember that the entire investigating team will be naked," Johnanthan responded.

"That's fine with us. Can we sign the contract today so we can get this ball rolling? We need to figure out what's going on with our house."

With that said, Samantha told them, "Sure thing. All I need you to do is sign here, then here, and put today's date in here."

After Mike and Destiny signed, Samantha and Johnathan signed the contract as well. "So now, let's get you guys scheduled." Samantha pulled up her appointment calendar. "Looks like we have next Saturday available. Would that work for you guys?"

"That would be perfect," the couple said at the same time.

As Samantha and Johnathan were taking care of Mike and Destiny, another prospective client walked in. This was the moment that the paranormal team has been waiting desperately for: getting as many clients as possible. Julia asked them to sign in and have a seat.

Julia took the clipboard and called back to the offices. "Ms. Samantha, we have two people here from the Aviation Museum."

"Julia, can you call back and let Amy and Watts know that we have clients waiting."

"Yes, ma'am," Julia said, still holding the phone receiver. She pushed a button that made the phone immediately hang up with Samantha and go directly connected to Amy and Watts office.

Watts picked up the phone and could see that the call was coming in from the front desk. "Yes, Julia," Watts said in a firm but gentle voice.

"Sir, we have two people here from an Aviation Museum that would like to speak to someone."

"I'll be right out." He immediately walked out into the waiting room. This time, unlike Samantha, Watts was completely naked. "Welcome. How can I help you?"

This was a shock to the clients, despite all the warning signs hanging around the office. They looked at each other, then the gentleman said, "I think we need your help."

"Come on back," Watts said, reaching out to shake the woman's hand. "My name is Watts."

"Hello, Watts. My name is Penny. I'm the curator of the Aviation Museum."

The gentleman then shook Watts's hand. "My name is Xander, and I'm the owner of the Aviation Museum."

Watts smiled. "Come on back to my office. Nice meeting you both."

Once they got back to Watts office, he invited them to have a seat. As they both took a seat in some very comfortable chairs, Watts asked them what he could do for them.

Xander started. "We've been having some paranormal activity happening around the Aviation Museum, especially around the B29 bomber from World War II."

"I'm not surprised as those planes have seen a lot of action in the war, and an object like that could hold onto a lot of energy." Watts took out the same packet that Samantha had used for her clients and started taking some notes. As Watts was writing down notes from what Xander was telling him, he asked what has been happening.

"We have nighttime tours through our airfield on Friday and Saturday nights. There have been sightings of what seems to be soldiers wearing leather jackets as if they were the pilots. Not only does our tour guide see it, but also our customers tell us the same thing. We even had customers fall down the aircraft steps, and they tell us that they felt like that they were pushed."

"That's not good at all," Watts said. He looked at Penny and asked her if she encountered anything.

"Yes, I did. When I'm in the museum building, I always get a creepy feeling, and I can swear that I've seen a shadow that goes really fast around all the display cases. I've also seen this black mist up in the corner of the ceiling over by the display that has information on the plane crash that happened in the Florida Everglades."

"That sounds like it may be demonic to me," Watts said. "There've been instances that something like that was not demonic, and that the entity just wanted to be acknowledged. We won't know until we get in there and investigate."

When Watts finished his note taking, he gave Penny and Xander the packet explaining about their company and their paranormal investigation techniques. Watts asked them to look at the packet that he gave them. This was the standard packet for all clients and nothing different on them. If something had to be altered, there was an amendment sheet. He went over the packet with them. "If you look at the first page, this page explains that the company was founded as a nudist paranormal investigative team, hence me being naked now. The second page explains what we do, third page about our equipment, and so on."

At this time, Amy walked into the office, and she was just as naked as Watts was. Amy introduced herself to the clients and told them she was one of the paranormal investigators.

Watts introduced them. "This is Penny and Xander. They're from the Aviation Museum."

"That's so cool," Amy said. "I've visited the museum before, but it's been quite some time. So, with knowing what you know about our paranormal team, are you still interested in having us investigate for you?"

Penny shifted uncomfortably in her chair, but Xander nodded. "I'm positively sure we want this you guys to investigate." Xander had already done his own research on this particular paranormal investigative team. "I'm ready to sign the contract."

Watts said, "So, what I'm going to do is read over the contract and explain everything for you. At the end, we both will sign it. Then, we'll get you scheduled for the investigation."

Watts was reading over the exact laminated copy of the contract. The first section was labeled, *The Nudist Contract*. The contract read, *This is a nudist paranormal investigative team and will investigate all locations naked. You must agree to these terms.* There was a section marked *yes* and a section marked *no*. Watts told Xander that he needed to initial one of those boxes, but if he should initial *no*, they would not be able to investigate. With that, Xander went ahead and initialed the box that was marked *yes*. Part two read, *We are a professional paranormal investigative team, and we use professional equipment. Do you agree to us using any equipment necessary for us to do our investigation properly?* Xander went ahead and initialed yes to that question. Part three read, *After our investigation, it may take anywhere from 48 to 72 hours for our team to gather all the evidence that we need to be able to give you a true report on our findings. Do you agree with the statement stated above on this contract?* Xander also initialed the yes box to this question.

"Awesome," Watts said. "Now, all I need you to do is sign the contract here and then here and date it here."

After Xander signed the document, Watts signed the contract, and he then gave a copy of the contract to Xander.

"So now, let's get you scheduled." Watts pulled up the appointment calendar, and he noticed that there was a scheduled investigation pinned for the following weekend. Seeing that, Watts told them that they were booked up for the weekend, but they did have an opening that week. He took two appointment cards, filled out the information, and gave one to Xander and one to Penny. "If you need anything from us in the meantime, please don't hesitate to get in contact with us."

Chapter Fifteen

Investigating Mike and Destiny's House

The day came to investigate the home of Mike and Destiny, so the paranormal team had gotten dressed and packed up since they could not be naked outside of the office. They all jumped into the company cars and vans and headed down to road towards the location of the home. The home was a very nice, located in a gated well-kept, gated community. They pulled up to the guard house located at the entrance of the development. There was only one way in and one way out of the community. As the team pulled up to the gate, the armed security guard in the guard house stepped out and asked the first vehicle who they were there to see. The first car was a black Toyota Crown that had a sign on each of the doors with *Pikes Peak Naked Paranormal Investigations* and the contact information. Samantha and Johnathan were driving that vehicle.

Samantha spoke to the guard. "We're here to see Mike and Destiny Anderson at 513 Cemetary Lane."

"Oh, yes. They told me they were expecting you." The guard stepped out, gesturing. "Follow this road to the end. Once you get to the end of the road, make a left. Then, follow that road down...their house will be at the very end. You'll know if you are in the right place because they're the only house on that road. There's a cemetery right next to the house."

Samantha looked at Johnathan, confused. "What the hell? That's one major detail they left out when they came to see us. That may be the issue that they're having with their house.

"I totally agree," Johnathan said. "I'm wondering what else we'll find on our investigation tonight."

As Johnathan and Samantha went through the gate, the security guard motioned for the rest of the team to follow them. The next paranormal team vehicle that went through the gate was a solid black Ford Transit van, and again, it had signs on each one of its doors. The command vehicle was next, and that vehicle was a Mercedes-Benz Sprinter van, but instead of having the paranormal team's signs on the doors, the information was decaled on each side of the van. Once all the vehicles were through the gate, the security guard put the gate boom arm back down. As the team followed each other up the road and to the house, they seemed to be leaving the development. Although Mike and Destiny's house was still considered to be in the gated community, it also seemed to be back in the woods, away from everything. As the paranormal team approached the house, Mike was standing outside totally naked waiting on them. When they stopped and got out of their vehicles, Samantha and Johnathan walked up to Mike and shook his hand.

Samantha smiled. "I didn't know that you were a nudist as well."

"I didn't want to say anything when we came to see you guys at the office because I wasn't sure if you would take our case or not. Destiny is a nudist as well, and that's one of the reasons that we hired you guys specifically."

Johnatha asked, "Mike, do you and Destiny want to investigate with us tonight?"

Mike looked excited. "I'd have to ask Destiny if she would be interested in doing that. Come on in and we'll give you a tour of the house."

The rest of the team stayed outside and started preparing the equipment that would be needed for the night's investigation. When Mike, Samantha, and Johnathan entered the house, Mike called out for Destiny and told her that the paranormal team is here.

Destiny came from upstairs, and she was naked as well. "Welcome to our home. Mike, have you offered them anything to drink?"

Mike said, "Not yet. How about a drink and maybe some snacks?"

Both Samantha and Johnathan said they were good, so Mike then asked if any of their team members would like a drink.

"Thank you, Mike, but we just ate dinner right before we got here. Ok, let's take a tour of the house," Johnathan said.

Mike led the way up the third floor and into the large room. "This is the master bedroom."

Samantha kept asking the questions while Johnathan was taking the notes.

Mike explained what all was happening in here. "Next, let's go to the second, and I'll explain what has been going on there." They made their way through the house one floor at time, ending in the basement.

Once Samantha and Johnathan did the walk through of the house with Mike, they met the rest of the team outside, who had already gotten all the equipment ready to go. Johnathan told the team that since it was a big house, they would start their investigation with two people at a time but to know that might change. When the briefing was done with the paranormal team, the everyone pitched in and set up the equipment. There were four static cameras set up, and once everything was in place, Ryker and Grayson went over the camera locations with Samantha and Johnathan. The two of them approved the camera locations, and they instructed the team to get naked and turn their lights out as it was 8:00 p.m. The entire team got naked and put all their clothes in their bins.

Mike and Destiny greeted them at the command center. "If the offer is still open, we would like to join you for your investigation tonight."

Samantha nodded. "That's awesome. We're glad to have them you in."

Of course, they were already naked since this was their home.

Samantha handed a SLR camera to Mike and explained to him what that camera actually does. "This camera will map out a figure if there is anything around us. We call it a stick figure since it actually looks like stick on the camera. Are you ready for this?

Mike responded, "We sure are! We're very excited."

"Don't get too excited just yet because we don't know what we are dealing with right at the moment." Samantha paused, turning toward her team. "Please stay outside while Mike and I go in for the first time."

Mike also asked Destiny to stay outside with the rest of the team. Although she had a little fit about having to stay outside, she agreed.

Mike and Samantha entered the dark house as all the lights were turned off. "Ok, Mike. It's your house, so where do you want to head to first."

"I think the master bedroom," Mike said. "Between the master bedroom and the basement those two areas seem to have the most activity."

As they headed up the steps to the master bedroom, Mike looked like that he stumbled up the step.

"You ok?" Samantha's voice was low.

"I guess. I didn't stumble. It felt like I was tripped. I don't think whatever is in this house wants us investigating."

She told Mike to not to show any fear as entities draw off of that energy. They finally made it to the master bedroom, and Mike entered first.

Samantha was right behind him with a voice recorder. "Mike, so what I have here is called a voice recorder. What this does is pick up voices that we can't hear. We ask questions and then play it back to see if we get a response. At the same time, we have to keep an eye on the SLS camera. Would you like to start asking questions?"

"Sure, I can start asking questions." Mike was quiet for a moment. "Is anyone here with us? Did you in the house? If you died in this house, how did you die?"

"Is there anyone else in this house besides you? If there is anyone beside you, who else is here with you?" After she asked the last question, she said, "We need to listen back to the voice recorder."

As Samantha rewound the voice recorder, it was making a squeaking noise as if it was a cassette tape, but voice recorders are digital and no tape is involved. Samantha hit play, and they could hear Mike's first question, *Is there anyone here in this house with us?* Right after that, a faint male voice that said *Yes.* Then they heard Mike's second question, *Did you die in this house?* The same male voice said *Suicide.* Both Mike and Samantha stared at each other in disbelief.

When they got to Samantha's question, *Is there anyone else here in this house besides you?*, the voice answered *Yes*, and there was a low growl.

"Did you hear that, Mike?"

"I did. Let's listen to it again."

Is there anyone else in this house besides you? Yes, and they confirmed the low growling. After that second time listening to the voice recorder, they let it play all the way through. Right after they both heard that growl, there was a demonic voice that said *Get out, kill you.* Mike and Samantha were stunned by that response.

Mike picked up the SLS camera. "If there are any spirits here, show yourself." He panned the SLR camera over to the king-sized bed. There was a stick figure showing up on the camera. "Look, look! There's someone there!"

Samantha was excited for Mike to have caught something on the SLS camera. The stick figure looked as if was sitting on the bed, and then it looked like it was laying down on the bed.

"This is great evidence," Samantha said. "Do you want to take a break and let some of the other team members come and investigate?"

"Sure, but can we come back?" Mike asked.

"Absolutely we can! But let's see what the other team members capture." Samantha radioed to the other team members that they were on their way out. "I want to send in Amy and Watts to the basement. Once we get outside, they can head in. I'll let Grayson and Ryker to save the footage that we captured."

Once Samantha and Mike were outside, Samantha handed the camera and digital voice recorder to Ryker and asked him to save all this evidence. Then, Amy and Watts headed into the house and straight towards the basement.

As they were walking down the basement stairs, Amy fell down the steps. Immediately, Watts ran to her and asked if she was ok.

Amy grimaced. "I'm fine, but check my back because it feels like it's burning. It felt like I was pushed."

When Watts turned on the flashlight, he immediately noticed three scratches, all very red, almost to the point of bleeding. He took his cell phone from his waist pouch and took a picture of the scratches and showed them to Amy. Then, he called in over the radio to Samantha and Johnathan that Amy was pushed down the stairs and has three very red scratches on her back. After they got to the basement, Samantha and Johnathan showed up as well. They both were concerned about Amy and wanted to see the evidence just in case the scratches would happen to disappear.

Grayson called Samantha over the walkie. "We've got a demonic image on the static X camera down with you guys. This thing looks like a goat head with ram horns. Do you guys see anything down there?"

Samantha radioed back that they did not see anything.

"Ok, just be careful because this thing is demonic. I don't want anything happening to you guys."

"We'll be fine," Samantha said. "I'm about to do an EVP session."

Samantha got the electronic voice recorder out of her waist pack and was ready to start the EVP session when the voice recorder went flying across the basement. All four of them were stunned.

Johnathan went over and picked up the voice recorder from off the floor. A he did, he yelled out to the demon or whoever had hit the recorder out of Samanthas hand, "You are not allowed to touch anything or anyone of them ever again!"

When he picked up the voice recorder, he accidently hit the record button. Johnathan handed Samantha back the voice recorder, and she had noticed that it was already on record.

She asked, "Are you a demonic spirit in this house? Why did you knock the voice recorder out of my hand?"

Then Watts said something smart to the demon and that made the demon even more angry. Watts was picked up and thrown against the wall. When that happened, Amy got mad as well and told the demonic presence, "Leave him alone! As a matter of fact, leave all of us alone because this isn't your house."

After that incident, all four of them decided to call it quits in the basement and head back out to command center. There, Samantha handed the electronic voice recorder to Ryker and Grayson so they could download any evidence that may have been caught. Once the evidence was downloaded, they decided to listen back to the recorder. When they heard Johnathan tell the demon he was not allowed to touch anyone, they heard a voice say *Fuck you,* and then there was a very loud and very distinct growl. Ryker let Samantha listen to the recording.

She immediately knew that they were not dealing with anything pleasant, which they already knew that from their experience in the basement. "I think we need to call in the psychic medium Amy to see if she can just do a walk around outside and inside. This investigation is going to take at least two days. Let's call it a night for tonight since it is already four a.m. The sun will be rising very soon. Can we leave the static X cameras set up to keep recording?"

Mike and Destiny gave them the ok to do so. The team packed up the rest of the things to secure them in the vehicles until the following night. Mike and Destiny invited the entire team to stay at their house. They got dressed, and then, they all got comfortable in the main living room. Around ten, Kimberly started making breakfast, and the bacon smell woke everyone up. Samantha and Amy jumped in to help.

After breakfast was over, the entire team helped clean up and then they wanted to revisit the evidence they caught the previous night. And as they looked through all the evidence, Samantha called Aria the psychic medium, talked to her for about five minutes and then hung up the phone. After hanging up, she told everyone that Aria said would meet them there at around 6:00 p.m., just as the sun is setting. She wanted to walk around the outside of the house first, and then, she would walk through the house. As she's doing her walk through, they needed to stay outside so she could get accurate readings without any of them interfering.

As four and five o'clock came around, the paranormal team met at the command center van. Once again, stripped off their clothes and waited for Aria to show up. At about 6:05, they heard a vehicle driving up the road. The vehicle was a jet-black SUV with Aria and her husband Jack was the driver. When they pulled up, both Aria and Jack got out and greeted the paranormal team. Samantha introduced Mike and Destiny to them, telling them they were the homeowners. Aria started her walk around the house, and Jack followed her videotaping and asking her questions as they went along.

Aria shivered. "There's a lot of energy here."

Jack asked, "Is it good or bad energy."

Aria thought through her answer. "A mixture of both. But the bad energy is not good at all. It is very evil. I'm picking up on a very good energy, and I'm thinking that it's the previous homeowner or the owner of the land."

Aria and Jack went inside the house and that was when Aria got a really bad feeling about the place. She immediately stopped walking and told Jack that she felt like she was being choked.

Jack was concerned. "Is it like your throat is closing up, or is it like there's an actual hand around your neck?"

"It's like a physical hand choking me."

They continued to walk through the house, hitting every room from the master bedroom to the kitchen to the basement. After the walk through, Aria and Jack went back outside.

Aria told her friend Samantha, "This isn't good. Finish your investigation tonight, and I'll be back tomorrow after I see an artist friend of mine."

The entire paranormal team was involved with the next night's investigation, including the homeowners.

Samantha gave them all directions. "There'll be two people working together at all times tonight since we now know that there's demonic presence in this house. Ryker and Grayson, of course, will be at the command center monitoring the cameras and the radio traffic. Tom, you will be with Julia and Destiny. Amy and River, why don't you take Mike with you. Johnathan and I will be paired up. Let's get to ghost hunting.

Tom, Julia, and Destiny entered the house first to do their investigation, and they headed right to the first floor. When they were finished there, they decided to head to the basement. The activity picked up again. This time, the three of them heard the growl, and it was not even on the digital voice recorder.

Destiny got scared. "I want to stop the investigation."

Tom said, "We need to keep going. We need to know what we're dealing with so that we can help you find a way to either cope with what's happening and or get rid of what is here."

Destiny agreed, even though that she was frightened nearly to death. Once down in the basement and investigating, Destiny got the same three scratches on her back side just above her rear end. She cried out in pain. Tom took out his flashlight to look at her back. The scratches were in a pair of three which meant that it was definitely demonic, which in three is considered a mockery of the holy trinity.

Time flew. It was soon 5:00 in the morning, and the sun was starting to peek up from over the horizon. Samantha called over the walkie to the entire team to wrap it up. Everyone turned all the lights back on and started packing up all the equipment, rolling up all the cables for the cameras and gathering all the other equipment up. Once again, Mike and Destiny invited the paranormal team to stay at their house once again, but this time they were free to be naked as long as they wanted. Johnathan gladly accepted for the entire paranormal team. The same as the previous morning, Destiny made everyone breakfast as the paranormal team was her and Mike's guest. This time around, unlike their exploration of Moon Bay Cottage, they did not have to review all the evidence as the evidence they collected and witnessed it first-hand. Ryker and Grayson, however, did download all the evidence collected onto a thumb drive for safe keeping so if anyone ever needed to look at any of that evidence, it would be readily available.

Aria the psychic medium went to see the artist at eight that morning. They sat down, and she described several images to him. The first image Aria had sketched was an older man, probably about in his early seventies with a beard and gray hair, wearing a hat. This was the gentleman she picked up on as the good spirit and believed that this was the previous home or landowner. The second sketch done was of this devilish looking creature, it had a goat head with ram horns that curled up alongside of its head. The eyes were solid black, and it had talons like an eagle or hawk would have. The sketches were completed, then put into a manilla envelope and sealed shut to make sure that no one opened them until Aria met with the paranormal team and the homeowners. After Aria was done with the sketch artist, she and Jack hoped into their SUV and headed back to Mike and Destiny's house.

The house had a video doorbell, so they saw and got the notification that someone was at their front door. Mike was not shy to answer the door completely naked. Aria was not surprised either, as she knew that they were all nudists.

"Come in. Let's go to the kitchen and we can discuss everything," Aria told Mike.

At the table, Samantha and Johnathan, Aria and Jack, and Mike and Destiny all sat across from each other. It was a huge table that sat eight people but could accommodate even more people if needed.

The rest of the paranormal team sat in the living room, listening in on the conservations that were happening in the kitchen.

Aria opened up the conservation. "During my walk, I saw several things. The first entity I encountered was a man, possibility in his early to mid-seventies. I believe this man is the prior homeowner or landowner, and he doesn't pose a threat to anyone. I believe he's here trying to protect everyone, as well as the house and property. My artist friend drew a picture of what I described to him."

Samantha opened up the envelope pulled out the picture, looked at it, and laid it on the kitchen table so that Mike and Destiny could see it.

Destiny said, "I've seen this guy around. I thought that he was the cause of everything happening."

Amy said, "No. It's not him, but when I walked through the house, I picked up on other entities as well. These entities don't pose a threat, either. I believe they are stuck between passing over and the space they are in now. When I got down to the basement, that's when things took a turn for the worse. I encountered this demon down there. This thing is here to cause a lot of harm and maybe even try to kill anyone that sets foot down there. I also had a drawing done of it."

Samantha picked up the second manilla envelope and opened it. After she took a good look at the drawing, she immediately knew that it was the same demon that Ryker and Grayson caught on camera. She told everyone that it was what they all encountered over the past two nights of investigations. After Samantha looked at the drawing, she placed it down on the table so that Mike and Destiny could see it.

She was horrified. "Oh my God. Are you serious?"

Once the initial shock was over, Samantha asked, "Is it safe for them to live here?"

Aria looked at them. "Yes, they can still live there, but there's work to be done. First thing, I need you to contact your church and tell them you need the house cleansed. You two don't need an exorcism done on yourself as this thing has not possessed you yet. Once that is done, you need to bring in a medicine man and have him move all the other dead people along. This medicine man can do that. Lastly, I need you to bring in a shaman, and he can get the previous homeowner moved along. But once the demon is gone, I suspect that the homeowner will pass over on his own. This shaman will be able to tell if that had happed immediately. When all this is completed, you should be able to live a happy and peaceful life without any fear of any entities around to bother you."

Samantha looked at Mike and Destiny and asked them if they were going to take Aria's recommendations to heart. They both said yes immediately.

Several weeks went by, and Mike and Destiny reached out to the paranormal team and Aria. They followed her advice to a T, and all activity had stopped.

"We want to thank your paranormal team and Aria as well for all the help that you provided. If we hear of anyone needing a paranormal investigation, we'll surely recommend you guys."

Chapter Sixteen

Investigating The Haunted Aviation Museum

Shortly after the paranormal team had done their investigation of the house of Mike and Destiny, it was time to investigate the museum. The investigation always took place on either a Friday or Saturday evenings, and on Sundays, the paranormal team took the day off. That way, the rest of the week the paranormal team could concentrate on obtaining clients for investigations. When the paranormal team arrived at the aviation museum, they were greeted by Penny and Xander.

"Welcome to the aviation museum," Xander said to the paranormal team.

"Thank you," Samantha said, looking around. "Wow! There are some very old planes here. This investigation should be very interesting."

"We've spent years and years collecting all these planes and artifacts that are currently in our museum. I'm going in the museum house and take care of some business really quick, so I'll let Penny give you guys the tour." Xander smiled and walked away.

Samantha asked Penny, "So, where would you like to start the tour?"

"Let's start the tour here at the airfield."

Samantha asked Amy and Watts to accompany her and Johnathan on this tour. "The rest of you guys can just hang out here until we get back."

Amy grabbed her notebook. As all five of them walked down the airfield to what looked like a runway, they stopped at a B-29 Super Fortress Bomber from World War II.

Penny explained, "This is a B-29 Super Fortress Bomber. This is the type of plane that dropped the nuclear bombs on Hiroshima and Nagasaki and was the only plane that was pressurized during World War Two."

Amy studied the plane as she spoke. "What type of activity you are having here?"

"We've seen apparitions of a person that looked like they were wearing a type of a leather jacket and a hat that looks like it's from this period. When we open the plane up for visitors, they've reported that they see someone sitting in the pilot's seat. They'll turn around, and when they look back to the front of the plane to ask a question, it's totally vanished. The only way that the pilots can leave the plane is coming back through the plane, and no one sees anyone come past them."

Amy furiously scribbled notes while walking, as Penny took them to the back of the plane. "Here in the rear of the plane, we've captured another figure, but this figure is in the gunner's turret. A lot of people call this a bubble, but the proper name of this area is a turret. This figure looks like that they have blood all over them, something like if they had been shot."

"Wow! Ok. Is there anything else happening here?" Amy stopped walking.

"No, not here, but let's go over to Douglass C-47 Sky Train which is two planes down."

Once they left the B-29 Super Fortress they walked past a P-52 Mustang, one of the greatest air dog fighters of World War II. They came up to the C-47 and walked around the plane.

Amy asked, "Penny, what's been going on here?"

"Here, it's been reported that the cargo area has a bunch of apparitions sitting in the cargo seats, like the plane is transporting troops. Again, they're there and then they're gone at a blink of an eye. This all that we had at these planes and in the airfield." Penny explained. "But let's go ahead into the museum house because there's some stuff happening there, as well."

Once inside the museum house, Penny took them to another World War II relic. "This item's a piece of shrapnel from one of the Germans anti-aircraft guns. We don't know who or how they actually retrieved this piece of shrapnel, but we did have it authenticated, and it came back as a real piece of shrapnel from a German anti-aircraft battery. Here, when we open up in the morning, we sometimes find this piece of metal either moved or find it laying on the floor. But if it's on the floor, it's not like it is close to the display…it's halfway across the room. We don't know how this can be happening because it's kept in a display case. We have tried to adjust our security camera on this object, but then sometime during the night, the security camera goes to all static, and we can't see anything. When that happens, we can actually hear the display case opening up, and we can hear the shrapnel like it's being thrown. And right after that happens, the security camera comes back on."

After Amy had taken her notes, she asked, "Anything else that we need to know?"

"Not that I'm aware of, but we can ask Xander if he knows of any other activity that I'm not aware of. Follow me to his office." They headed down to his office space in the building.

"Mr. Xander, I gave them the tour on everything that I know of with the ghostly hauntings. Do you have anything that you can tell them about any other hauntings?"

Xander asked Penny, "Did you tell them about the piece of shrapnel?"

"Yes, and I explained to them what's been happening to our security cameras when we try to catch what has been happening."

"Great. Thanks, Penny. I don't have anything else to add."

Right after the tour and taking notes for the aviation museum both inside and out at the airfield, Samantha had the team to start unpacking all the equipment and start to set everything up. "In the meantime, Amy, why don't you and Watts go do some research on these planes? Julia, why don't you see what you can dig up anything about a piece of anti-aircraft shrapnel that they have in the museum in the display case?"

When Amy, Watts, and Julia left, the rest of the team started setting up the cameras and testing out the rest of the equipment. It was still early afternoon, so there was still plenty of time to get whatever research was needed on the planes and shrapnel. Once all the cameras were set and all the recording equipment was checked, all they were doing was just waiting for Amy, Watts, and Julia to come back so they all could go get dinner together. Another half hour went by, and finally, the three of them finally showed back up at the Aviation Museum.

"Finally!" Johnathan said. "I'm starving, so let's get some dinner."

"I agree," Julia said. "And while we are at dinner, I'll tell everyone what I found in my research."

The paranormal team went to a very nice Italian restaurant, and the hostess seated all of them but had to put together a couple tables to make one big table to accommodate all of them. As they took their seats, the waiter came over and introduced his name to them. "Welcome! My name is Carlos, and I will be taking care of you tonight. Can I start everyone off with drinks?"

After all of them gave Carlos their drink order, he said, "I'll be right back."

When Carlos left to retrieve the drinks, Julia started off pulling copies of paper out of her bag. "During my research, I found that this piece of shrapnel is truly from a German anti-aircraft gun battery. The battery was located in the Pacific Ocean Islands. The markings on the shrapnel indicate that this particular piece is from a direct hit on a US warplane, and the plane ended up in the Pacific Ocean. After the war, when they retrieved the plane from the ocean, they found that piece of shrapnel still in it. According to the historical records, the pilot did survive and was able to parachute from the plane before it went into the water. Whoever retrieved the plane from the water saw that piece of shrapnel and took it as a souvenir. That's where the story ends, and I couldn't find any more information on this artifact. No one knows about the person who took it, and how it even ended up in this particular museum. What did you guys find?"

Amy started. "During our research, we uncovered some information on the Enola Gay. Now, the Enola Gay was the B-29 Super Fortress that dropped the very first atomic bomb on Hiroshima,

Japan. The pilot named plane after his mother. We found out that the Enola Gay is still around. Although not able to fly anymore, it's in a museum somewhere, which is very exciting that it's actually still around. In order to load the atomic bomb onto the aircraft, they had to modify the bomb bay because the bomb was super fat. The weight was no obstacle for the plane, but the size was. In fact, they had to dig a hole and put the bomb in the ground, then drive the plane over the bomb to load in into the bomb bay. Anyway, do you remember seeing anything different when we took the tour of the plane with Penny?"

Each one of them said no. Watts said, "I wouldn't know what I would be looking at or looking for. When we go back after dinner, let's ask if we can look into the bomb bay again. In the meantime, while we're here at dinner, I'll try and pull up what a normal bomb bay looks like and what the bomb bay would look like after a modification for the nuclear bomb."

Carlos came back and took everyone's food order, some ordered spaghetti and meatballs while some ordered fettuccini Alfredo. After Carlos took the order, Watts pulled out his phone and searched for what the B-29 Super Fortress looked like in the bomb bay and then what a B-29's bomb bay looked like modified for the nuclear bombs. There was a huge difference between the two. He shared the information until the food arrived. Samantha was excited to finish eating and get back to the Aviation Museum. It took everyone about an hour to eat, pay the check, and get back to the museum.

Once back at the museum, Samantha and Watts headed into the museum house to have a talk with Xander and Penny. When they walked in, Xander was surprised to see them as he thought that they were going to start the investigation.

"We came to ask if we can look in the bomb bay on the B-29. We need to see if the bomb bay was modified in any way."

"Sure," Xander said. "Let me grab the special tool specially made to enter the B-29's." After a minute of being in the back, Xander came back out with what he needed. "Let's go on out there, but hop in the golf cart, and we'll drive out."

Once Xander, Watts, and Samantha drove out to the airfield, Xander took the special tool and opened the entire B-29 so that Samantha and Watts could look through the entire plane again. They went through the inside first to see if they could find anything out of the ordinary. The inside looked standard issue, but once they exited the plane and looked in the bomb bay, the bomb bay looked exactly like the modified picture found during research. They both were all in shock but excited at the same time.

"Could this be it? This is amazing." Samantha said.

"Absolutely! I'm getting more and more excited about what we are finding. Of course, there were only two B-29 bombers that had to be modified to be able to fit either one of the two nuclear bombs into the bomb bay. One was the Enola Gay, and the other B-29 was the Bockscar that sometimes was called the Bock's Car. From what we are looking at, this had to be one of those planes. Let's walk around the outside of the plane and take a look."

Once they walked around the plane, the noticed a black spot on the left side just behind where the aircrew sat, but the rest was silver. Samantha asked Xander if he knew what that black spot was all about.

Xander did not know what that black spot was. "It was there when I acquired the aircraft. The records I received with the plane just say that this was just one of the B-29 bombers that fought in the war. It was one of the air raid planes that dropped incendiary bombs over Japan before the atomic age was born. Other than that, I have no other information on this particular plane."

THE NAKED PARANORMAL INVESTIGATORS 149

"That's cool," Watts said and thanked Xander for letting them look through the plane once more before the investigation took place.

As nightfall approached, Samantha gathered the rest of the team for a meeting. Smantha and Watts started the meeting with what they had seen, about the bomber that was modified to accommodate the nuclear bombs. Little Boy, which was the nuclear bomb that was dropped on Hiroshima, and Fat Man, which was dropped on Nagasaki.

"From what Watts and I saw, this is probably one of those planes. Julia, after the investigation tonight, can you see if you can get any more information on the Enola Gay and the Bockscar?"

"Absolutely. I'll also try and get information on Paul Tibbits, the pilot of the Enola Gay."

"Sounds great," Samantha said. "Now that the sun's down, let's get this investigation going. Since we preset the cameras earlier, we're ready to rock and roll."

As with all the investigations they did, they stripped off all their clothes, put them in their storage containers, and were" ready.

"Let's start here at the B-29. Amy and Watts, why don't you start with the inside of the plane? Julia, why don't you and River start in the museum house? Pay close attention to that piece of shrapnel," Samantha said.

"Sounds good," Julia said. She and River grabbed an electronic voice recorder and a SLS camera and headed towards the museum house.

As Amy and Watts were inside the plane, they wanted to do an EVP session. They sat on some of the plane's seats, which was made of nylon netting. "Wow! These seats are pretty uncomfortable, especially when you're naked, even with a towel on the seat," Amy said.

They adjusted the towels they had brought with them on their seats several times before finding a comfortable position.

Amy started the EVP session. "Is there anyone here with us?" She waited about thirty seconds then continued, pausing between each question. "If there's someone here, who is here with us? Did you fight in the war? Did you die in the war?"

Once Amy was done asking questions, Watts took a shot at asking some questions, also pausing between each one to allow time for answers. "Are you one of the crewmembers of this plane? If you were one of the crewmembers of this plane, what was your job?"

Once Watts asked the last question, Amy wanted to view the recording in real time, so she rewound the recorder and pressed play. After Amy ask her first question about if anyone was here with them, then they could hear a faint *yes*. Both Amy and Watts jumped with excitement. Her second question was asked and once again, then another faint answer, *the crew*.

Amy paused the recording. "Woah. This is fascinating!"

On the record, Amy asked if they were in the war, which some said very pronounced, *YES*. On Amy's last question the answer came through the EVP recorder as a distinct, *No*. Right after Amy's questions were Watts questions. Watts first question was answered as, *Yes*. Watts' second question about the ghost's role was answered very faintly but could still hear clearly, *Pilot*.

"Wow! We got an answer to every one of our questions. Let's break out the cameras and see if we can capture anything on video." Watts moved towards the cameras.

Once the cameras were out, they immediately pointed them towards the cockpit. There, they caught a glimpse of an apparition sitting in the pilot's seat.

"Look, look!" Watts was as excited to see something on camera as he was with the voice recorder. Right after that, Watts hit the save button on the video camera to save that video.

Meanwhile back in the museum house, Julia and River were conducting their investigation. They also carried in an EVP recorder and a digital camera. As Julia started the EVP session, River was operating the camera.

Julia asked about the piece of shrapnel that was in the display case. She, too, was careful to pause to allow time for an answer. "Is this piece of shrapnel from a German anti-aircraft gun from World War Two? Is there an attachment to this piece of shrapnel?"

All the while as Julia was asking questions, River did not capture anything on camera. There was also an X camera set up recording the piece of shrapnel. Julia decided to rewind the EVP recorder and listen back to see if she had captured anything on the voice recorder. Once she asked the first question on the electronic voice recorder, they could clearly hear a response, but the response was in a different language that either Julia or River could understand. The response for Julia's second question was the same as the first, as it was an answer that no one could understand. As Julia and River were messing around with the EVP recorder, the display case top seemed to have lifted life up by itself and was set down on a table fight next to the display. Neither Julia nor River had noticed it until they both heard the tap of it being set down. This phenomenon had never been witnessed in person except those two. After that incident, they wanted to go see Samantha and Johnathan and let them hear the evidence for themselves.

Once the four of them met up at the command center van, Julia played the recording back for the both of them, and Samantha had to listen to it a second time. She heard the recording again, but she could not figure out what the answer was or what language that was in.

Johnathan, on the other hand, knew exactly what it was. He didn't know what the answer was but definitely knew what the language was. "That's in German."

River asked, "How do you know that's German?"

"I spent three years over in Germany in the Army," Johnathan responded.

"Can you tell us what the answer is?" River asked.

"Unfortunately, no. I don't speak German. I picked up a little bit of German words here and there, but I'm not fluent in speaking the language."

"I see. So you mean to tell me that you don't speak German, but you know that's German that you heard on the EVP?" River said sarcastically.

"Yeah," Johnathan said.

Samantha stepped in. "River, don't be disrespectful to Johnathan. We're all on the same team here."

"Yes, ma'am," he said, then turned back to Johnathan. "I'm so sorry...I don't know what's gotten into me. I never act like this at all."

"I know," Johnathan said. "I forgive you...it's just this place has everyone on edge."

As Johnathan, Samantha, and River at the command center talking, Ryker was monitoring the static cameras and then noticed on the monitor that was viewing the shrapnel. The shrapnel went flying out of view of the camera. He immediately told Samantha, and she reviewed the footage as well.

Samantha wanted a different team to investigate the B-29, so she sent Julia and Tom over to see if they could capture any evidence at all in the plane. At this point, Samantha and Johnathan only wanted to concentrate their investigation on the B-29 Super Fortress and the museum house and not worry about the other plane.

Once Julia and Tom got to the plane, they immediately went inside the plane and up to the cockpit area.

Tom started an EVP session but only asked one question. "If you are the pilot of this aircraft, what is your name?"

After a few seconds, he rewound the voice recorder, hit the play button, and listened in. It took a few seconds to hear the response, and the response was *Tibbits*.

"Holy torpedo!" Tom yelled out.

River came running. "What was what? What did you hear?"

"I just got a response that said Tibbits." Tom explained to River that Paul Tibbits was the pilot of the B-29 bomber named after his mother Enola Gay, and that he was the pilot of the plane that dropped the very first atomic bomb. They sat in silence for a long time.

As the sun started to rise in the Eastern sky, Samantha called quits on the investigation. "Let's all get dressed and get ready for reviewing all the evidence."

After everyone was dressed, Xander and Penny came out to the B-29 to meet the paranormal team.

Xander said, "Well, the sun's up. I was wondering if you guys were able to catch anything for us."

Samantha said, "Yes, we did catch some things, but we need to go over a lot of evidence. We'll be back in touch with you on what we find in our evidence. I have your number. I will definitely give you a call to set up an appointment with you, and we can explain everything in detail with you."

"Sounds good," Xander said. "I can't wait to hear back from you guys and see what is up with this museum."

"We can't wait to see the evidence ourselves because it's not always visible evidence what we catch or see when we do our investigations. Sometimes, we can visibly see evidence, and sometimes, we don't see it with our naked eye, no pun intended. It's often only caught on our equipment. Just give us a few days so we have time to go over everything and be able to save all the evidence on a thumb drive for you. We also need to do a little more research on the B-29, as well as the piece of shrapnel."

Chapter Seventeen

The Aviation Museum Evidence Review

When the paranormal team got back to the office, it was only nine in the morning. They had stopped the investigation of the Aviation Museum at around 5:30 a.m. The museum was not all that far from the office, approximately fifteen to twenty minutes away. They all had heard of the museum, but none of them had ever been there before. As the team got back to the office, every one of them took their clothes off and put them in their personal lockers. After that, they all grabbed towels to sit on, as was nudist etiquette. Their chairs were leather, so they also didn't want to stick to the chairs when they stood up. Each of the team members had a job to do, and they started immediately reviewing the evidence.

In the meantime, Julia went out to do the research that she was asked to do by Samantha last night. As the team started the evidence review, they started with the voice recordings. Tom hooked up the voice recorder to the computer so that they could listen to the recordings while also getting rid of any static that may have interfered with the recordings. After the electronic voice recorders were hooked up, Tom played the recordings. The first set of recordings was from the team that initially went to the B-29 Bomber. After adjusting some controls, the recording was louder and clearer when played back. What they all heard was crystal clear evidence of all the questions and answers. Every question that was asked was answered.

Then they got to the EVP recordings of inside the museum house. As with before, the answers to the questions were in a foreign language. Since no one there spoke German, they needed an interpreter to tell them what was said on the recordings. Samantha knew a professor named Steve at the Colorado State College that taught foreign languages, so she had given him a call.

After Samantha hung up the phone with Steve, she told the crew that he was on his way. "While we wait for him, let's continue the evidence review and take a look at our video evidence."

"Sure thing," Grayson said. "Let's go into the viewing room."

After the team went into the viewing room and got situated around the table, Grayson and Ryker started the video review on the fifty-inch-high-definition viewing monitors. As the video was playing, all of a sudden there was an apparition sitting in the pilot's seat in the B-29. They could see that it was a male in a bombers jacket and a hat that matched the pilot's uniform from the 1940s. Then, the apparition vanished, and another apparition showed up in the bombers seat. Just as fast as it showed up, it disappeared.

That was all that the paranormal team had captured in the B-29, so Ryker disconnected the camera from the monitors and connected the camera that was used in the museum house. After Ryker hit the play button, they could see Julia and River enter and walk around the piece of shrapnel with their recorder. As they walked around the museum house, there was a total black image that showed up right behind them. The image had no features. Neither Julia nor River had seen this shadow figure and did not notice anything on their hand-held camera. The image was caught on the X camera that was stationary.

The shadow figure seemed to be just observing Julia and River walk around. However, it also looked as if it was in a fighting stance, as if it was in a combat situation. Julia and River during that time had the fine hairs on their neck stand straight up but did not say anything about that during the investigation. As paranormal investigators, that happed quite often. It was normal for them, so they barely noticed.

As they were reviewing the aviation museum house video evidence, the door buzzer went off. This let them know that front door opened. Once that buzzer sounded, River immediately went out to the waiting room. "Hi. Can I help you?"

"Hello, my name is Steve, and Samantha called me."

"Oh yes! Samantha told us that you were on your way. Hang on one second, and I'll go get her." River walked back into the viewing room and told Samantha that Steve was here.

"Great! I'll go bring him back." Samantha walked out completely naked. "Hi, Steve. Come on back, and I'll let you listen to the audio that we got on the recording."

Steve followed Samantha back into the office area. He didn't seem surprised that they were all naked.

"Have a seat near the computer, and I'll have Tom play the recording for you. Maybe you can tell us what you think or let us know what it says."

"Sure thing. Go ahead...let me hear what you have."

Tom hit the play button, and the first thing they heard was the investigator asking the question. A few seconds after the question was asked, the response was clearly, *Fliegerabwehr*.

Steve said, "Yep. That definitely German. That means anti-aircraft, so yes, Johnathan was correct. What part of the museum that was recorded in?"

Samantha told him that was from around the piece of shrapnel. Right after, they could hear the investigator ask another question, and again a couple seconds later, they heard a voice say, *Strosstrupp-Hitler*.

Steve told them that *Strosstrupp-Hitler* means Hitler's guard. Hitlers guard was also known as SSH.

There was no other evidence on the voice recorders. This was very possible a piece of the anti-aircraft battery that was protecting Hitler.

"Do you know where exactly they acquired this piece of shrapnel?" Steve asked as Julia walked in.

"Steve, this is Julia, our researcher." Samantha nodded toward her.

Julia heard Scott's question, so she jumped right in the conservation. "This piece of shrapnel was recovered from a US plane that was shot down, and the shrapnel was still in the plane. This plane, of course, did not survive but the pilot did. The pilot had jumped out and parachuted to safety."

"That's totally amazing. I would love to visit this museum. Where is it?" Steve said.

"The museum itself is about thirty minutes away from here, give or take, depending on traffic," Samantha said.

"Cool. I'll definitely have to go."

The team was still looking through the video evidence, when all of a sudden, they watched the shrapnel display case lid lift up and get set down gently on the table right next to the display case. That was the moment when Julia and River heard the display case move. Right after

Julia and River walked away, the piece of shrapnel went flying across the room.

"Who was doing that? I know that it's not a living person moving it. There was no one else in the room." Julia said.

Grayson said, "Wow! I've never seen anything like that before. I know we've caught evidence before, but nothing like this at all."

Meanwhile, while everyone was talking to Steve, Julia asked Watts to come with her to do research, since he was in the Army and knew a little bit more than what she would about military things. Watts agreed and got dressed, then they left to go do their research to figure out where the Enola Gay was actually located. Once they arrived at the library, they walked up to the information desk and asked where they could find the historical records on World War II and specifically the Enola Gay. The lady at the information desk asked if there was anything in particular they were trying to find out.

Julia told her that they were researching the Aviation Museum. "We kind of know that the B-29 Super Fortress that is there on display had its bomb bay altered, and that it could be one of the two planes that dropped the atomic bombs on Japan at the end of the war. We are almost certain that is either the Enola Gay or the Bockscar."

"Sure thing. So everything that we have on the Enola Gay is down in the basement in our historical files. Follow me, and I can show you where exactly they are." When they all went down into the basement of the library, Julia and Watts saw rows and rows of historical data on shelves. The basement looked bigger than the main library for some reason. As the lady from the information desk walked down the aisle with all the World War II information, Julia and Watts followed her. 'Here we have all the information about World War Two and the Enola Gay. We don't have much on the Bockscar since that plane is not well known. I believe it is because the Enola Gay was the very first plane the dropped the very first nuclear weapon ever, so maybe that's why the Enola Gay is well known. I have to go back upstairs, help yourselves looking through whatever you need. If you have any questions, please don't hesitate to ask."

As the information clerk left to go back upstairs, Julia and Watts started looking through all the material that was available to them. They took their time.

After about an hour and a half, Julia said, "Hey, Watts. I think I found something here. Take a look at this."

Watts took the piece of information from Julia and was reading through it. "Wow. Looks like the Enola Gay was repainted and shipped off to a museum in Colorado. There is only one Aviation Museum in Colorado. So according to this information, it is extremely possible that the B-29 at the Aviation Museum is the one and only Enola Gay. Look here. The article says that the Enola Gay was repainted, so if the plane was repainted, it's very possible that they covered up the name of the plane. Wasn't there a black spot on the plane just behind the pilot's seat and then it was all silver?"

As Julia and Watts continued their research, they uncovered more information. Julia said, "Well, it looks like we have gotten all the information that we need here, so let's go back and tell everyone what we have found."

Watts said, "I have a very strong suspicion that the plane at the Aviation Museum is the one and only Enola Gay."

They put all the information that they used back where it belonged and headed back upstairs to the main library. Julia walked over to the information desk and thanked the lady that let them use the reference are. After Julia and Watts got back to the headquarters, they immediately went back into the offices. The rest of the team had finished with the reviewing of the evidence and were back in their perspective offices.

They asked Samantha and Johnatha to meet them in the conference room so they could give them the information they had found. After Samantha and Johnathan got to the conference room, Julia and Watts presented their research.

Watts started with the information that the Enola Gay was repainted and was shipped to an Aviation Museum in Colorado. "Now, we also checked on how many Aviation Museums were in Colorado, and this is the only one. We need to figure out which plane this is at the museum."

After giving the other information about the pilot Paul Tibbits and the information about the bomb bay having to be altered to fit Littleboy and Fat Man in the bay, it was time to contact Xander and Penny to reveal all the evidence.

Samantha thanked Julia and Watts for their hard work researching and said she would schedule Xander an appointment to come back. After Samanth left the conference room and went back to her office, she immediately called Xander on the phone.

Xander answered the phone. "Aviation Museum. This is Xander. How can I help you?"

"Xander, this is Samantha. We've gone over all the evidence that we had caught on our equipment, and we did some research as well. We'd like to set up a time to meet with you and go over everything."

"That's awesome," Xander said. "Can we meet tomorrow at nine a.m.?"

"Sounds great. We'll see you tomorrow at nine. Oh, before I let you go, we noticed there was a black painted spot on the B-29 just behind the pilot's seat. Is there any way that you can get someone to see what's behind that? We have a suspicion that the logo was covered up."

"Sure," Xander said. "I'll get the restoration team out here today and start working on that."

"That would be great," Samantha said. "We'll see you tomorrow morning at nine."

After Samantha hung up the phone, she started putting all the evidence together for tomorrow. She assembled the team members that were going to accompany her and Johnatha to the reveal. "So tomorrow, the team members that are going to the reveal with me and Johnathan will be Julia, Watts, and Tom. Since Tom is the tech ops person, we would like to take you just in case any of our equipment should fail. That way, you can fix any issues that may come up. Ok team, it is now four. Let's call it a day, and everyone is dismissed. Enjoy the rest of your night, and I'll see everyone at seven am tomorrow, bright eyed and bushy tailed."

So, everyone got dressed and left for the day. Samantha and Johnathan stayed back for a few more minutes before they set the alarm for the night.

Chapter Eighteen

The Reveal

The next morning at seven, the paranormal team started to arrive at the office. Everyone got naked except for the ones that were going to the reveal at the Aviation Museum with Xander and Penny. That just didn't make any sense for them to get naked and then turn right around and have to get dressed again. The reveal crew wanted to leave a little earlier so that they could get the equipment set up and tested before they invited Xander and Penny in to review everything. As they loaded up the car with the laptops and other equipment, the rest of the team started doing their daily duties which were looking for more clients, researching other places that may be haunted, and advertising for their paranormal team.

Once the reveal team got to the Aviation Museum, Samantha walked into the office and immediately saw Penny. "Hi. Where can we set up the equipment?"

Penny asked, "How much equipment do you have? Is there anything special that you will need?"

Samantha said, "We just have a laptop computer and a thirty-four-inch flat-screen monitor. We'd like to do a test of the equipment before we have you and Xander come in to go over everything with you guys."

"Nice," Penny said, leading them to a conference room. "And Xander and I have something to tell you guys as well, but we want to wait until we can see what you have to tell us first."

Johnathan said, "This is so interesting, and we can't wait, either."

As Tom set up the equipment for the reveal, the rest of the team walked around the museum house to look at all the artifacts they had on display. The museum had a lot of interesting things, mostly artifacts from World War II. Once Tom got the equipment set up and running, he joined the rest of the team in the museum and told them that he was ready for everyone.

Johnathan went to the museum office and told Penny that they were ready for them. Penny called over the walkie-talkie for Xander to meet in the museum's conference room. Penny followed the rest of the paranormal team into the conference room, waiting for Xander to show up. Ten minutes later, Xander arrived, apologizing to everyone and told them that he was out on the airfield with the restoration crew.

"Ok," Samantha said. "Let's start with the video evidence that we caught. First, let's start with the B-29. If you watch right here, you can see a slight apparition of someone sitting in the pilot's seat. What we know is that this is the actual pilot of this particular aircraft. I'm not going to put out a lot of information until we get the audio reveal. Let me replay that for you."

Tom replayed the video, and Samantha took her stylus pointer and made a circle right where the image showed up.

"Wow!" Penny said.

"Now, let's move over to the bombardier's seat. I'm sure you're aware that on the B-29, the pilot co-pilot and navigator sit behind the one that actually releases the bombs. I don't know why they made the plane like that, but it is what it is. As you can see...Tom, pan the camera to the right...in the aircraft from the pilot's seat you can also see that there is a ghostly figure that is sitting in the very front of the cockpit. We believe this is one of the crewmembers of this plane, naturally, because who else could it be but a crewmember? The next video evidence that we are going to show you can be disturbing, so prepare yourself. As we move from the airfield to inside the museum house, we caught some shadow figures on the footage. These shadow figures do not look friendly at all. Look right in this area." She took her stylus pointer and made a small circle up in the left corner of the computer screen down the left side. "As we go walking into the museum house, take a look at this. There was a shadow that seemed to be floating off the ground, and you can see very faintly that this totally looks like a German soldier. We didn't know if this entity was friendly or evil, as we didn't see or hear anything from this particular entity until we reviewed our footage.

"Moving inside the museum house where the shrapnel is, we actually caught it flying across the room. At first, we had some team members in the museum house. During their investigation, they didn't catch anything whatsoever. After a while of investigating, they heard a small clank as if someone moved something. It kind of startled them at first, and they didn't know where it actually came from. Upon looking around, they saw the top of the display case had lifted off and was set down on the table right next to it. Unfortunately, they didn't physically see this happening, but upon investigating to see where the sound came from, they noticed that the top of the display case was moved. The team members then tried to do an EVP session, and they did catch something on the EVP recorder. We will get to that a little later on, but for now, that's all we have on video. So now comes the interesting part: our EVPs. First, let's talk about the B-29 Super Fortress."

Watts took over this reveal. "Remember how we showed you the figures that were in the cockpit of the plane?"

Xander and Penny nodded.

"Well, we also did an EVP session, and if you don't know what an EVP is, that stands for Electronic Voice Phenomena. That's something we can catch on a recorder when we ourselves cannot hear anything. As we were doing the EVP session, you can hear where we ask a question, and then, we wait a few seconds to see if we get a response. We were astonished by the answers we got. We will play the entire session for you...are you ready?"

Tom hit the play button on the computer and played the entire session. Both Xander and Penny were wide eyed and covering their mouth with their hand.

"Do you know who Tibbits is?" Watts asked them.

Penny said, "He was one of the pilots of the B-29 Super Fortress."

"Yes," Watts said. "But there's more to that. Tibbits entire name is Paul Tibbits, and he was the pilot of the B-29 Super Fortress that dropped the very first nuclear bomb on Japan. As a matter of fact, Paul Tibbits named his plane Enola Gay, which he named the plane after his mother.

"Over at the museum house, we also caught another EVP, but this session is very brief. During this session, we actually had to bring in help from the Colorado State College. We had to ask the professor from the Foreign Language department to come in and tell us what it actually said. But before we tell you what was said on this session, I want to play it for you."

As Tom set the computer up for this EVP, Watts told Xander and Penny, "Watch the lines at the bottom of the screen. You'll hear our investigators ask a question, and then, you'll hear an answer. You have to listen really close to hear it." After the investigator asked the question, Watts pointed to a certain part of the line. "Listen to this, and then a German voice came through. Did you hear that, we can play it for you again."

Tom replayed the recording.

"Wow!" Penny said.

Watts continued. "There's one more that we need to play for you, and it's just as amazing."

Once Tom played the second recording, it was almost just like the very first recording from the museum house. Watts asked if they wanted to hear it again, and both Xander and Penny said yes. Tom replayed the EVP recording for them.

"Now that you have heard the EVPs, what do you think? Can you make out what the EVP says?"

"Not at all," Xander said.

"So this is the one that we had to get some outside help with since we didn't understand what it said. Johnathan knew it was German just from spending three years over in Germany in the Army. So are you ready for the answers?" Watts asked.

"Yes, we definitely want to know what it said." Penny looked anxious.

"You did understand the Hitler part, right? Well, the entire answer is *Strosstrupp-Hitler*. That means Hitler's Guard. Next one is *Fliegerabwehr*. That means anti-aircraft. So, there you have it. There's a German soldier that was in an anti-aircraft unit that was also part of Hitler's Guard. We believe that the soldier that's attached to this artifact must have died in the war and his spirit didn't move on and got attached to this particular piece of shrapnel. During the firing of this anti-aircraft weapon, we found out that there was an air raid happening, and the

US dive bombers saw the position of this guard and dropped a bomb on the position. We don't think that this German soldier is going to hurt anyone but is just causing havoc in the museum. Maybe he just doesn't want to leave his job, even though the war is long over, and the guns and equipment have changed dramatically. Do you have any ideas for Penny and Xander on how they can cope with this entity?" Watts looked at Samantha.

"Ok, so you have several options here. One option is that since this soldier hasn't hurt anyone, you can try and live with it. You may have to keep picking things up off the floor with this option. The second option is to just get rid of him. I know a team that can do this for you. In this team, there is a psychic medium and a shaman. Both of these people will come at the same time and do a ritual. After they get this soldier to move on, they'll give you instructions on what you can do to keep your museum house free of any other entities that may want to come in. Now, with the soldiers on the B-29, I would just leave them alone because they haven't done anything wrong. With the information that I gave you, what would you like to do?"

Xander immediately said that he wanted to get rid of the spirit in the museum house.

Samantha said, "Right after we get done here, I'll call the team, and they can set up a time that will be convenient for you."

Once the paranormal team was done with their reveal of the Aviation Museum, it was time for Penny and Xander's surprise.

"You know when you asked me to see what is under the paint on the B-29 out on the airfield? Well, we have a huge surprise for you. If we are done here, let's all go out the airfield. Some can ride in the golf cart with me, and some of you can ride in the golf cart with Penny."

They all got up from the table and followed Xander to the garage to get the golf carts. Once the garage door was halfway open, Xander hit the gas pedal and zoomed out of the garage. Samantha and Johnathan were certain that they were going to hit the garage door, but the golf cart cleared the door by an inch. Penny waited until the garage door was completely open before she drove out. Halfway to the B-29, Xander stopped and asked the team if there were ready for what they were about to see.

"Of course we are! Not much surprises us since we are paranormal investigators," Samantha said.

Xander and Penny drove a different way to the airfield than before so that they would come straight into the aircraft hangar so the team could not see the side of the aircraft. Once they all got to the aircraft, Xander and Penny stopped the golf carts right in front of the plane.

"Remember you told us to see what is under the paint a few days ago? Walk around the plane and see what we have found.'

As the team walked around the aircraft, they did not bother to look at the side of the aircraft but instead examined the bomb bay and landing gear.

Xander smacked his forehead as to say what in the world. "Will you look up at the side of the airplane?"

When they looked up, they saw big, black lettering with the words, *Enola Gay*. The team could not believe what they were seeing.

"Are you serious? Holy cow!" Samantha said. "This is awesome, but are you playing a joke on us?"

"Not at all," Xander said. "This is what was uncovered by our restoration crew. I couldn't believe it myself when they came running in to share this. I don't know how we got so lucky and how this was even possible that we ended up with the Enola Gay."

Johnathan asked for either Xander or Penny to drive him back to retrieve the Geiger counter in the car. He wanted to measure if there was any radiation that was still attached to this airplane. It had been years since the war, but there could still be some radiation on the aircraft. Penny took Johnathan back to his car, and he grabbed the Geiger counter out of a protective case and got back into the golf cart. They returned to the Enola Gay so Johnathan could take a radiation reading. He turned it on and walked up to the airplane, and the Geiger counter had a small reading on the gauge. The reading that was showing on the meter was one mg. Johnathan knew immediately that was the real Enola Gay. He reported to Xander and Penny that there was still a small amount of radiation on this plane, but the levels are so low that everything is safe to be around. Since the plane was so high when the atomic bomb was dropped, it only picked up a slither of radiation from the bomb. It was still safe to keep this exhibit open to the public.

Samantha told Xander that the crew and pilot Paul Tibbits was still here at the plane.

"Like I said before, I'd just leave them alone. They're not hurting anyone or anything and he just wants to be with his plane. I feel that he's still very proud of helping to bring World War Two to an end," Xander said.

As they wrapped up their meeting, Xander asked the team if they were hungry since it was close to noon.

"We're starving," Watts said as he was young, and his metabolism was running wild.

Xander laughed and said that the team can come back to the museum house for some lunch. Once inside, Xander ordered a couple pizzas for lunch and talked more about their findings. "I still cannot believe that we have the one and only Enola Gay at our museum. This is so wonderful."

Right after the pizza arrived, Xander got out some paper plates and plastic cups and invited everyone to dig in. While they were eating, the piece of shrapnel went flying across the room again.

Xander said, "Here we go again. Samantha, how soon can the team come and get rid of this thing?"

Samantha told Xander that she would call and see if they can put a rush on coming over here. After the call, she had good news for Xander. The team could come over tomorrow evening at around eight.

"What a relief," Xander said. "I can't wait to get rid of this German soldier once and for all."

Samantha asked Xander if he wanted her and a couple of her team members to be here when this procedure takes place, and he immediately accepted. After lunch, the paranormal team left for the day.

The next afternoon, Samantha said to Johnathan, "Watts and Amy are going to the Aviation Museum later tonight, so we can be there for Xander and Penny when she calls the exorcism team. But they are meeting us here with any new information they can find first."

Once they arrived, they went through all the information that was available at the library, but none of them could come up with anything new. They had spent the entire day at the library. They sat around the table, discussing the events of the previous day. At around 7:30, they headed over to the Aviation Museum. The exorcism team arrived shortly after. Samantha guided them over to the piece of shrapnel and explained to them what was happening. When they were finished, the air seemed lighter and there was even more calmness. in the area. The exorcism team told Xander that the entity is gone, and they should have peace now. Xander thanked everyone, and right after that, everyone left for the night. The next morning when Penny arrived at the museum, the piece of shrapnel was still in the display case and not on the floor.

Chapter Nineteen

Mike and Destiny Join the Team

Shortly after the paranormal team investigated the Aviation Museum, all of them were sitting in their offices, with Julia at the front desk. The front door buzzer sounded, and Mike and Destiny walked into the office.

As they approach the front desk, Julia recognized who they were and greeted them. "Hey guys! How are you all doing? What can I help you with today?"

Destiny said that she wanted to speak to Samantha and Johnathan.

"Can I ask what this is about?" Julia picked up the headset of her phone.

"Sure. We're looking to join the team since we are nudist as well. We had a good sit-down discussion with each other, and we both decided that because you guys are not only nudist but are professional as well. There may be a lot of people out there that may not believe that you guys are professional just because you investigate naked, but we saw it firsthand."

"Sure. I'll let Samantha know."

Samantha went to use the rest room, but Johnathan was there and picked up the phone and asked Julia, "What can I do for you?"

"Sir, Mike and Destiny are here, and they would like to talk to you and Samantha."

"Ok, Julia. I'll be right out." He hung up the phone.

Julia told them to have a seat and that Johnathan will be right out with them. As Mike and Destiny had a seat in the waiting room, they noticed that there were some old, outdated magazines sitting on the end table in the corner of the room. Mike went over to the table, sifted through the old magazines, found one that said *Paranormal* with the date of the magazine August 1979. After picking up the magazine, he sat down next to his wife.

Mike was flipping through the magazine and found an article that caught his eye, *Workplace Paranormal Witness*. Bending the magazine in half, Mike started to read the article but did not get far into it before Johnathan came out to greet them

Johnathan was completely naked, one would not suspect otherwise as this company was called The Naked Paranormal Investigators. "Nice to see you. Come on back to our office and make yourselves comfortable."

Samantha had returned met them. "Everything still ok at your place? What can we do for you?"

"Well, Destiny and I were talking the other night, and we would like to ask you guys if we can join your team? We are nudist ourselves, and we had seen first-hand how skilled you guys are. Even investigating totally naked, you guys are so professional, and we absolutely love that about your team. We'd would love the opportunity to join, and I know that we can be a vital part of your team."

"We will love to have you on our team, but first, the both of you need to take this small test." Samantha reached into her desk file drawer and rumbled through some file folders. After about a minute, Samantha found what she was looking for and pulled out two sheets of paper that had a test on them. She handed the tests to them, along with a pen for each of them. "This test isn't a pass or fail test, but the intended purpose is just to see where you stand at on different topics. The test is not timed, so take your time. If you have any questions, please don't hesitate to ask Johnathan or me. And since you guys are married to each other, we won't separate the two of you. Just answer the questions with your heart. Once you are done, just let us know, and we can talk about you joining us. Also, if you guys want to get comfortable, you are more than welcome to go naked as well."

"I think we will, since we may be joining the paranormal team anyway, so why not?" Destiny said.

Samantha and Johnathan left the office and left Mike and Destiny alone to take their little test. Mike asked his wife if her test was the same one that he had.

She read off the first question. "Do you believe in the paranormal?"

"That's the same one I have. I'm sure Samantha and Johnathan know that we are going to answer the questions together." Reading the directions at the top, Mike read out loud, "*Please read all questions and answer all questions. On every question, write down the reason why you answered that question the way you did, no matter if you answered yes or no to that question.* Maybe we can alternate reading the questions and can come to an answer together."

Mike said that he would start it off. "First question. Do you believe in the paranormal?"

Immediately, they both checked yes, and the reason is they both put down was that they had paranormal activity in their home and this paranormal team did an investigation. Both of their answers matched up for question number one.

She read the second question. "Do you believe in unidentified flying objects?"

They tried to answer in unison, but Mike said *yes* and Destiny said *no*.

"You don't think UFOs exist? How come?" Mike asked.

"I just don't believe in UFOs. How come you do?"

Mike said, "When I was younger, my father and I were out in the country doing some naked camping, and we saw some strange lights in the northern sky. Until this day, we still don't know or can explain what we saw that night."

Destiny nodded, seeming satisfied with the answer. She continued. "The third question. What types of sound is most frequently captured on EVPs?"

They discussed it, and they both decided that the noises were possibly speaking or growling, as that was what they had experienced themselves at their own investigation.

The fourth question was, *Are shadow figures a figment of the imagination?*

Both Mike and Destiny answered this question as a no, since they both saw shadow figures in their own house, and that is what they put down as their reason.

Mike finished writing, then read on. "Can objects be possessed by spirits?"

Once again, neither one of them knew a good answer so they quietly discussed the answer. They both came to an agreement of yes because they watch paranormal shows on tv and there were a lot of shows that have that scenario on and that is where they get most of their information, except for when their own home was haunted. Their home did not have haunted objects, just the home was haunted.

As they wrapped up the little test that they were taking, Destiny walked out into the hallway to get Samantha and Johnathan to let them know that they were done the test. The first one she saw in the hallway was Johnathan, so she told him that she and Mike were done.

"Cool beans," Johnathan said. "Let me grab Samantha, and we'll be right in."

After Johnathan got Samantha, they went back into the office and sat behind their desks. They took the test back and looked over the answers briefly before they started their interview.

Johnathan said, "Ok. Let's get this interview started. Why do you want to be a part of this paranormal team?"

Mike answered first. "I know that you are naked paranormal investigators. You guys are legit. As you know already, we have seen you in action when you investigated our home."

Johnathan turned to Destiny. "What about you?"

"As Mike said already, we're nudist as well, and we've seen you guys in action. At first, we thought you guys were some fly by night paranormal group being naked investigators. We weren't expecting how professional you guys are. You really help people. We'd both love to be a part of this group."

Samantha asked the second question. "I know you guys are nudist as well, as we have seen when we investigated your house and here now since you guys are naked. Would you be ok with being naked in other places as well, possibly naked in front of others while walking around in the pitch black of darkness looking for ghosts?"

The couple eagerly nodded. "Absolutely! We think that would be so exciting."

Johnathan looked down at the test that they had taken. "Destiny, why do you think that UFOs aren't real?"

She thought for a moment. "I don't believe that UFOs were real because I've never experienced anything of the sort. And another reason is that our government has not said anything or came out and told us that they're real."

Mike, on the other hand, told Johnathan the story of camping with his father he had just told Destiny.

Samantha asked the next question. "This question was about EVPs. I see your answers about EVPs here on your quizzes. Can you tell me anything else that you can captured on an Electronic Voice Phenomena? There are other things that can be captured so can you name a few more besides a yes and a no."

"We haven't had much experience with EVPs, but maybe a name, maybe other noises like a growl, and things like that," Mike explained.

"Awesome," Samantha said. "That's all the questions that I have for you at the moment. Johnathan, do you have any other question?"

"No, I don't have any other questions for them right now."

"Let us go into the other room, and we'll come to a decision. Then, we'll come back and let you guys know our decisions. In the meantime, do you need anything? Water, the restroom, anything." Samantha stood.

Mike and Destiny both said that they were good to go, and Samantha told them to look around the office while they discussed the decision. As Samantha and Johnathan left the office and headed back to the conference room, Mike and Destiny got up and started wondering around the area, both were still naked, looking at all the pictures and diplomas of the people that already worked there. They were really impressed about who had diplomas and worked in the paranormal field. Tom, for instance, had a diploma in Information Technology.

Julia had a degree in Research Methodology. Samantha and Johnathan came out of the conference room fifteen minutes later while Mike and Destiny still walking around and looking at everything that was hanging on the walls. Johnathan told them that him and Samantha had made a decision if they could accompany them back into the office.

As everyone walked into the office and had taken a seat, the couple held each other's hand.

Samantha started. "We've decided that we'd like to welcome the both of you to our team."

Both Mike and Destiny had huge smiles on their faces.

"But before you get started, we'd like to put you two in some training. Everything is here, and it's just to get you familiar with our rules, our equipment, and our team expectations. We are going to set you up with a couple of our team members: Tom, Julia, Ryker, and Grayson. These team members will explain everything you need to know about our equipment and some other things that may help you guys out in the long run. This will only be a one-day training for a total of eight hours. When will you two be available for this training?"

As Mike and Destiny were really excited, they both agreed that the sooner the better, and that they will be available whenever Samantha scheduled them. Samantha pulled up her appointment calendar on her laptop and could see that the next available date was for Friday, which was two days away.

"That would be perfect," Mike said.

When Samantha plugged in the appointment for the training, Johnathan said that he wanted them to meet the team. Of course, they already knew the entire team from their home investigation.

"Let's start out front and work our way back." Johnathan, Mike, and Destiny walked out of the office and walked to the front where Julia was sitting. "Do you remember Mike and Destiny?"

Julia answered with a grin on her face as she saw they were naked along with the rest of them. "Yes, of course."

Johnathan told Julia they were now part of our team and would be attending some training on Friday. Julia welcomed them aboard and went back to doing her work.

"Next up will be Amy and Watts." Johnathan entered their office and told them to welcome the new member to the team. Amy and Watts welcomed them and congratulated them. Then, they were off to get reacquainted with Riker, Grayson, Tom, and the rest of the team.

Once Johnathan took Mike and Destiny around the office, he took them back to his office to for some paperwork. They completed the required paperwork for taxes, received a copy of the paranormal team and employee handbook, and signed a non-disclosure agreement to not talk about anything that they found on an investigation. Samantha asked what size shirts that they wore as the paranormal team now had shirts as part of their advertising. Mike wore a large and Destiny wore a medium.

"You guys are lucky. We just received these shirts in, and you two are the very first ones to get theirs. We haven't even given them out to our team members yet!"

"Wow, we are the lucky ones," Destiny said.

Samantha had asked Tom to bring her two shirts, one large and one medium. When Tom returned with the shirts, he handed them to Samantha, and then Samantha looked at the tags to check the sizes and handed them to the couple. After Mike and Destiny finished signing all the paperwork and signed for their shirts, Samantha congratulated them once more and told them they could either go home for the day or hang around and help out. They both decided that they wanted to hang around and help out where needed.

"Once you go through your training on Friday, Johnathan and I will have to put you into a position. Are there any certain positions that you're interested in?" Samantha asked.

Mike said that he was interested in tech, and Destiny said that she would like either front desk or research.

"Cool. Let's get you through the training first and then you can reevaluate, and if you still are interested in those positions, we can make that happen. We like to wait until after the training to be sure that we place people in the field that they want. The last thing we want is for anyone to be placed into a position and absolutely hate it. Of course, we can always change their positions, but we want people to get placed right the very first time. But like I said, one size does not fit all, and we'll be glad to move someone into a different spot on down the road. The only thing is that when we go out on our investigations, we expect everyone to do the investigation, except for maybe Ryker and Grayson, as they always man the command center. That's their strength. So, if Samantha and I see that you are good at something, don't be surprised if we want to move you into that position. You'll always have options. Welcome aboard."

Chapter Twenty

The Naked Paranormal Team Promotions

Once Mike and Destiny joined the team, Samantha and Johnathan were able to move and promote some of the team member. First, however, they had to modify some of the offices to be able to make room for the new hires to be able to have their own office. Once the renovations were done, they would call a company meeting for everyone. The renovations that had to be done seemed to be minor, so Johnathan was able to do the renovations himself, with the help of the rest of the team. All they needed to do was put up a wall in the bigger office, add a door, and run internet cables. The renovations should only take about maybe a week, as long as they did not run into any problems. All the while doing the renovations, inside of the building everyone was naked except for Johnathan and Watts. They needed to run in and out of the building, cutting wood and assembling pieces outside, as to not make a mess with all the saw dust and chemicals that they needed to use.

After three days of work, the renovations started to take shape. Initially, it looked like a mess, and Samantha was starting to wonder if that was the right choice to let the team do all the renovations themselves. Johnathan kept assuring her that everything will be ok and that the project had just started and to give it some time. She was very nervous and kept asking him if he knew what he was doing. Johnathan assured her that he knew exactly what he was doing. Before Johnathan had joined the Army, he owned his own handyman company.

"Really?" Samantha said. "I didn't know that, and we been dating for some time now. Now I know why you are good at managing the team."

After day four and five, the new office was just about completed except for having to run the internet cable and put in a couple power outlets. While Johnathan and Watts were finishing up in the new office, Samantha, Julia, and Amy went out shopping for two new office desks and chairs. There was an office furniture outlet just a few miles down the road, so they decided to stop there first as they may have something that was decent at a discounted price. Once they ladies got to the office furniture outlet, also known as Office Furniture Depot, Samantha parked the car, and the girls got out and walked into the store.

There was an employee by the door who greeted them. "Welcome to Office Furniture Depot. If you need help with anything, please don't hesitate to ask one of our team members."

"Thank you," Samantha said. "We'll definitely let you know if we need any help. Oh, I do have one question. Where can I find office desks and chairs?"

"All the desks are directly in the back of the store, and all the chairs will be back there as well."

"Thank you," Samantha said, and all three of them started walking towards the back of the store.

While they were in the back of the store looking at the desk, Samantha received a text from Johnathan for her to stop by the hardware store and pick up two power outlet face plates. Samantha texted Johnathan back and told him that she would and that they were at Office Furniture Depot right now, looking to see if they would have anything that she could get there. They walked around, looking at the desks that were sitting on rubber mats to protect them from getting scrapped up on the bottoms. Amy spotted two of the same exact desks sitting side by side. Samantha looked at the price tag, and for one desk it was $700. On the bottom of the tag was a note that said they were available for $1,100 for the pair. Samantha told her companions that if she bought them as a pair, there was a $300 discount. While it was a good deal, she wanted to look at chairs before she made a decision.

When the three of them walked over to look at the office chairs, Samantha immediately saw two brown leather chairs that would match perfectly with the two desk that they had just seen in the desk section. These chairs were genuine leather and were $300 for one chair. Unlike the desks, there was not a special on a purchase of two. Once Samantha made her mind up, she decided to purchase the desks and the chairs, so Julia went to get the sales associate that was working in the desk section.

"How can I help you ladies?" he said.

Samantha said, "I want to purchase the two desks and the two chairs to go along with the desk. Are desks on display are the ones we will get?"

The salesperson told her no. "These desks are for display only. You'll receive brand new ones."

"That's even better," Samantha said. "I'd like to purchase these two desks as a pair, and I'd like to purchase two of these office chairs to go with them."

As the salesperson was writing up the ticket, there were some add-ons was available. He asked Samantha if she wanted a five-year warranty on everything, and with the five-year warranty, they covered all defects, even if it is your fault, with no out-of-pocket costs to her. The five-year warranty on the desk, it will be an extra $80.

"Yes, I'll add the warranty. How much would delivery be?"

"Delivery will be $70, and with that service, we will deliver, assemble, and place the desks where you would like them."

"Sure," Samantha said. "Go ahead and add the delivery."

Once the salesperson finished writing up the desk order, they went over to the office chair section.

Samantha showed the salesperson the two office chairs that she wanted. "Is there a special pair discount on the chairs like the two desks had?"

"Unfortunately, there is no option like that on the office chairs," the salesman responded.

"That's a shame," Samantha said. "It would have been nice to have that option as well."

"Tell you what," the salesperson said. "Let me get the order form finished, and I'll see what I can do for you since you are spending a lot of money here with us." The salesperson then asked the same questions about the warranty and delivery. "With the office chairs, the delivery fee would be $50."

Of course, Samantha opted in to all that again with the office chairs. Once the salesperson got the order written up, he told the ladies that he would be right back, as he needed to speak to the store manager for a minute. The salesperson walked away towards the front of the store where the offices were. He was gone for approximately ten minutes and then returned. "I have some good news for you. One, we'll combine the office chairs as a pair for $450, and we'll also waive the delivery fee for the office chairs since you are having the two desks delivered. It wouldn't make sense to have to pay for a separate deliver fee for the chairs."

"That's awesome!" Samantha said. "Thank you so very much."

Once everything was written up, the salesperson gave Samantha the order form and told her to take it up front and they would take care of everything. As they checked out, the total price of everything seemed higher than what was expected. Of course, Samantha questioned the price. The cashier read off everything that was rung up in the computer system. The total price the cashier had included a delivery fee for the office chairs and the regular price for each of the chairs, not the discounted price that she was quoted. Samantha told the cashier that the total was incorrect, and she explained the discounts the salesperson offered.

The cashier sighed and put her hand on her hip. "I don't see anything about that."

Samantha smiled. "Can I please see the salesperson that waited on us and the store manager?"

The cashier rolled her eyes, then called back to the offices and asked the store manager to come out. When the store manager came out, the cashier explained to him what Samantha had told him. The store manager said that Samantha was correct and walked the cashier through how to edit the sale. Once everything was corrected in the computer system, Samantha took out her corporate credit card and paid for her order.

Once Samantha signed the paid receipt, the manager went into the scheduling system to schedule the delivery. He told Samantha, "The furniture can be delivered as early as tomorrow. We have these in stock at our warehouse here in town.

"That would be fantastic. I can't wait to get them." She put her card and the receipt into her purse. The cashier shot her a look, but she ignored it.

After the three of them were done at Office Furniture Depot, Samantha walked down to the hardware store for some power outlet face plates. In the hardware store, it was very easy to find what she needed because there were signs hanging on the ceiling on where the different departments were. Once they were in electrical department, the power outlet face plates were hanging right there on the wall. There were different size packages of them, one single, one double, and a pack of three. Samantha grabbed the pack of three and headed up to check out. They paid for the face plates, then headed back to the office to see how much progress Johnathan had made on the running of the wires and cables. She handed Johnathan the power outlet face plates so he could quickly complete the job.

When Johnathan was done, he asked Samantha to come back. "So do you like it?"

"I love it. You did a great job. I'm impressed." She admired the new office and absolutely loved how it looked, with freshly painted walls, brand new carpet, new outlets, and a forty-two-inch mounted monitor. "And completion is perfectly timed. We'll be getting two new furniture tomorrow between nine and eleven."

The next day came, and Samantha, Johnathan, Mike, and Destiny were eagerly waiting for the new office furniture to arrive. At 9:45, the delivery truck finally arrived. The delivery driver walked in and told the front desk that he was there to deliver new office furniture.

Julia immediately called back to Johnathan and Samantha that the new office furniture was here. Johnathan came up to the front and greeted the delivery driver.

"Where do ya want 'em?" The driver asked

Johnathan told the driver to follow him, and he would show them where it was going. As the delivery driver was walking back, he was stunned that most of the people there were running around the offices totally naked. The driver raised his eyebrows and asked, "Why's everyone naked?"

Johnathan gave a little laugh and explained to the driver that they were naked paranormal investigators, and this was what they did. "We also investigate naked. When we are outside in public, we don't go naked."

When they reached the new office space, Johnathan told the driver that everything would go in there. After the new desk and office chairs were set up and the delivery person left, Samantha wanted to call a team meeting.

"Julia, can you ask everyone to come back to the conference room for a meeting in ten minutes."

As Samantha and Johnathan went to the conference room to wait for everyone to come in, Johnathan took his stack of papers that he had made to hand out to everyone. One by one, the entire team entered the conference room, including Mike and Destiny, as they were now official parts of the team.

Samantha opened the meeting up. "Good afternoon, team. I've called this meeting because Johnathan and I are making a few changes. These changes are good changes and will benefit most of you. Before we get started, Johnathan needs to hand out some papers."

As Johnathan handed out the papers, the team members couldn't help but look at them. The top of the paper read, *new promotions and changes*.

"Now that everyone has the paper, I wanted to let everyone know of some promotions and changes that Johnathan and I are making. As of today, I am the Chief Executive Officer of the *Pikes Peak Naked Paranormal Investigations*, and Johnathan is now the Chief Operations Officer. I have always been the CEO of this team because I am the founder of this group, but we are making everything official.

"With Johnathan and I out of the way, I would like all of you to congratulate Tom on his promotion to Manager. Tom will still be charge of tech operations until we can hire some more people, so if any issues arise, go to Tom first and he will come to us. Now, we have a couple more promotions to announce. Effective immediately, Amy is now the Field Manager. She's in charge when we go out to the field for investigations, and Watts is now the Assistant Field Manager. Again, Amy and Watts are in charge. If there are any problems out in the field, they're the ones to go to for help. If they can't solve the problem, then they can come to me or Johnathan. Grayson and Ryker are still at command center as they love doing that job. Maybe later on down the road, they'll be interested in receiving a promotion. I definitely want to make sure that everyone is happy in their positions. Julia is now Research Coordinator, and I'm going to place Mike and Destiny in the research department. But don't worry guys, you'll still go out and do investigations with us. All research will be done before we hit the location that we'll be investigating. That is all the changes that I have for now. Does anyone have any questions?"

No one said anything or asked any questions, as they were all friends and were happy for the ones that got the promotions.

"A couple more things before everyone goes back to work. As you all know, we hired Mike and Destiny. I'm sure you remember that they were clients, and we went and investigated their house. Right now, I'd like to turn the floor over to Mike and Destiny. Guys, go ahead and introduce yourself, tell us a little about yourself, and explain why you wanted to join our team."

Mike started. "Hello, my name is Mike, and I am very happy to be a part of this team. I was an engineer for the National Park Service, and I was originally assigned to Gettysburg, Pennsylvania. I never believed in ghost until I had an encounter at the Gettysburg Battlefield. I was working one night, and I was walking past one of the display cannons. I had physically seen an apparition walking around the cannon. This apparition was dressed in a union soldier uniform. I could see through it, but it was defined enough that I could definitely tell what it was. After that, I still denied that ghost existed until one time on a different night roughly around the same area, I heard what sounded like a cannon going off. It startled me, and I know there was a field artillery national guard unit that was close by. But they wouldn't be shooting their cannons in a garrison environment like that. Then, I felt this pain in my leg as if I got shot. It hurt so bad but didn't break the skin. I looked down, and I saw a musket ball rolling by. That's when I started to believe that ghosts are real. Shortly after that moment, I got reassignment orders to come here to Colorado. I didn't want to come here because I really love history, especially Gettysburg. But once I got here to Colorado, I met Destiny. A couple years later, we got married, so I can say that fate brought us together. Now it's your turn, Destiny."

"Hello, everyone. As you all know, my name is Destiny, and just like Mike, I never believed in any ghosts or that hauntings existed. I was a very practical math teacher. I never believed any of that until I had an experience at The Stanley Hotel. If you don't know this is the hotel gave the inspiration for that horror movie. I was told about the hauntings in the hotel when I checked in but just blew them off as nonsense. Well, sometime in the middle of the night when I was sleeping, I had my covers pulled down. I know that I wasn't dreaming, nor did I do that myself. And once I was awake, I heard a squeaking noise outside in the hallway, like it was a tricycle. I could remember that odd squeaking noise when I was a kid riding my tricycle outside. I still played it off as my mind was playing tricks on me. After I checked out of the hotel, I went to visit Central City Masonic Cemetery. It was starting to get dark, and I was walking around the cemetery when I noticed that there was this solid black figure standing right behind one of the gravestones. Unlike how Mike could see features on his, mine there was no features at all, not even a face or eyes. I really got scared, and that was the time that I started to believe in ghosts. I kept walking, and I all of a sudden got this burning sensation on my arm. This burning sensation came out of nowhere, and as I looked at my arm, I could see three scratch marks that were deep enough that they were bleeding a little bit. I got home, then did some research and found out that three scratch marks are a sign of a demon. After I did the research, I totally became a believer of ghosts, demons, and hauntings. Mike and I are also nudists, so that's why we think that we would fit right in with you guys."

'Thank you for those introductions. We're very happy to have you guys on the team. As you can see, there's always room for advancement here at *Pikes Peak Naked Paranormal Investigations*. We would still like to grow our team, so if you knew of anyone that would like to join, please send them to us. We don't make you get naked because we feel that's a personal choice that each individual makes, but if they are nudist, that'll be a plus in our book. The person has to believe in what you just said, Destiny. They have to believe that there are ghosts and hauntings and that there are demonic entities out there. What we don't see does not mean that there aren't things out there. That is why ghost hunters use specialized equipment to capture the evidence. Now that you guys introduced yourself, I'd like to turn the floor over to Johnathan."

"Hello, everyone, and congratulations to those that got promoted. I would like to share that I have gotten a call from a man named Zack, who is the owner of Moon River Brewing Company located in Savannah, Georgia. I had a long conservation with him about his place. Now, just a little information about The Moon River Brewing Company. The Moon River Brewing Company is now permanently closed to the public as a bar and grill, but they still give tours of the place on the weekends. They had tour guests report some ghostly happenings when they finished the tour. Some people have expressed they were extremely frightened during the tours. The tour guide gives two tours a night, one at eight and the other is at midnight. It didn't matter which tour they were on. There was definitely some paranormal activity. The midnight tour seems to have the most activity. Zack said that he may or may not fly out to us and maybe look for local paranormal investigators. We shall see in a few days if he shows up or not."

Chapter Twenty-One

Traveling to Savannah, Georgia

A few days had passed since the meeting and the promotions at the paranormal investigator headquarters. Johnathan and Samantha were still waiting to see if Zack from the Moon River Brewing Company would show up or not. On Friday afternoon as everyone was in their offices, the door buzzer sounded. No one was sitting at the front desk as they went on a restroom break.

Mike was the first one that walked out into the foyer and saw a gentleman standing there. "Hello. How can I help you?"

"Hello," the gentleman said back. "I'm Zack. I called a few days ago and spoke with someone by the name of Johnathan about Moon River Brewing Company in Savannah, Georgia."

"Oh yes! We were informed that you may be coming. Have a seat and let me get Johnathan for you."

As Mike went back, he knocked on Samantha and Johnathan's office. They both of them looked up as he spoke. "Zack from the Moon River Brewing Company is here."

"Really?" Johnathan said. "That's so awesome. Please let Zack know that we'll be out in a few minutes."

Mike walked back out into the waiting room to let Zack know that they would be right out to get him while Johnathan gathered all the paperwork that they would need for the contract to investigate. There was no guarantee that they would land the contract to investigate, but he was optimistic. After a few more minutes, Johnathan came out to the waiting room and greeted Zack and introduced himself, shook his hand, and asked Zack to come back to his office. As Zack was walking back to the office, he knew to expect Johnathan to be totally naked but was surprised the entire team was.

Zach asked, "So are all of you always naked?"

Johnathan explained as they walked. "That's why we're known as the naked paranormal investigators. In order to work for us you, have to be a nudist. Doesn't affect our work, though. I wasn't sure you were going to come pay us a visit today."

"Yea. It took a few days to be able to get my flight booked to fly out here and to make arrangements for someone to be able to run the tours of the brewery."

"I see," Johnathan said. "Well, thanks for giving us the opportunity to talk about an investigation for you."

Once they were in the office, Johanthan invited Zack to have a seat at the chair that was placed in front of both Samantha's and his desk. She greeted Zack with a handshake and told him nice to meet you. Samantha was sitting there totally naked, and for some reason Zack couldn't keep his eyes off of her, as he was not used to seeing everyone naked.

"I'm sorry if this our dress code is a little jarring for you. Please take your time to get comfortable," Samantha said.

Zack visibly relaxed and finally started to get more comfortable with everyone being naked. "I'm good."

Johnathan handed Zack some papers. "First and foremost, Zack, we want to thank you for giving us the opportunity to talk to you about doing an investigation. If you look at the very first page, you'll see all the details about our company and how we were founded then started with the paranormal investigations. Samanth is a nudist and had a paranormal experience while at a nudist resort. She never had an experience until she stayed at this particular nudist resort. After she left and got home, she had to figure out whether or not she was dreaming or going crazy. And if it was real, maybe a combination of all three. After a few days, she came up with the idea of starting a nude paranormal investigation company. Thus, Pikes Peak Naked Paranormal Investigations was born."

Zack nodded in silent understanding, beginning to flip through the paperwork.

"Now, if you look at the second page, it explains about all the equipment that we use, and as you can see, we're not some fly by night paranormal company. Just because we are nudist and investigate naked, we take our work very seriously. We have all the modern, up-to-date equipment. We spare no expense on our equipment. So, do you have any questions so far, Zack?"

"None at this time," Zack replied, flipping to the third page.

"If you read through this page, it explains everything that we do on an investigation. If you notice, down in the third paragraph, it explains that we do not do any type of summoning or use of a spirit boards to try and get activity. We don't believe in that. Investigations like that can bring in negative energy or maybe even a demon, and we definitely don't want that for our clients or ourselves. Now, if there's any kind of negative energy or a demonic entity, then we do bring in professional help from the church. The rest of the contact is pretty self-explanatory, so I'll give you a few minutes to read through the rest. If you have any questions, please ask. We are very transparent on everything, and we don't hide anything from our clients. Go ahead and read through the rest of this pages, and please let me know if you have any questions."

After several minutes, Zack was finished reading through the page and asked what a spirit board was.

Johnathan explained. "It's a board that you use to summon spirits. A spirit board comes in several styles. You can even buy these in the toy section at your local department store. I don't know why they sell these boards like that because they can definitely bring in all types of negative energy and or even demons. Do you have any other questions on this page?"

"No, I understand everything now." He remembered kids in his neighborhood growing up playing with them, although he was forbidden by his parents to do so.

"The next page explains all of our fees. As you can see, we have a fuel fee for traveling in vehicles and in the use of our generator to power our equipment if there is no power available. This fee fluctuates depending on how far we need to travel. Does the Moon River Brewing Company have power?"

Zack nodded. Yes, we still have power to the building. We still have some hotel rooms we use for special visitors and also have our offices there."

"Now, there's a payment fee that goes to us for our time and energy to investigate. That is one set fee per hour and with that being said, we normally spend 24 to 48 hours on each investigation. That gives us time to investigate and review the evidence the next day. We then do a reveal to our clients that afternoon. We also have a fee if we need to fly out to a location, although parts of our team will be driving in order to accommodate all of our equipment. We request a $1,500 deposit before we do any type of investigation. That deposit is fully refundable if our client has to cancel. That deposit also goes towards the total amount due at the end of all investigations. So, if your total amount comes to, for example $13,000, we'd subtract the $1,500. Your total would be $11,500."

"I understand perfectly."

"Now that we went over all the paperwork, what do you think? Would you be interested in us doing an investigation at the Moon River Brewing Company?"

"I think I made the right choice by coming here. Yes, I'd love for you to do the investigation."

"That's great!" Johnathan said. "We need a few minutes to get the contract written up, and we'll be right back to you."

Johnathan stepped out of his office and went into Mike and Destiny's office. "Since Julia is away from her desk, can you put together a contract for the Moon River Brewing Company? Please add all the fees associated with having to go to Georgia. Include the plane tickets for half the team and all the fuel cost to be able to drive as well. Make sure that there's a $1,500 deposit required, as well."

"Sure thing, Johnathan. We will get that entered right now and price the flight We already have the templates saved in our computer system." Destiny picked up the phone to call the airline.

Shortly after, the contract was ready. Johnathan got the notification on his computer, and he printed it out. Johnathan went over everything with Zack, and after everyone signed the contract, all that was left was the down payment. Zack took out his corporate credit card and handed it to Johnathan, who ran the card through his point-of-sale system. Once the receipts were printed, Zack signed one for the paranormal teams copy and one was stapled to the customer copy of the contract. Now everything was set, all they needed to do was get everything together and get to Georgia. Samantha told the team to let their families know that they will be going to Georgia for a week for an investigation. They were so excited that they were finally going out of their hometown for an investigation.

On Thursday, Ryker and Grayson left to drive the command center, with Samantha and Johnathan following in the company sedan. This trip was going to take roughly 24 hours to drive, so they hit the interstate and were on their way to Georgia. After several hours on the road, Samantha decided that it was time to stop for gas and to eat. She had Johnathan look on his phone to see what places are close and to make a decision on where to eat. As Johnathan was researching places that were close, Samantha got on the walkies to let the rest of the staff know what the plan was. Not only were they going to stop and eat, but they were also just going to top off with fuel even though they were only about at a half a tank. They did not used much within a few hours but decided to top off with fuel anyway. Johnathan found a fast-food restaurant that was ten minutes away, so he decided that they would stop there as he absolutely loved that restaurant's roast beef sandwiches. First, they would stop at the next gas station. Samantha pulled into the station and up to the first gas pump, the command center van pulled in right next to Samantha and Johnathan at the next pump over. Johnathan got out and inserted the corporate credit card and filled their gas tank up. Once he was finished, he walked back to the command center van and did the same thing, topping them off. Once everyone was full of gas, they then got back on the road and headed to lunch. It only took four minutes before they pulled in and found a parking spot. After getting out of the vehicles, they walked into the restaurant and all hit the bathroom. After that, they went to the counter and ordered their lunch. They all got the same meal: roast beef sandwiches, mozzarella sticks, and drinks.

The staff that was flying left on Friday, as their trip is only going to take two-and-a-half hours. Tom drove the company passenger van with the staff inside to the airport to catch the flight. Once the team got through the security process, they stayed together and headed for the departing gate 23, which was on the complete opposite side of the airport. Luckly for them, they arrived early at the airport, with time to spare before the plane actually departed. This meant that there was time to stop at one of the airport restaurants and grab a bite to eat before heading to the gate. As the team was walking through the airport, they finally arrived at the food court section. There were a lot of restaurants that they could choose from. There were fast food places, as well as sit down places and little corner bakeries for desserts or sandwiches. Amy suggested that they stop at one of the fast-food places to just get burgers and fries. The rest of the team had agreed to that, ate, and continued walking to the departure gate. As they sat in the chairs, they faced out the huge windows to watch the planes coming and going. Finally, the time had arrived for the plane to dock at the passenger boarding bridge, and about twenty minutes later, the gate attendant announced the flight over the speaker that all first-class passengers were welcome to board. This was the paranormal team's moment to board as Samantha had purchased all of them first class tickets because she wanted them to be comfortable on the flight.

The paranormal team were certainly enjoying the first-class flight. They were getting alcohol drinks free of charge with snacks. The flight attendants gave out hot towels. They had to be careful when they used it because it was so hot. Soon enough, the plane starting to make the descent into the Savannah/Hilton Head International Airport.

The pilot came over the speaker and told the passengers that the weather was sunny with a high of 80 degrees. "I'm going to turn the fasten seat belt signs on, and I would like to ask everyone to stay in their seats during our approach into Savannah. Once we land, I'll allow everyone to roam about the cabin when we dock at the gate. Thank you for flying with us. We hope you had a great flight, and we hope that you choose us again in the future."

The plane came closer and closer to the runway and finally touched down. It was kind of a hard landing. As the plane touched down, it bounced back up slightly when the front landing gear hit the runway. The pilot put the engines in reverse and hit the brakes. The plane shimmied and was slowing down very fast, and a few seconds later, the plane was at a crawl, heading to the gate. The pilot came back over the speaker and announced that they were going to be at gate 13 and they could pick up their checked items at baggage claim 10. Once docked at the gate, the pilot shut the engines down completely and turned the fasten seatbelts off. Just about everyone began to stand, and they could hear the seatbelts unclick and the overhead compartments opening up. Right after that, the passenger bridge maneuvered to the door, and the flight attendants invited all the passengers to disembark the plane.

After the paranormal team disembarked the plane, they headed down to the car rental location as they did not have any luggage to pick up at baggage claim. They mostly had a small, carryon bags with personal hygiene items. Once at the car rental desk, they asked for a van to rent as they just needed to get around town until the other team members arrived with their vehicles. Fortunately, the team was in luck as the rental place had one 8-passenger van left to rent out. Amy signed the contract and got the keys and headed out to the parking lot to get the van. They got in the van, then headed out to the Moon River Brewing Company.

The Moon River Brewing Company was built as a hotel before it opened as a brewing company, so the upper floors were still hotel rooms. The owner offered a couple rooms to the paranormal team to stay in, if they were able to deal with the hauntings that were happening there. Of course, the team agreed as they were paranormal investigators and delt with the paranormal on an almost daily basis. That was their job, and they were very excited to spend a night in a location that was totally haunted. They would always go and investigate a location and then leave to review their findings and then come back and do a reveal.

It was eight p.m. when the owner of Moon River Brewing Company showed everyone to their rooms up on the third floor, gave everyone their keys, and then wished everyone a good night and good luck. The team walked into their rooms, got naked, and went to bed to try and get some sleep before busy days ahead of them. At about three in the morning, there was a loud banging noise that woke everyone up. Each one of them jumped out of bed and ran into the hallway. They all were totally naked, and they tried to investigate the noise that they had heard but no one could figure out where it came from. Mike made a suggestion that this was an old building, and that it could possibly be the building itself just making noises. That seemed very unlikely, though. They decided to go back to bed and start fresh in the morning.

Early the next morning as everyone was starting to wake up, Mike went out into the hallway just to stretch out and wake up fully. He noticed there was a folding chair sitting up in the hallway. This chair was not there the previous night, so he went and woke everyone else up to tell them that something happened last night and for them to come and take a look. As everyone else got out of bed, none of them got dressed so they all walked out into the hallway naked to see what Mike was talking about. To everyone's surprise, the chair was totally gone. Mike swore up and down that there was a folding chair sitting in the hallway. By this time, the sun was up, so everyone decided to get dressed so they could head out for some breakfast. After they had gotten dressed, they headed downstairs and were in luck as the owner's wife of the Moon River Brewing Company was in the kitchen already making breakfast for everyone. She greeted them and asked everyone to take a seat at the bar area as breakfast would be ready very soon.

Once breakfast was finished cooking, Sierra, the owner's wife, set all the food out as a buffet. She placed a stack of plates and a basket of silverware near the food. There was sausage, bacon, scrambled eggs, pancakes, and French toast, as well as a mixed fresh fruit bowl.

"Please help yourself to whatever you guys want to eat. I've got some freshly squeezed orange juice here. If you want something different to drink, I can get that for you." She busied herself pouring coffee.

"Thank you," Samantha said. "After breakfast, we would like to sit down with you and your husband just to get a little background on the location and get the information on what's been going on with the hauntings."

"Sure thing. Just let me get everything cleaned up after everyone is done, and we can definitely sit down to chat. Gene, Jose, and I would love to sit down and explain everything to all of you."

After everyone was done eating breakfast and had their bellies full, Sierra quickly gathered the leftovers while some of the team stacked plates and cups, carrying them to the kitchen. The other members of paranormal team were exploring the restaurant area as they waited. As they were walking around, Watts thought that he saw a figure in the mirror that was hanging on the wall. Upon glancing again, the figure seemed to have disappeared. This was nothing unusual with this location. After Sierra finished cleaning up from breakfast her, Jose, and Gene went into the dining area and told the paranormal team that they were ready whenever the team was ready to have that sit down.

Chapter Twenty-Two

Investigating the Moon River Brewing Company

After Sierra had gotten all the dishes done and put away from breakfast, she called her husband Gene and his partner Jose downstairs to have a meeting with the paranormal team. After Jose and Gene got to the dining area, Sierra invited the entire paranormal team to have a seat at the party table which was actually three tables pushed together. Julia, the researcher, took out her note pad to take notes of the meeting.

Sierra started the meeting off. "The Moon River Brewing Company was constructed back in 1821 by Charlston native Elazer Moon as a hotel and has gained quite a reputation for being haunted since. It was also home to one of the very first post office locations in Savannah. In

1851, a man by the name of Peter Wiltberger purchased the property and renovated it. He actually had live lions on display so that he could bring in the wealthy to come and see the charming city. During the Civil War, General Sherman conquered Savannah, and the once-great City Hotel closed and never reopened. As with other buildings in the area, the old City Hotel was used as a makeshift hospital during the yellow fever outbreak that totally devasted Savannah. After the old City Hotel was used as the makeshift hospital, the building sat empty until the next phase of its existence.

"During the turn of the century, the building was used as a warehouse for both lumber and coal stores. Unfortunately, coal slowly died off, so the building was used for general storage. Back in the 1960s, the building was renovated again and was turned into an office supply store with a printing shop. Then, Hurricane David hit Savannah, and that forced the new office and warehouse to shut down in 1979 because the hurricane took the roof off. The building was then bought by us, and thus, we turned it into the Moon River Brewing Company. Back in 2010, we won an award for having an original beer. Even though we have spirits at the bar, we also have other spirits.

"Now getting to the spirits—and not the ones at the bar—I want to start off with the basement. There is a ghostly spirit down there that hides in the shadows, and we call him James. There are random cold spots throughout the basement, and others have reported seeing someone or something in the darkest corners of the basement. Staff have also claimed they heard disembodied voices there. As we go to the upper floors, this is where we have the most activity. There's a lady up there, and she's The Lady in White. The Lady in White is a floating apparition that people have seen go through walls. Back in the early days, it was also rumored there was a deadly shooting in the building between two gentlemen by the names of Alexander Stark and

Phillip Minas. Stark was shot by Minas, who was a physician. Written history doesn't support this part of the story, but it is rumored that Mr. Stark roams around, looking for the man that took his life too soon. The fourth floor has the darkest energy because this was the floor that was used for the poorest patients when this was a makeshift hospital during the yellow fever pandemic. The top floor was the one hardest to get supplies up to, and staff often ignored them in favor of people on the other floors. Of course, people have died there. Visitors have heard unexplained coughing and disembodied voices asking for help and patches of icy-cold spots. That is pretty much the history of Moon River Brewing Company. Most of this is oral history, so if you try to do research on this location, I don't know if you'll find much information on the place."

"Thank you for all that information, Sierra. That's some intriguing history. I'll have our researchers Julia and Destiny try and get any more information that they can on the place. We'll be back this evening at around six to start setting our equipment up. We're going to take a walk around town in the meantime to look at all the history of Savannah. There seems to be a lot of history here," Samantha said.

"If you wanted, I could go with you guys and definitely show you around the place and introduce you to others that have had paranormal encounters," Sierra offered.

"That would be so awesome, Sierra. We'd love for you to join us. In the meantime, Julia and Destiny, why don't you guys go to the local library and Hall of Records to see if you can dig up anything else about the place, and the rest of us will go and get more history about Savannah."

As Sierra got ready to go with the paranormal team, Julia and Destiny headed out to do their research. Five minutes, later Sierra came back down and said that she was ready. They all headed out the door, and Samantha told Sierra to lead the way because none of them knew where they were going.

After a day of exploring the Savannah area, at three p.m. the paranormal team met up at a popular restaurant on the river. They went in, and the hostess seated them and poured everyone a glass of water. Their waitress came over to the table and introduced herself and asked if she could start off with getting anyone drinks. They all placed drink orders and looked over the menu to see what they wanted to order to eat. After the waitress came back with the drinks, she asked everyone if they were ready to order, and everyone was ready. After the food order was taken, the conservation started about what was going to happen tonight during the investigation.

"Well, Sierra. I'm sure by this time you know we're naked investigators. Even though we do investigate naked, we're very professional with our investigations." Samantha smiled at her client.

Sierra said, "We think it's pretty neat there's actually a group that investigated the paranormal naked. That's fine with us. More importantly to us, we can't wait to see what you guys are able to get on record. We've had different paranormal teams come and investigate the location, with varying results. Some say there's demonic presence there, and others say that there aren't any demonic entities there."

Samantha sighed. "Well, we're as real as we can be. I'm sure it's been hard to not know. There aren't always demonic entitles. If there are, we'll disclose that. If not, we'll explain that as well. Either way, we tell the truth. That's one thing that we do not want to compromise with our clientele. Lying just discredits all of us."

After dinner was over, Sierra and the paranormal team walked back to the Moon River Brewing Company to start preparing for the night's investigation. Sierra, Gene, and Jose headed out and left everything to the paranormal team. This time around, the paranormal team decided to set everything up naked, so they all took their clothes off, placed them in their totes, and grabbed all the equipment. Tom started running the cables throughout the building for the static X cameras, while Watts, Amy, and River grabbed the cameras and tri pods to set the cameras up. Julia, Mike, and Destiny started taking all the other equipment out and started testing them to make sure that everything was working properly. After setting the cameras in place, Ryker and Grayson were directing over the walkies where to point the cameras. One was down in the basement; one was on the main floor, looking directly at the bar; one was on the second-floor hallway; and the last one was near the steps on the fourth floor. Ryker and Grayson also directed the fine tuning: slightly up, slightly down, a little to the left, or a little to the right. After all the cameras were placed and ready, Samantha called for a huddle at the command center for a team meeting.

When everyone finally got to the command center, Samantha started the meeting for the night's investigation. "Welcome to the mysterious The Moon River Brewing Company. Who is excited to be here to investigate this place?"

Just about everyone all together replied, "We are!"

"That's great to hear. I know that we all were at the briefing that the owners gave earlier today, but I just wanted to put out a few more things. We need to be careful this evening because it's been reported that the entities on the upper floors are not very nice to people. There've been reports that people have been shoved, scratched, or felt cold spots. One report even said that someone was actually possessed and had to have an exorcism performed. If anyone of you isn't feeling right during this investigation, please let one of know, and we can get you out and away from the building."

Samantha read the list Johnathan had made, dividing the team into groups. "Ryker and Grayson, of course you guys are going to man the command center like always. This time, we'll have Destiny join you, and that way, you can teach her about watching the monitors. Halfway through, we'll switch you out with someone else. Tom, why don't you team up with Mike and take the fourth floor to start. Julia and River, go ahead and take the second floor. Amy, Johnathan, and I will start down in the bar and dining areas. We'll explore the basement later. Does everyone have their walkies on?" She paused to wait for their responses.

"Right now, I want to do a comms check to make sure that we are able to communicate back and forth with each other. Does everyone have on their waist pouch and the equipment that they need? If so, let's get this party started!"

After a brief check, everyone headed out to their perspective areas to start the investigation. Tom and Mike headed to the fourth floor. As they first stepped off the elevator, Mike looked like he tripped and fell on the floor.

Tom asked, "You ok? What did you trip over?"

Mike responded, "I didn't trip. It felt like someone—or something—pushed me in the back and made me fall. That's crazy. We're only just now starting the investigation. If things are starting already, then we're going to be in for one heck of a ride tonight."

After Mike got back up off the floor, they headed down the hallway with the digital voice recorder in hand. Tom told Mike to go ahead and start an EVP session. Since Mike was very new, he stumbled on questions that he wanted to ask.

Instead, Tom started the EVP off by asking the very first standard question and pausing between each question. "Is there anyone here with us? Why did you push Mike down? We didn't do anything to you for you to do that. What is your name?" After a minute, Tom told Mike to ask it some questions.

Mike then asked, "Why are you still here? If you're here with us tonight, please make a sound so that we know that you're here."

Right after that, they both could hear a loud bang coming from the next room. It was clear as day, and they could actually hear it without the digital voice recorder. Mike asked Tom if he heard that, and Tom acknowledged that he did.

"We need to go find out where that sound came from." Tom said, then started walking down the hall towards where the sound came from. Mike followed close behind. Upon arriving where they thought the sound came from, both of them noticed a very cold spot that made the hair on their arms and back of neck stand straight up.

Meanwhile back at the command center, Destiny noticed something on the monitor for that area. The camera was having some static interference and was losing connection. Destiny pointed it out to Ryker, and he immediately called over the radio to Tom and Mike to let them know what was going on with the camera in that area.

Tom radioed back. "There's a very cold spot where we are...the only cold spot on the entire floor."

Right after Tom had mentioned the cold spot, Mike felt like there was something that went right through him. His whole body got freezing cold, and he felt paralyzed for a few seconds and could not move anything. He couldn't walk, move his head, or even raise his arms. This sensation only lasted for two seconds. Tom was beginning to worry about Mike, as this last incident seemed that Mike was being personally attacked. He radioed Samantha and Johnathan to let them know what was going on with Mike. While Tom was talking to Samantha and Johnathan, Mike started dancing around like he just stepped on something.

"What's happening?" Mike reached for his friend.

"My back feels like it's on fire!"

"Turn around so I can look." Tom said, pulling the back of Mike's shirt up. There were three deep scratch marks going diagonally across Mike's back. These scratches were deep enough that all three of them were bleeding.

Tom picked up his radio. "Samantha and Johnathan, Mike's been attacked. He's bleeding."

Johnathan responded. "Get out of that area immediately. We'll meet you back at the command center."

Once back at the command center, Samantha asked Mike to turn so that she could look at the scratch marks on his back. By this time, the scratch marks were deeper and darker then when Tom saw them, and there was enough blood that it was running down Mike's back. Samantha quickly got the first aid kit to treat the wounds. As she was taking care of the injury, Johnathan told both Tom and Mike that he did not want either of them to go back to the fourth floor. There was something very demonic in that area, and it was taking it's anger out on Mike.

Johnathan then called on the walkie. "Ryker and Grayson, why don't you two do some investigating? I'll have Mike and Julia watch the monitors at the command center. Mike needs to rest."

Ryker and Grayson agreed and climbed out of the command center. Mike and Julia took their place. Mike handed the electronic voice recorder to Ryker, and Johnathan instructed them to head to the fourth floor. As the two of them were getting off the elevator, there was a distinct growling noise and a deep voice that said, *get out*. It was extremely low, but they could definitely make out what exactly it said.

Grayson asked Ryker, "Did you hear that?"

Ryker having a little bit of hearing issues. "I didn't. What did it say?"

As Grayson went to repeat it, the voice said it louder. "Get out! Kill you."

Grayson went pale. "I think there's something evil going on. That's not good at all. I think we should take the advice and head back."

Down on the second floor, Destiny and River had started their EVP session. During the meeting with the owners, the second floor did not seem to be as bad as the fourth floor. The EVP session was all the typical questions, things like, *Is there anyone here with us? What happened to you? Can you give us a sign that you are here with us?* The static X camera that was placed on the second floor caught a white mist over in the corner, something that was not seen with the naked eye. Mike noticed it on the monitor, and once he had saw that, he called over the radio to ask if they had seen anything strange. Destiny told Mike no, that they did not see anything at all. Both Destiny and River had a very peaceful feeling on the second floor. The entity there almost seemed calm and protective of everyone.

Down in the bar and restaurant area, Samantha and Johnathan were still doing their investigation. They had tried numerous times to get the presence they knew was there to throw the glass off the bar. After a few tries, both Samantha and Johnathan turned away from the bar area. All of a sudden, the glass flew across the bar and shattered as it hit the floor.

"Are you kidding me?" Johnathan yelled out as he was not expecting that to happen. "Why didn't you do that when I asked the first time?"

While using the Electro Magnetic Field detector, Johnathan did not get any readings until he approached the bar. Once at the bar, the meter spiked to twenty megahertz. That was enough to cause hallucinations and to think that something was there in the room.

While at the bar, there was no reason for any EMF to register as there were no power outlets around or any type of equipment that was in operation anymore. Any reading had to be the paranormal. After a few more tries to communicate with the spirit, they gave up as there was no further activity that was happening. Samantha decided to call it a night as it was two in the morning. They wanted to get everything wrapped up, taken down, and put away before the sun came up in the sky.

Johnathan called over the radio, "Let's call it a night. Get the lights back on and everything packed up and put away. Then, we can head out to breakfast and go over all the evidence that we had captured."

While at breakfast, the team was talking amongst themselves about the events that occurred that night and what experiences that they all encountered.

Johnathan said, "After breakfast, we need to sift through all the evidence so that we can present it to our clients. At least we don't to travel anywhere to review the evidence since we are staying there."

Once they got back from breakfast, they got all the equipment together that they needed to review hours upon hours of evidence. They set up in the bar area, got naked, and started the evidence review.

The first piece of evidence that they came across is an EVP recording that was taken up on the fourth floor. This EVP came out as an extremely dark voice saying *Get out*. The team heard that and jumped in surprise. None of them should have been surprised because they all knew what went on the night before. It was just so clear. Then right after the voice on the EVP recorder, there was another voice that said, *Kill you*. Now the team knew that they were dealing with a dark presence up on the fourth floor. In the next piece of evidence, the team actually saw was the demonic figure on the static X camera. This figure was hard to see, but they could still make out the features of it. It looked exactly like a ram's head with horns curled on top of its head. The eyes were completely black, then all of a sudden glowed red. Destiny put her arms around Mike and held him close.

"We're definitely dealing with something evil here, and I believe that's what attacked Mike last night. I'm just thankful that no one got possessed and needed an exorcism. But I'll contact the church and have a priest come and bless the location, as long as it's ok with the owners."

The second-floor evidence was a lot nicer than the fourth floor. The image that was caught on camera was a white mist. During the investigation, not one person had a bad interaction or a bad experience. That entity seemed like it was there only to protect whoever was around. On the electronic voice recordings, they could hear a female voice faintly say, *Hello*. There was another EVP caught on the electronic voice recorder that said, *Evil upstairs*.

"Whoa!" Watts said. "That's so cool that we have that recording."

Julia chimed in. "That must be Callie. She died here on the property back in 1825 when a gun fight that broke out in the bar area of the building. Several innocent people were shot, but only one died. She had been struck by a bullet in the head, and it killed her immediately. I'm going to explain all of this to the owners once we do the reveal."

The next footage was the bar area. "Samantha and I tried our best to get any response out of anything that may have been there. We didn't get much but take a listen to the EVP that we have. There's no voice, but listen and see if you can hear anything out of the ordinary."

Johnathan hit the play button. They could hear Samantha and him ask several questions to provoke a spirit to throw a glass off of the bar. After several attempts, they heard Samantha say, *Well, we aren't getting anything here, so let's move on*. Once Samantha said that, there was a scraping noise and breaking glass.

Johnathan chimed in. "When we weren't looking, the glass we'd placed on the bar hit the ground. Unfortunately, we both looked away at the same time and did not catch the glass being thrown. When we heard it hit the floor and break, we immediately looked at each other, then at the bar. The glass that we'd put there was missing, and then we saw it broken on the floor a few feet away."

After all the evidence was reviewed and placed onto a thumb drive, Samantha called the owners to check and see if they were available to meet up and go over the evidence. Sierra asked Samantha if they could wait for another half hour so all three of them would be available, so the paranormal team just chilled out for a bit. Just before the half hour was up, Sierra called Samantha and told her that everyone was read. The team grabbed the laptops and the thumb drive and towels to sit on and headed downstairs. After getting to the dining room area, Sierra and her husband, along with their partner, were sitting at the long table that was put together yesterday.

"Hello, everyone. Give us a minute to get the computer set up and ready, and we'll explain everything to you," said Samantha.

It took less than five minutes to get the laptop turned on and signed into and the thumb drive placed into one of the USB ports.

Johnathan started the meeting. "First and foremost, the entire team and I would like to thank you for this opportunity to come and investigate this historic location. We've caught a lot of evidence last night during our investigation. Tom and Mike start off on the fourth-floor investigation, and as they were getting off of the elevator, Tom thought Mike had tripped and fell on the floor. This wasn't the case, as Mike was actually pushed and fell. If you watch the screen right here, you can see here they are walking off the elevator, and right here, you can see Mike actually fall down. He wasn't hurt, but like I said, Tom thought he certainly tripped. When they were walking to the location to do an EVP session, Tom ran directly into a cold spot. He immediately asked Mike if he noticed it, and Mike confirmed. Mike felt the cold spot run right through him. Right after that, Mike said he had a burning sensation, so Tom looked. Mike had three scratches, and these scratches were deep enough that they actually started bleeding. During the EVP session, they caught a voice on the recorder. I want you to listen and see if you can tell what it is saying."

Johnathan handed Sierra the earphones and told her to listen carefully, then he hit the play button.

Sierra nodded. "Yep. That's what we heard."

Johnathan told Sierra because Mike had gotten three scratches, a sign of a demonic presence. The three scratches is a mockery of the trinity: Father, Son, and Holy Spirit.

"Down on the second floor was much better and a nicer area. We caught a white mist on camera. If you look right here in the corner, it goes quickly."

Samantha asked if they had seen it and pointed right at the corner of the screen. "We can play it again. Are you ready?"

Gene sucked in a breath. "I see it!"

"Not only did we catch that on video, but we got an EVP as well. I'm going to play the EVP." Johnathan handed Sierra a set of headphones, then hit the play button.

"Wow." Sierra handed the earphones to her husband and told him to listen.

"You know, I was a true skeptic until this. We definitely don't think this entity is evil. We believe this spirit is here to protect people from the evil presence. Later, Samantha and I were investigating the bar area, and had a spirit down here to throw the glass on the floor. We caught it on camera and also on a voice recorder. Take a look at the glass on the bar, and you can see it start to move slightly. Then, it just goes flying off the bar. I know that there's no sound on the video but listen to the EVP. This EVP doesn't have anything talking, but you can clearly hear the scrapping of the glass on the bar. Take a listen." Johnathan hit the recording play button for them to view.

"We feel this entity down here is a poltergeist, which is a ghost that moves and manipulates objects. While most poltergeists are on the evil side, we don't feel that's the case here. However, we feel that it can turn negative on a dime, so we may have a solution you may want to consider. We know of some psychic mediums that are in the area, and we can send one over to sage and bless the property. This psychic medium can get rid of the evil spirit on the fourth floor, and she can get rid of this poltergeist as well. Naturally, it's up to you since it's your property." Samantha waited for their response.

Sierra asked, "The spirit on the second floor...will that interfere with her staying here?"

"That's something that you can ask the psychic medium. We believe if the evil entity on the fourth floor and the poltergeist on the main floor leave, The Lady in White on the second floor will most likely leave on her own. What do you think?"

After a careful discussing with Sierra, her husband, and their business partner, they decided not to have any cleansing of the building because they liked having The Lady in White around. "We offer ghost tours on the weekends. This will give us the business to keep the ghost tours running."

"That's fine. If you ever change your mind and decide that you want the location cleansed, you know exactly how to get in contact with us. We'll gladly help you out. Once again, we want to thank you for letting us come out and investigate this great location and for your hospitality." Johnathan stood to shake their hands.

With that, the team closed the laptop and gathered everything up to take back upstairs. They were packing up to go home when Samantha got a phone call from the Maryland Highway Division. They asked if the team was available to come to Leonardtown and investigate Crybaby Bridge.

Chapter Twenty-Three

Crybaby Bridge

Once everyone got back to the rooms at The Moon River Brewing Company, Samantha assembled the team and informed everyone that instead of going home to Colorado, they were heading to Maryland.

"I just received a call from the Maryland Highway Division, and they're asking us for help to investigate Crybaby Bridge. All of us will be driving up to Maryland so we all can be together. Julia, I know that you don't have any libraries at your disposal, but can you see how much information that you can get on Crybaby Bridge on the way to Maryland?"

Once they all got dressed and packed the equipment up, they started to load everything up in the vehicles so that they could get on the road. The drive to Maryland would take eight-and-a-half hours, maybe longer for restroom breaks, eating, and refueling. Samantha and Johnathan once again went with the owners of The Moon River Brewing Company and thanked them for their hospitality. When everyone got into the vehicles, the first thing they did was head towards the nearest gas station so all the vehicles can get topped off with gas and get refreshments for the road.

They were on the road heading to Leonardtown, Maryland, and Samantha came over the walkie talkies to let everyone know their plans. "First, we are going to stop at the Maryland Highway Division office in Leonardtown. While talking to the area supervisor, he mentioned there was an urban legend about Crybaby Bridge. Crybaby Bridge is on a back road called Old Indian Bridge Road. In the story, back in sixties, there was a lady carrying a baby and walking down the road at night. When they reached the wooden bridge, a vehicle came by and struck them. Unfortunately, they both died. People have reported driving over the old wooden bridge at night and claimed they've heard a baby crying. The cars would stop and look around, and they couldn't find any babies. They would look all over the bridge, down around under the bridge, and around the stream that the bridge goes over. They would call the police and report what they have heard. Even the police would come out and look around. The police also couldn't find anything. When the police got back in their cars and started to drive off, they could hear the baby crying. This is why the bridge was called Crybaby Bridge. Julia, I know that you don't have a lot of material to work with, but please just see what you can come up with." After Samantha gave the briefing about Crybaby Bridge, she put on some good music, and they were rocking down the highway.

An hour later, Juia had done some research. She found some information on Crybaby Bridge and what was reported. She picked up the walkie talkie and asked everyone if they were on channel. Everyone had responded so she knew everyone was listening in. "So, I have found some information on this bridge, and if everyone's ready, I'd like to give you the information."

"Go ahead," Johnathan told her. "This should be interesting."

Julia continued. "Back in 1950, there was a lady was walking down the road with her baby at about eleven p.m., and once she got to the bridge, she threw her baby over the bridge. Once she did that, she took her own life as well. So, the story of getting hit by a car isn't true. But the story about people hearing a crying baby is true. Also, this happened in Prince George's County. Leonardtown is in Saint Mary's County. Are you sure the supervisor told you the right area, Samantha?"

"I could've sworn he told me Leonardtown. But let me verify the location." Samantha picked up her phone and dialed the supervisor's phone.

After three rings, he picked up. "Maryland Highway Division. Shawn Healy speaking, how can I help you?"

"Hi, Shawn. This is Samantha from the Pikes Peak Naked Paranormal Investigations."

"Oh hi, Samantha. What can I do for you?"

"I know that I spoke with you a few hours ago, but our research shows that Crybaby Bridge is located in Prince George's County. I thought that you said it was in Leonardtown?"

"No, it's in Prince George's County. I may have accidentally said Leonardtown because I was located in Leonardtown but transferred to Prince George's County. I'm sorry if I told you Leonardtown. But yes, it's definitely Prince George's County, and the road is Old Indian Bridge Road. It's a backwoods road with a lot of turns and hills. There's one section that's flat, and that's where the bridge crosses over a stream. I'll text you an exact location," said Shawn.

"We're about a few hours away from Maryland, so we should be there by three p.m."

"Sounds good," Shawn said. "Be careful, and I'll see you soon."

Samantha got off the phone with Shawn and immediately got back on the walkie talkie. "We had a miscommunication. The location is definitely Prince George's County, not Leonardtown. Thank you, Julia, for finding that information out. We should be there in a few hours and arrive at the Maryland Highway Division in Prince George's County by three."

Finally, the team pulled into the driveway of the Maryland Highway Division field office. Once parked, Samantha and Johnathan told the team to hang out while they went in and speak with Shawn.

Upon entering the office, the secretary greeted them. "Good afternoon. What can I help you with?

Johnathan said, "We're here to meet with Shawn."

"Sure," she said. "Go ahead and have a seat, and I'll let him know that you are here. What are your names?"

"We are Samantha and Johnathan form the Pikes Peak Naked Paranormal Investigations."

"Ah yes, he has been expecting you. I'll let him know that you are here." The secretary called back on the intercom, an old model that looked like it has been in use since the seventies. "He'll be right up to get you guys."

"Thank you," Johnathan said.

A few minutes later, Shawn came out and greeted both of them. "Come on back to my office, and I'll explain a little bit more about what has been happening." Once back in the office, Shawn said, "Please have a seat."

There was a leather loveseat and a recliner. This was extremely nice furniture for being in a Highway Division Office. "First of all, I want to thank you guys for coming all the way here to Maryland, home of the Blue Crab. I called you guys out here to investigate Crybaby Bridge. Lately, we've been having reports of a baby crying throughout the night. Police have been called, and they can't find anything or anyone that would even remotely sound like a baby crying. This only happens at night. We've gotten six reports in the last month. What I would like you guys to do is see if you can get any type of evidence at the bridge. I'm going to have the police block of the road from both ends when you do your investigation, so there will be no traffic to disrupt your investigation. Are you guys going to investigate tonight?"

"Yes, we are," Samantha said. "We'll start about eight since it'll be dark at that time."

"Let me go ahead and contact the state police and let them know what time we are going to need them. Thank you." Shawn handed Samantha a gift card for $300. "Take your team out for dinner. Since you're in Maryland and our specialty is crabs, I know a great place that makes awesome crab cakes."

"That sounds delicious. We'll definitely take you up on that offer." They waited patiently for him to finish his call.

"The State Police said that they'll be blocking the road off at 7:30. If you're not there by the time they are expecting you, all you need to do is let them know who you are, and they'll let you through." Shawn then told Johnathan where the best local place for crabcakes was and that he couldn't wait for the results of the investigation.

Right after the meeting with Shawn, Samantha and Johnathan went out to the rest of the team members, then explained the plan for the night and that the Maryland Highway Division was treating them to dinner.

"Let's head to dinner. We're going to a seafood restaurant, and he recommends trying the crab cake dinner platter," Johnathan said.

At the restaurant, the team walked in and was seated at a big party table, and the waitress came over and took all their drink orders. Once back with the drinks, everyone ordered the same thing: the crab cake platter with a side of fries. The orders came, and they gobbled the crab cakes down like it was no tomorrow. Shawn was right: the crab cakes were out of this world.

"These are easily the best crab cakes I have ever eaten in my life," Mike said.

Samantha chimed in. "Welcome to Maryland, home of the blue crab. This state knows how to cook seafood, from steamed crabs to crab cakes to even shrimp. But back to business. We're going to investigate a bridge tonight out in a deeply wooded area. The State Police are going to close down the road for us. The temperature tonight is supposed to be chilly here. So, it's going to be up to you if you want investigate outside totally naked. "

"The State Police said that they will be closing the road down at 7:30. It's now seven, so I think we should pop smoke and head on out to Old Indian Bridge Road. If the police are there before we get there, they'll let us go through," Johnathan said.

The team gathered up their things and headed out to the vehicles so that they could get to the bridge before 7:45. Samantha and Johnathan wanted to start the investigation by eight. Once they got to Old Indian Bridge Road, the state police were already there. They pulled up right behind the police cruiser, and Johnathan got out and walked up to the driver's side window. The police officer looked up and asked Johnathan if he needed help with something.

"Good evening, sir. My name is Johnathan, and I am one of the leaders of the paranormal team that will be investigating Crybaby Bridge this evening."

"Ah yes," the police officer said. "We're waiting for you. Head on through." The police officer pulled forward to let the paranormal convoy through and then backed back up to block the road with his cruiser.

A mile down the road, the paranormal team came to Crybaby Bridge. Since the entire road was blocked off, they did not have to worry about pulling off to the shoulder of the road. They were able to park right there in the travel lane. Crybaby Bridge was a single car bridge. When the team first got out of the cars, the team walked onto the bridge to look down at the creek that was running through. The creek was about 80 feet wide, and water was running through like rapids. The depth of the creek was only about three to four feet. On the side of the bridge was an embankment that was pretty steep, as the bridge was 100 feet above the water. This was to prevent the bridge from getting flooded when there were rainstorms and the water surged.

"Let's see how we're going to investigate tonight. Let's all meet back over at the command center." Once they all got to the command center, Samantha said, "First things first. If you want to, strip down and stow away your clothes. Keep your shoes on as we'll be walking in the woods as well as down in the creek."

Almost everyone got undressed and put their clothes in their storage bins.

Johnathan gave a safety briefing. "As you know, this is Crybaby Bridge. Did everyone listen to the briefing about the bridge? Great, so tonight we're going to be out here in nature, and unlike investigating in a building, there are other safety factors. Safety is paramount tonight. You must be with someone at all times. This is not an option. It is going to be extremely dark out here, so everyone has to have a walkie on them. If any issues arise, you are to call into the command center immediately. Someone will be at the command center at all times. The water's moving swiftly, so no one is to enter the water for any reason. You can go under the bridge, but don't step into the water whatsoever. If I catch anyone stepping in the water, I'm immediately going to pull you from the investigation. We don't need to have anyone swept away and be a liability.

"Next thing on the safety is that we'll still be using handheld cameras and voice recorders, but we will not set up static X cameras, so as you are walking around with the camera, be very cautious where you are stepping. We don't need anyone tripping and breaking a camera, and we definitely don't want anyone getting hurt. It looks like the sun is down behind the trees, so let's rock and roll. Mike and Destiny, I want you guys to start on the bridge with a mapping camera as well with an electronic voice recorder. Amy and Watts, I want you to head down the embankment with a mapping camera and an electronic voice recorder. Julia and River, I'd like for you guys to head down the embankment with the thermal camera and an electronic voice recorder on the other side of the bridge. The rest of us will stay here for a while. If you catch anything on camera or the voice recorders, notify us immediately. Either Samantha or I will contact you when it will be time to switch teams. Have fun guys."

As Mike and Destiny headed to the bridge. Once they got to the center, Destiny started her EVP session. She started to ask questions, and the first question that she asked was naturally, "Is anyone here with us?" She waited for a few seconds. "If you are here with us what your name is? Why did you throw your baby over the side of the bridge?"

After a few minutes, Destiny rewound the voice recorder to listen back to see if they caught anything. Sure, enough a voice was on the recorder, and for the first question there was a female voice that said, *Yes.* They clearly heard Destiny's next question. The same female voice came over the recorder and said *Leslie.* For the next question about why she threw her baby over the bridge, and the same female voice came back and said *Father.*

Under the bridge and down by the creek, both teams were getting evidence as well. Amy and Watts were getting evidence on the mapping camera. The mapping camera was picking up a very small stick figure that was in the water, although the water was rushing by the stick figure did not move at all. This stick figure was very small, just like a baby size. On the other side of the bridge, Julia and River heard a baby cry out loud, without the use of an electronic voice recorder.

"I bet this is why people always hear a baby crying at night and not during the day. At night, it's much calmer and hardly any traffic. This must be why people stop their cars and look around," River said to her.

Shortly after that, Johnathan called everyone back up to the command center so he could change teams out. Back to the command center, he told everyone that he had a surprise. He pulled out an SB-7 spirit box. He asked the team if they knew what a SB-7 spirit box was, but no one knew except for Samantha. Johnathan explained that a SB-7 spirit box was a device that makes white noise, and it scans through different channels at a high rate of speed. This allows the spirits to be able to communicate in real time. "If you all want to come with me and Samantha, we'll put it to the test."

Everyone followed them to the bridge, and Johnathan turned the spirit box on. It sounded like nothing but static, which it was supposed to.

Johnathan asked, "What your name was."

The statice crackled, and then they heard a voice come through, saying, "Leslie."

"Leslie, my name is Johnathan. We want to ask you some questions. Why did you throw your baby over the bridge."

The spirit box crackled, "Father."

"Did your father make you throw your child over?"

The box was quiet for a moment before conveying, "Yes."

"Leslie, so you did not get hit by car, correct."

"No."

"Then how did you die?" Johnathan asked gently.

"Hanging."

Amy said, "That's terrible. Can I ask a question."

"Of course you can. Go for it," Johnathan responded.

"If you died by hanging, did someone hang you?"

The box seemed to switch channels for a long time before conveying, "Myself."

Amy had one more question. "Why did you hang yourself, Leslie?

"Baby."

"So you were so distraught over your baby's death that you took your own life right after, is that correct?"

The spirit box came back but only with static. After a moment, the flashlight Amy held turned off by itself.

"It's ok, Leslie. I believe we've gotten the answers we need. We just wanted to know what happened. We hope that you and your baby find peace. You don't have to stay here anymore, Leslie. Go and be with your baby." Amy's voice trembled at the end, and out of the corner of her eye, she saw a figure on the side of the bridge furthest from them. This figure was dressed in a white dress and was not scary at all. The figure looked at the paranormal team, then just vanished. Amy started to cry when that happened and hoped that she was able to move Leslie along to where she needed to be.

"This was so sad," Julia said. "Tomorrow, I'd like to come and give an offering to Leslie and her baby."

The team walked back to the command center. Samantha asked everyone if they were ok, and even though some of the staff brushed away tears, everyone was fine. "Tomorrow, we'll go back to the Highway Division office and let Shawn know what we have learned about the bridge and what took place. This happened so long ago I don't think that the police would have much left to investigate."

Once everyone was dressed, the team headed out to town to see if there was a hotel available for the rest of the night. At the end of Old Indian Bridge Road, they stopped and let the State Trooper know that they were completed with the investigation and that they can open the road back up. He called in to dispatch and let them know that the road was back open. Johnathan told the trooper that he was more than welcome to come to the office tomorrow if he was inclined to hear all the evidence that the team captured. The trooper accepted the invitation.

The team headed into town and found a cheap motel to be able to stay in the rest of the night. The next day, they woke up around eight, had some coffee, and headed to the Highway Office. On their way, they contacted the State Trooper from the previous night and told him that they were going to be at the office at around nine. Once the paranormal team and the State Trooper got to the Highway Division Office, the team revealed what they caught as evidence.

"Now what we are about to reveal is pretty sad. The first thing is that I broke the team members up in pairs. We had one team on the bridge and one team at each end of the bridge down under by the creek. We caught a SLS figure on our mapping cam, and you can see it right here in the water. It looks to us like a tiny like a baby. Next, we had one team actually hear a baby crying without any equipment. Our team on the bridge caught some EVPs as well.

"After about an hour or so, I called the team back up to the command center and told them that we had a new SB-7 spirit box. Do you know what a SB-7 spirit box is?"

"Not really," Shawn said.

"It's a SB-7 spirit box is a device that makes white noise, and it rapidly scans through different channels. Spirits can communicate in real time with this device. I had one of my investigators record our spirit box session, and I'd like you to take a listen." Johnathan started the recording.

After playing it, Shawn and the police officer agreed that was a very sad situation.

"For our investigation, we believe that this girl Leslie threw her baby over the bridge because her father made her do it. She was so upset and depressed that she went back to the bridge and hung herself. Just before we ended our investigation, we all saw a young girl as a ghostly figure that was in a white dress look at us and then vanish into thin air. We believe these spirits are not here to hurt anyone. They're stuck here, so what we would like to do before we head back to Colorado is to go back there and give an offering. Typically, we don't do these types of things, but this story broke everyone's heart. I'm not saying this will get rid of them, but hopefully it'll give them peace and know they aren't forgotten and are still loved to this day," Samantha said.

The State Trooper and Shawn agreed and wanted to go with them. "I'll drive you to the location in my cruiser, Shawn, and we can escort the team as they go and make peace."

On the way, they stopped at the store and picked up a baby toy and flowers to leave at the bridge. Once at the bridge, the Trooper pulled over and turned his emergency lights on just to warn cars when they come around the turn. After they got out, they went down to the creek and tied the baby toy to one of the bridge support beams and threw the flowers in the creek.

Amy chocked up. "Leslie, you are not forgotten, and you are loved. We brought your baby a toy as well, and she is loved and not forgotten. May you have peace from here on out."

As the flowers floated away, there was a calm silence before everyone walked back up the embankment to the police cruiser and vans. They said their thanks and goodbyes before starting out for home.

Chapter Twenty-Four

Back Home

When the paranormal team got back home to Colorado, the vehicle drivers pulled around back of the headquarters to unload all of the equipment and put everything away. Once parked in the special spots at the front of the building, they went into the headquarters.

Samantha and Johnathan told everyone to go home. "Go home. See your families and take the next two days off. We'll close up shop...spend some time at home. We'll see everyone back here in two days, bright and early."

With that, everyone left the headquarters and headed back home to their families, looking forward to hot showers and relaxing. During their stay at home, all their spouses and partners made them homemade meals for breakfast, lunch, and dinner. None of the team members had homemade meals in a long time, even when they were back here in Colorado doing investigations. The ones with children were able to go out to play and go to parks. Tom even took his son and daughter to the naked planetarium because Tom was raising his children as nudist as well. He wanted to teach them to not be ashamed of their bodies and taught them proper nudist etiquette. After two days of what the military calls R&R, which is Rest and Relaxation, Wednesday morning, everyone was back at the office bright and early at eight since they needed to transfer all the evidence to thumb drives and file the evidence properly. They had to check messages and email messages to see if any more clients would come in for other investigations.

On Thursday morning, Watts and Amy happened to be looking out the office window at ten and noticed there was a line to get into the planetarium. Neither one of them knew what was going on, so they got dressed and headed over to see what was going on. They, of course, had a key to get in because they were the owners, so they squeezed through the crowd and headed to the front door. They told the crowd that they would be letting them in soon and closed and locked the door behind them. Upon entering the planetarium, they immediately headed back to the offices since not one person was up front. They walked into Jennifer's office and saw that the entire crew was naked.

Watts asked, "What in the world was going on outside with all the people?"

Jennifer was shocked to see both Watts and Amy. "We are having a special nudist event. We advertised the event through several media outlets, as well as social media channels. We raised over $25,000, and the event is titled *Full Moon and Milky Way*. We're going to show two different shows: one is on about the moon and how the Apollo 11 landed, and one on the Milky Way. We even contacted the NASA Kennedy Space Flight Center down in Cape Canaveral, and we were able to get a real astronaut to come and give a speech. Then, we're having lunch, but the guest is not to enter the planetarium until 10:30.

The show starts promptly at eleven. We'll let people in after 11 as long as they have a ticket or purchase a ticket at the door for this event. Most of our ticket sales were online, and we purchased a scanner to be able to scan the QR codes from the app."

Amy and Watts could not believe that Jennifer had put together such an event. "How in the world did you come up with the idea of putting on such an event, and how in the heck were you able to get in contact with NASA to be able to schedule a real astronaut to come and give a lecture?"

"Most of the tickets we sold were family tickets, and everyone, including us, are going to be naked as well. The only one that we are not requiring to be naked is the astronaut, but with that if he or she wants to get naked, they may do so. It's just not mandatory for them. As for your question about getting ahold of someone from NASA down in Florida, my cousin actually works for NASA down there. He's an engineer. I contacted him, and he was able to talk to the person in charge of all the astronauts. I was able to get him to agree to get one of them to come and give a lecture. I made it very clear that we are a nudist planetarium and to make sure that whoever they send is perfectly ok with that. So, they're sending someone from one of the most talked-about missions. I cannot wait to hear his story. It's going to be awesome to hear it directly from the man himself."

After Jennifer gave Watts and Amy the run down, it was close to 10:30, and it was time to open the doors for the day. Jennifer had two of her other employees at the entrance, scanning the QR codes and security searching anyone that had a carryall, backpack, or any type of bag. Those that did not previously purchased tickets online were directed over to the counter where they could buy tickets for the event. Since this was a special event, the planetarium was closed to the general public just to come in and see a planetary show. As people were directed to the locker room where they could strip down and put their clothes, the projection room was filling up. The projection room had 500 chairs, which was the max compacity for this particular planetarium. This was a huge planetarium, and there were 400 tickets sold online, and another 80 tickets sold at the counter. The turnout for this one particular event is awesome, and Watts congratulated Jennifer for the effort to put this event on.

As the planetarium projection room was filling up, Jennifer put on a headset and started talking to all the guests that were filing in. "Good morning. Thank you for coming to our very first Full Moon and Milky Way event. Today, we are going to feature two different shows: one will be about our moon, and the other one is going to be about our Milky Way. There are two separate shows, so we are going to feature the moon first and then the Milky Way. After the two shows, we'll take a short break, and we have something special planned for you. We are going to keep that secret until after the shows and the break. Do we have any children in the audience?" Jennifer asked.

There were at least twenty kids that raised their hand, if not more.

"Wow. We have a lot here. That's great!" Jennifer asked the kids in the audience some questions about the moon and asked them about some space missions to the moon, then explained some answers to them. "Now without further ado, it's now eleven o'clock. Enjoy the shows!"

The operator of the projector turned the lights that were around the dome off, hit the play, and the show about the moon started.

The moon program ran for an hour and a half because it had a lot of valuable information about the moon and the manned moon missions. Since the first program went for over an hour, Jennifer got back on the headset and announced that they were going to let everyone take a fifteen-minute break to stretch their legs and use the restroom. "Everyone, please be back here no later than 12:50."

Everyone got up and started walking out to stretch but not everyone left the projection room. After everyone took their break, they started returning back to the projection room, and once everyone was back in, Jennifer got back on the pa system and welcomed everyone back in. Once again, she started asking the kids some questions but this time about the Milky Way, questions about the Big Dipper and The Little Dipper and Orion's belt. Jennifer kept the question-and-answer session to ten minutes because they still had another program to go through, then Jennifer told everyone to enjoy the show.

Once again, the projector operator turned the lights off, hit the play button, and the program about the Milky Way started. The program about the Milky Way was 15 minutes longer than the moon program. When the Milky Way program was over, Jennifer came back on the pa system and asked everyone in the audience what they thought. There was loud applause from everyone.

"That good to hear, because we aim to please!" Jennifer gave a full-hearted laugh. "Has everyone heard of that infamous mission to the moon in 1970?"

There was a mixture of yeses and noes from the audience. Most yeses were from the slightly older crowd.

"Now, without further ado, I would like to introduce our very special guest speaker, please welcome the astronaut and the commander of that mission, Tom Wilkes!"

That is when the audience roared out loud and stood up and clapped, whistled and just welcomed him like no other.

After the crowd finally settled down, he put on a headset and started speaking to the audience.

THE NAKED PARANORMAL INVESTIGATORS 237

"Thank you everyone for coming out. I want to thank the nudist planetarium for supporting the nudist lifestyle. I'm not a nudist, but I certainly don't mind others for partaking in the lifestyle." Then, he started his speech about what happened on the mission and what the three of them had to do to stay alive. "During our launch, we had our main booster alarm sound off. I silenced the alarm and asked mission control what was happening. Everyone having a great time and even broadcast live on tv. Right after that, mission control asked us to give our tanks a stir, so we did. That is when all hell broke loose. We were getting alarm after alarm and shimmies and bangs. Our instruments were just going crazy as well as mission controls. After five minutes of trying to silence every alarm that we had going off, I looked out the port window and I saw this gas coming out of the spacecraft. I immediately told mission control, and that's when I figured it out. After that, the moon mission was off, and we were in survival mode. The wonderful people down there at mission control came up with a device that we had to build with just the materials that we had onboard."

Tom went on to recount every detail of the mission. He was an engaging storyteller. When he was done, it took another hour and fifteen minutes for everyone to ask the questions that they had. That story was very sad and intriguing at the same time.

Jennifer then came back and gave another little speech that took maybe five minutes. Right after that, she invited all the guest down to the cafeteria area to eat. "Tom will be joining us, and he agreed to have pictures taken with him. Yes, you can stay naked, but the pictures you take are not to be posted to any social media platform whatsoever. He even has a book for sale and will sign it for you."

Tom was at a table with a stack of books. After everyone ate, chatted with Tom, and got their books signed, it was close to three pm. Everyone was getting dressed and slowly started heading home for the day. Watts and Amy went to Jennifer and congratulated her on an amazing event and offered her a raise because she had done a phenomenal job. Since this event was a huge success, Watts and Amy started thinking about leaving the paranormal team and just putting on events at their nudist planetarium. It was a huge decision to make because they loved both jobs. They decided to talk it over for the next week and make a decision then. After the week was over and having a talk with Johnathan and Samantha, Watts and Amy decided to not quit the paranormal team all together, but they would split their time between the nudist planetarium and the naked paranormal investigators.

Chapter Twenty-Five

Epilogue

As Pikes Peak Naked Paranormal Investigations continued to draw in business more and more because of some advertisement. Their best advertisement, though, was word of mouth. They were looking to add to the team with more team members. Samantha and Johnathan placed advertisements on job search website, as well as on their website.

We are hiring! Positions include Tech Operations, Investigators, and Front Desk Associate. Send your resume and cover letter to Pikes Peak Naked Paranormal Investigations, 2323 Pikes Peak Drive, Pikes Peak, CO 12356, or digitally upload your information using our website. Just click the link below and upload your resume and cover letter.

The job advertisement was very professional and was developed by Tom. When Samantha first saw the ad, she loved the design and approved of the design almost immediately. While Watts and Amy were now splitting their time half with the nudist planetarium and half the time with paranormal team, they definitely needed more employees to fill the empty spots. Not only that, Samantha and Johnathan also wanted to hire more investigators so that if needed to investigate two different places at one time, they could. Johnathan would go with one team and Samantha would go with the other team.

During the next three weeks only, a few applications trickled in sporadically, which may have been because the team were nudists.

"I guess there are not a lot of people that are comfortable with being a nudists and investigating haunted locations totally naked. That is why we are called Naked Paranormal Investigations. Among the seven applications we received, maybe three out of the seven were worthwhile.

Samantha had called in the three applicants that she and Johnathan wanted to look into more deeply. Samantha called one of the applicants while Johnathan called two of the applicants. Asher and Elijah were to come in for an interview on Thursday at ten, and Kelly would just a little later. Johnathan and Samantha made sure that they asked the applicants if they were aware of and ok with the team of nudist. Kelly, Asher, and Elijah all said that they were aware and each of them said that they were ok with that. Kelly had told Samantha that she had gone skinny dipping with her boyfriend from time to time, and both Asher and Elijah told Johnathan that although they have not gone naked anywhere, they were not ashamed and was excited especially about joining a paranormal team.

A few days had passed, and it was Thursday and time for the interview. Elijah showed up first. As he entered the building, he went up to the front desk and noticed that Destiny was sitting there naked.

She looked up and asked, "How can I help you?"

"My name is Elijah, and I'm here for a ten am interview."

"Yes, sir. If you can have a seat, Johnathan will be right out to get you."

Just as Elijah was just sitting down, Kelly and Asher had walked in together even though they did not know one another. As they walked in, they said hi to Elijah then walked up to the front desk.

Destiny greeted them. "Are you here for interviews?"

"Yes," they said in unison.

Kelly smiled. "I knew you guys were nudist when you did your paranormal investigations, but I didn't know that you were naked here as well."

"Yes, we are naked here, as well. Are you ok with being naked in the office as well as in the field investigating naked?" Destiny asked.

"Oh, yeah," Kelly said. "I'm perfectly fine with all that."

"Great. Have a seat, and Johnathan and Samantha will be out shortly to get you."

A few minutes later, Johnathan walked out completely naked. "Come on back."

Johnathan showed them into his and Samantha's office and invited them to have a seat. Once the applicants were seated, Samantha joined them.

Samantha said, "I know that we have spoken with you over the phone, but 'd like to introduce myself. I'm Samantha, and this is Johnathan. We are the owners of this company, and we wanted to thank you for your interest in this position. What we are going to do is alternate asking questions, so are you guys ready? Don't be nervous."

Johnathan started. "Explain how you stay focused for long periods of time? Kelly, you can go first. One thing I'd like to mention is just try not to repeat what the person said that was ahead of you. We'll alternate who goes first. With that said, Kelly, you go first this round."

The questions kept coming, and the candidates did their best to share their answers. Johnathan said, "You all did very well. I now want to tell you a little bit about us. I'm going to let Samantha start, so Samantha, the floor is yours."

"I started this company five years ago because I was a nudist, and I was also interested in the paranormal. So, I wanted to start a naked paranormal team that investigates the paranormal totally naked. The people that are working for me now were all nudist to start. Then, I started buying bigger and better equipment, and this is where we are today. There are a couple more pieces of equipment that I would like to purchase, like a laser grid and rem-pod, but that will eventually come soon. Now, I'm going to turn it over to Johnathan."

"I was actually in the US Army, and I was a section chief for a Field Artillery unit. We have another veteran as well...Watts. You'll get to meet him. I joined Samantha in her endeavors, and we actually met at the NCO Club on Fort Carson. I've always been interested in the paranormal, so this is right up my alley. So that is a little about us and our company, and now we would like to give you the opportunity to ask us any questions that you may have."

Once Johnathan gave the three applicants the opportunity to ask questions, Asher said that he had a question. "I see that when we came into the office and that everyone was naked. Is everyone naked all the time?"

Johnathan answer. "We're absolutely naked all the time in the office and when we do our investigations. Naturally, we can't be naked once we leave this build and outside of the area that we investigate. With that answer, I want to ask you if there is going to be a problem with you guys being naked?"

Kelly was the first to chime in and say that she didn't have an issue with being naked as she had done some skinny dipping from time to time with friends. Then Asher and Elijah said that they also did not have an issue with being naked.

Samantha said, "There are always room for promotions and raises, so just because you start in one area at a certain rate that does not mean that you will stay in that position. Are there any other questions that you guys have?"

Each one thought about if there were any other questions, and none of them could think about any right off the top of their heads.

"Awesome," Samantha said. "If you guys wouldn't mind waiting here for a while, Johnathan and I need to go and discuss everything."

Samantha and Johnathan left the office and left the three of them in their office. They asked Tom to join them in the discussion. Johnathan was very pleased with the way each of them had handled themselves during the interview and discussed everything with Tom and Samantha. After fifteen minutes of discussion, Samantha and Johnathan agreed to hire all three of them, so they headed back to their office.

Once back in the office, Johnathan was the first to congratulate them. "We'd like to offer you positions with Pikes Peak Naked Paranormal Investigations. Do all of you accept the job offer?"

All of them accepted the job offer.

"Great. We'd like to start you guys tomorrow, so can all of you be here at eight?"

The three of them agreed to be there bright and early the next day.

When the interview was over, Samantha and Johnathan walked the applicants around the office and introduced them to the team and told everyone on the team that they will be starting the next morning. They worked their way around the office and finally out front where Destiny was sitting at the front desk. Johnathan asked her if she could get the new hire paperwork together.

"Absolutely, Johnathan. I'll work on that right away. By the way, we had a phone call from a group that was in West Virgina, so I will give you guys the details once I get their paperwork ready."

It took Destiny five minutes to get all the paperwork for the three new hires. "You can fill them out at home. Just put it back in the folder and it back with you tomorrow. Have a good rest of your day."

Once they left, she went down to her bosses office. "I had a kind of a weird phone call while you guys were back doing the interview. A group located in West Virgina goes out and hunt for cryptids throughout the Appalachia. They asked if we had a branch to investigate cryptids, and I told them that we don't, but I'd have one of you guys call them back. Here is the phone number."

Johnathan went back to his office and immediately called them back. After a short discussion, Johanthan asked Samantha to come in because he wanted to talk to her about the phone call. "Samantha, I just got off the phone with the Cryptids of Appalachia, and they are interested in joining our team with a cryptid division. I think that is a great idea. What do you think?"

Samantha did not have to give it hardly any thought. "Go ahead and call them back. Let them know that we accept the offer and set up a meeting with them. We can start a brand-new division of our team!"

Later that week, Johnathan and Samantha took a trip to West Virgina to meet up with the cryptid team. It was way out in the hills. When they walked into the meeting, Johnathan and Samantha noticed that these guys were a bunch of hillbillies whooping and hollering. Johnathan could not help but bust out laughing at these guys. They were funny and were goofing on each other but in a fun way. The meeting with these guys went well over two hours, and by the end of the meeting, a brand-new team was formed with ghost hunters and cryptid hunters. Samantha and Johnathan had to come up with a new name to add to the company. And thus, that was how The Naked Crypted Investigators was formed.

www.ingramcontent.com/pod-product-compliance
Ingram Content Group UK Ltd.
Pitfield, Milton Keynes, MK11 3LW, UK
UKHW040831110825
7325UKWH00040B/307